RIVER *Wild*

OTHER CONTEMPORARY NOVELS BY SAMANTHA TOWLE

Under Her

Unsuitable

Sacking the Quarterback (BookShots Flames/James Patterson)

The Ending I Want

When I Was Yours

Trouble

THE GODS SERIES

Ruin
Rush

THE WARDROBE SERIES

Wardrobe Malfunction
Breaking Hollywood

THE REVVED SERIES

Revved
Revived

THE STORM SERIES

The Mighty Storm
Wethering the Storm
Taming the Storm
The Storm

PARANORMAL ROMANCES BY SAMANTHA TOWLE

The Bringer

THE ALEXANDRA JONES SERIES

First Bitten
Original Sin

SAMANTHA TOWLE

Visit my website at www.samanthatowle.co.uk
Cover Model: Andrew Biernat
Photographer: Wander Aguiar
Cover Designer: Najla Qamber Designs
Editor and Interior Designer: Jovana Shirley,
Unforeseen Editing, www.unforeseenediting.com

ISBN-13: 9781793353139

AUTHOR'S NOTE

DEAR READER,

I have always been a believer of not putting warnings onto my books because I like the element of surprise when it comes to storytelling.

But I do also understand that not everyone is like me and that triggers are a very real thing, and the last thing I would ever want to do is cause anyone distress, hence the reason for this note.

River Wild is ultimately a romance novel, but it does also cover the difficult subjects of child abuse and sexual and domestic violence.

This story is one of survival, redemption, and healing, encapsulated by love.

My whole heart and soul went into this book. I hope, if you do read on, that you adore River and Carrie's story as much as I do.

Much love,

Samantha

Monsters lurk in plain sight.
They wear ordinary clothes.
Have ordinary faces.
Work ordinary jobs.
Live ordinary lives.
But the monster is always there.
Lying in wait, beneath its ordinary skin.
Waiting for its moment.
And when its moment comes.
And it breaks free.
You won't see it coming.
But I will.
And I'll be ready.

—River Wild

PROLOGUE

River
Eight Years Old

It's Sunday.

I hate Sundays.

Sundays are when Mama goes to her weekly book club meeting. Sundays between five and seven p.m. are when Mama isn't home.

Sunday between five and seven p.m. are when *he* hurts me.

But I can't tell my mama that he hurts me.

He told me that he'd hurt her, too, if I told. He said no one would believe me anyway. Because he's important.

My stepdaddy is the person you tell when someone hurts you.

He is a policeman.

The police are supposed to be good

But he isn't good.

He's bad.

I'm in the backyard, playing with the new basketball Mama bought me for my eighth birthday last week.

She left five minutes ago.

I know what's going to happen.

He's going to make me go inside soon.

He's going to make me do things that I don't want to do.

He's going to do things to me.

I throw the ball at the hoop that hangs on the side of the garage wall.

It goes in. Hits the concrete floor with a thump.

I walk over and pick it up.

I throw it through again.

Thump.

"River, come inside," he calls from the kitchen.

I hate his voice.

I hate him.

I shut my eyes.

No.

The ball rolls back to me, bumping against my foot.

"Now," he barks.

I take a breath. Open my eyes.

I pick my ball up, hugging it to my chest. I slowly walk inside, into the kitchen.

He's standing against the kitchen counter.

"Shut the door," he tells me.

I obey, turning and closing the back door.

"Come here."

I don't want to. Please don't make me.

"Don't make me tell you twice. You know what will happen if you do."

I turn and walk over to him. My stomach starts to hurt.

I hold the ball tighter to my chest.

I stop a few feet away from him.

I don't look at him. But I know he's looking at me.

He reaches out and takes the ball from me, placing it on the counter behind him. There are the usual empty bottles of beer on there.

I see his gun belt lying on the counter, too.

His gun is still in it.

He never leaves it out like that. It's always in his safe.

Why is it there?

My heart starts to beat faster.

"We're going to play a new game today, River."

My new daddy came and sat beside me on the floor in my room. "Do you want to play a game, River?"

"A game?" I asked excitedly. "I love games! What kind of game?"

He leaned closer to me. He smelled like stinky beer and sweat. I didn't like the way he smelled.

"Well, this is a secret game," he whispered. "Only good boys can play it."

"I am a good boy! Miss Clarke says I'm the best behaved boy in her class."

Miss Clarke was my teacher in first grade. I liked her. She smelled nice. She was pretty, too, but not as pretty as my mama. No one was as pretty as my mama.

"Okay, but if we play this game, you have to promise not to tell your mama that we played."

"Why not?"

"Because it's a secret game. One that mommies aren't allowed to know about."

"Okay."

"Do you pinkie promise?"

"I pinkie promise. So, what's the game called?"

He starts to unbuckle his pants.

I turn my face away. I stare at the picture tacked to the refrigerator. I drew it at school on Friday for Mama. It's a picture of a puppy.

I really want a puppy.

I hear the clang of his buckle. The zip lowering.

My body starts to tremble.

"River."

Please don't make me do this.

His hand takes hold of my arm and pulls me to him.

His usual stench of beer and sweat hits me. I feel sick.

"Look at me, boy."

I force my face his way. I stare at the wall behind him. I can't look at him.

"We're going to do something different today. You know how, when you're a good boy for me, Daddy gives you that special treat."

I shut my eyes.

"Well, you're going to do that for me."

"P-please … I-I d-don't want to," I whisper.

He slaps me across the face.

I start to cry.

He slaps me again, harder this time. He grabs hold of my face, fingers pinching my cheeks.

"Open your eyes, boy."

I do as I was told. Tears run down my face.

"Stop fucking crying. Only babies cry. Are you a baby, River?"

"N-no."

"Then, stop acting like one." His face is bright red. His eyes are bulging. His fingers squeeze my face, hurting me more. "You will do as I tell you, boy. Because, if you don't, you know what will happen."

"I-I d-don't want to play this g-game anymore," I whispered. "I-I d-don't think I like it."

"Do you know what happens to little boys who break their promises, River?"

I shook my head.

"They go to jail, and they never see their mamas again."

"I don't want to go to jail! Please don't take me to jail!"

"I won't so long as you do what I tell you. Will you do exactly as Daddy tells you, River?"

I looked down at the floor. My hair fell into my eyes. It got wet from my tears.

"Yes, sir," I whispered.

"What will happen, River?"

I force myself to look him in the eye. "I'll go to jail. I'll never see Mama again. She'll be left alone with you, and you'll have no choice but to hurt her."

He smiles. It makes me hate him more.

"Is that what you want? You want me to hurt your mama, River?"

I take in a breath. "No, sir."

"I didn't think so."

He strokes his fingers down my cheek. I clench my teeth.

"Now, I'm going to go and sit down at the kitchen table. You're going to get me a beer from the fridge. When I'm done drinking it, our game will start. Understand?"

"Yes."

I turn and walk over to the refrigerator. My hand shakes when I open the door. I clench it to make it stop. Then, I reach inside and get a beer from the top shelf. I twist the cap off and put it in the trash, trying to prolong the inevitable.

When I turn back around, I catch sight of his gun again.

It's just sitting there, on the counter.

I look at him. He's sitting on *my* chair at the table.

My chair.

He's moved it out from under the table and turned it, so it's facing me.

He's also taken his pants off. He's only wearing his shirt.

My insides tighten.

The bottle trembles in my hand.

My eyes go to the gun on the counter again.

"What are you waiting for, boy?" he barks. "Get over here."

"River, get over here." His hand thumped against the bed he was sitting on.

Mama's bed.

He'd never brought me in here before to play his games.

It was always in my room.

I didn't want to do this. Not in here.

My hands started to shake. They did that a lot now. Especially on Sundays.

I curled my fingers into my palm until my nails started to hurt my skin.

"Now, River."

I walked over to the bed and stood in front of him.

He smiled.

I dug my nails deeper into my skin.

"River, I won't tell you again! Get your ass over here! Now!"

"No!" I yell.

It's like a thunderbolt has just hit the room.

I've never said no to him before. My whole body shudders with fear.

He stands up. "No?"

"I-I …"

"You dare to tell me no, boy?"

I open my mouth, but no words come out. My heart is beating so fast. I'm so scared. I dig my nails into the palm of my free hand until I feel the skin break.

My eyes dart to the gun on the counter.

"River, it's time to play, and Daddy has a brand-new game for us today."

"I didn't fucking think so. Now, get your ass over here, boy!"

My hand tightens around the beer bottle. I bring my eyes to his. "No," I say again.

His face turns to stone. His head tips to the side. "The rules have changed, River. You tell me no one more time, and I'll kill your mama the second she steps through the door. And, instead of you going to jail … I'll keep you here with me. It'll be just you and me here, alone, in this house. And I'll do what I want to you, whenever I want. Just think … I'd be able to hide my baton in your holder every single fucking day if I wanted to." He brushes his finger over his lips, smiling. "Actually, I like that idea more … so maybe I'll just kill your mama anyway—"

"No!" I yell.

Then, the beer is on the floor and his gun is in my hands.

And I'm pointing it at him.

His eyes widen for a moment. Then, he laughs.

The sound hurts my ears.

"And just what do you think you're gonna do with that, huh?"

My hands are shaking like an earthquake. The gun is so heavy.

"I-I …"

"*I-I,*" he mimics. "You what, boy? Speak up." He cups his ear, making fun of me.

"I-I w-want you to l-leave!" I cry, lifting the gun higher. My arms are aching.

His head tips to the side. "Leave? I'm not leaving, River. I'm never leaving you. You're my special boy. And Daddy loves his special boy so very much."

"You're so good, River. So special. Time to play a new game."

"Stop! Just stop!" I scream. My head hurts so much. Everything hurts. I just want to stop hurting. "I just want you to stop! Leave me alone!"

"I-I d-don't … w-want to p-play anymore."

His hand grabbed my head, and he pushed my face into the pillow. "Be quiet. You're spoiling the game."

There wasn't any air. I couldn't breathe.

Mama, help me, please.

His hand released my head. I turned my face to the side and gulped in a breath.

"I don't like that you made me do that." He ran his hand over my hair, smoothing it down. "Will you be a good boy now?"

A tear rolled down my cheek. "Yes, sir."

"You're not going to shoot me, River. So, just put the fucking gun down."

"I-I …"

The smell of beer …

Hot tears on my face …

Can't breathe …

I'm scared …

Make it stop …

"Put the fucking gun down, you little shit!" he yells at me, taking a step closer.

"D-don't c-come any c-closer!" I cry out. I hold the gun higher.

It's hurting my arms.

But I can't put it down.

If I put it down, he'll … he'll hurt me again.

He'll hurt Mama.

I'm so scared.

I don't know what to do.

"I-I d-don't w-want to do g-games with you anymore! Please just leave me alone!"

"*Just leave me alone*!" he mimics. "Stop being a fucking crybaby. This is what boys do for their daddies. This is what I did for my daddy when I was your age, and I didn't cry about it! Do you have any idea how hard my life is, boy? I'm out there, risking my life every fucking day, earning money to put clothes on your back and food in your ungrateful belly! Now, you do what your father tells you and put that gun down!"

I'm so scared …

Can't breathe …

"That's my good boy, River. Daddy loves you. Daddy loves you so much."

"You're not my dad!" I scream. "I hate you! I hate you! I hate you!"

I feel the gun slip in my hands. I grip it tighter.

Bang!

My body jolts backward.

My stepdad … he's just standing there, staring at me. His hand is pressed against his stomach.

He moves his hand away, and there's a red stain on his white shirt. He stares down at it. "Y-you fucking shot me," he stutters. He never stutters. "I'm going to fucking kill you!" He lurches forward.

Bang! Bang! Bang!

My stepdad is on the floor now.

There's blood everywhere.

The gun drops from my hands.

I look up, and Mama is standing in the doorway.

She looks scared. She starts to cry.

"What have you done, River?" she whispers.

I saved us, Mama. I saved us.

Annie

I glance at the man sitting across from me at the kitchen table. The man I married seven years ago.

The man I hate.

I stare at him with every ounce of my hidden contempt and hatred.

I'm leaving you.

The words echo in my head.

I wish I could say those three words out loud.

But I can't.

Fear and a hundred other terrifying reasons keep them safely locked inside my head.

My finger lifts to my face, gently touching the swelling on my cheekbone, moving down to my split lip.

He sees me touching my face.

He frowns.

I drop my hand.

Last night's beating was bad. He hit my face. That happens less often nowadays.

He doesn't want people questioning bruises on my face.

So, when he beats me, the hits are to my body. Usually, the only violence that happens during sex is when he chokes me. He likes to do that often.

But, last night, he hit me while having sex with me.

Or, as I should call it, raping me.

Because that's what it is.

In the beginning, I didn't realize it was rape. I thought, to be raped, you had to say no. Maybe even tried to fight back.

I've never done either of those things.

But it wasn't like I could say no. I was too afraid to. And, if I had told him no, he would have taken what he wanted anyway.

But I'm glad he beat me the way he did last night because I can't risk a hit to my stomach.

Not now. I'm pregnant.

Pregnant with a baby that he will never know about.

I only found out a few days ago that I'm pregnant. That's why I'm finally leaving. Why I finally have the courage to leave him.

Because it's not just me anymore.

I have a child to protect.

I know people will think I should just call the cops on him. Have him arrested for what he's done to me.

But Neil is the police.

Detective Neil Coombs. Highly respected and admired by his peers. Expected to make Chief of Police one day. He got a Medal of Valor last year.

Yet he regularly beats his wife.

I did try calling the cops once, a long time ago, in the beginning. And they didn't help me.

Because they're all as dirty and corrupt as he is.

So, I'm doing this the only way I can. I'm changing my name, and I'm going to disappear.

The only good thing about having an abusive bastard of a husband, who is a cop, is when he's a dirty cop who gets paid by criminals to turn a blind eye to what they do.

Neil thinks I have no clue what he does on the side. But I know more than he realizes.

And that dirty money that he gets paid, which he can't put in the bank, as it would raise questions, he keeps in the safe that he has hidden in the desk in his office.

The safe he thinks that I don't know about.

But I do know.

And that's going to be my way out of here.

I don't want to take his money. I wish I didn't have to.

I wish I could be ethical and moral, but I don't have any other choice.

I don't have my own money.

Neil has never let me work. At first, I thought it was because he loved me and wanted to take care of me.

I quickly realized that it was just another way for him to control me.

If I didn't have money, then I couldn't leave.

So, I'm taking his money, and I'm leaving.

Neil gets up from the table. I see the gun on his belt, like I do every day, and it still makes my stomach tighten.

Neil gets his suit jacket from the back of his chair and puts it on.

I stand and follow him to the front door, as I do every morning. Because I've been conditioned to do so.

But not after today.

Never again.

He stops at the door and turns to face me.

I brace myself.

His hand lifts to my face.

I flinch.

The satisfaction in his eyes slithers through me, and I hate him more in this moment than I've ever hated him.

"I'm not going to hurt you, Annie." He grips my chin with his thumb and forefinger.

I tense up as I watch his eyes trail over the bruise on my cheekbone. My split lip.

Once upon a time, there used to be remorse in his eyes.

Now, there's nothing.

"I got carried away last night. Stay home today. I'll pick dinner up on my way home tonight."

"Okay," I answer.

"Good girl."

He presses a punishing kiss to my lips, the cut on my lip stinging painfully, but I don't react to the pain, and I hide the revolt inside me. The sick feeling I get whenever he touches me.

I just respond to his kiss as I always do. It's more important right now more than ever not to screw up. I don't want him to get a scent of anything being different with me.

He steps back, releasing his hold on my chin.

I hate you.

"Have a good day." I smile. Forced but practiced.

He opens the door to leave. "I mean it, Annie. Don't go out today."

"I won't. I promise."

Just go.

He steps through the door. Anticipation lifts my heart rate.

Then, he stops and turns back to look at me over his shoulder.

My stomach tightens with fear.

Not for myself.

I stopped fearing for my own life a long time ago.

When you no longer fear death but wish for it, you have nothing to lose. But, now, I'm having a baby; it's not just my life anymore. I owe it to my child to give him or her the best chance in life.

"Aren't you forgetting something?" he speaks in a harsh voice, brow raised.

Fudge. Fudge. Fudge.

"I love you," I tell him, swallowing nervously.

He stares at me for what feels like forever, his expression questioning.

I hold my face and body as still as possible, wishing my heart to slow down its racing beats.

Then, finally, after what feels like forever, he speaks, "I love you, Annie. Till death do us part."

"Till death do us part," I echo the lie with ease.

Never, ever again.

The door closes behind him.

I let out a quiet breath. One that I've been holding all morning.

I stand here, listening. Waiting.

His car engine starts.

I hear it pull away.

I wait a beat to be sure he's definitely gone.

And then I spring into action.

I run upstairs and dress quickly into a pair of jeans and a T-shirt, and then I slip my feet into my sneakers. I grab my old beaten-up brown leather duffel bag from the closet. The one that I brought my clothes and memory box in when I moved out of my foster home at eighteen and moved in with Neil.

I don't have any family. I'm a foster kid. I was taken from my drug-addicted, prostitute mother when I was a baby and placed in foster care. It was never known who my father was. Probably one of her johns.

I guess that's why I fell into Neil's arms and lies so easily.

He was older. Mature. And I was desperate for stability. A family of my own.

I was eighteen. Fresh out of school and hoping to start community college. I was mugged one night, walking home from the subway. Neil happened to be walking past when it happened. He was off-duty at the time.

He caught the guy and arrested him. I got my purse back and a date with an older, handsome cop for the following night.

I moved in with him a week later.

My nightmare started six months later when he beat me for the first time.

The night after we were married.

Before that, he had been so wonderful. I couldn't believe that this amazing guy wanted to be with someone like me.

Now, I realize that I was an easy target.

Easy to manipulate and control.

I'd thought I was lucky to get him when, in reality, it was the worst thing that had ever happened to me.

I go into my closet and get my memory box. It has a few things inside, like our wedding certificate. A ticket stub from our first cinema date. The champagne cork from when he asked me to marry him.

All those things can go in the trash for all I care.

I open it up and take out the two things I need that will help me disappear. The identification card and birth certificate with my new name.

I put them in the inside zip pocket of the duffel bag and zip them safely up.

Then, I get the clothes and underwear I already planned to take with me and put them in the duffel bag. There's no point in taking too much with me. Less to carry, and I won't fit in those clothes soon anyway.

I tie my long blonde hair up into a tight bun, and then I pull on a baseball cap over it.

I go into our bathroom and get my toothbrush, toothpaste, and other toiletries and put them into my cosmetics bag. That goes in the duffel bag with my clothes.

I carry the bag downstairs and go into Neil's office. The silence is eerie. I hate this room the most.

Even though I know I'm alone, a shudder still runs through me.

I'm still afraid that he's going to show back up at home and catch me.

I walk quickly over to his desk and crouch down, putting my duffel beside me. I open the door on the desk.

I move the folders stacked in front of the safe, putting them on the floor.

I slip the key to the desk from my pocket. The key I had to steal from him, copy, and put back before he knew it was gone.

The day I did that was one of the scariest I'd had, and I'd spent the last seven years being afraid. I was terrified that he was going to find me out, and that would be it for the baby and me.

But he didn't, and this is happening. I'm going to get the money and get out of here, and everything is going to be okay.

A fear hits me.

What if the money's gone? What if he took it out for some reason?

I guess there's only one way to find out.

Well, either way, I'm still going. I'm not spending another day here with him. I'll just have to figure something else out.

Holding my breath, I unlock the safe.

And exhale.

The money is still here.

I don't know exactly how much money is in here. Hundreds of thousands, I would guess.

All I need is enough to get me out of here and pay my rent until I can get a job, which I worked out to be about six thousand. I know I'll probably have to pay at least six months rent up-front because I won't have a reference to give them.

But ... what if no one will hire me because I'm pregnant? What if I run out of money, no one will give me a job, and I can't pay my rent?

God.

I hate myself for what I'm considering doing. I take a deep breath, holding it in.

It's not like you aren't owed, Annie.

I know. But I didn't want it to be like this. I wanted to be able to take care of the baby myself. Earn my own money.

And you will, but right now, you need money, no matter where it comes from.

I let out the breath I was holding and take ten thousand from the safe.

I'll donate whatever I don't use to a women's shelter.

I shut the safe door, locking it. Put the folders back in front and close the desk door.

I carry the duffel out to the hallway, putting it down. I get my jacket from the coat closet and slip it on. I pick the duffel bag back up and hang the long strap over my shoulder.

My cell is still on the bedside table. It can stay there. I won't need it anymore. If I took it with me, Neil would put a trace on it to find me.

I walk out the front door, leaving Annie Coombs behind, and become Carrie Ford.

Carrie

The real Carrie Ford died five years ago in an automobile accident. She was twenty-five. The age that I am now. We look similar—same pale skin, same blue eyes—but she had gorgeous long red hair, whereas mine is blonde.

But women change their hair color often, so I can pass for her.

I never knew her, Carrie.

She was the granddaughter of the only friend I have. The friend my husband doesn't know I have.

Neil has never allowed me to have friends.

But I needed someone, and Mrs. Ford is amazing. She lives in the house three doors down.

She's in her late seventies and the sweetest lady you've ever met.

We became friendly when I was out, tending the front garden, and she would stop to chat.

One day, she invited me in for a slice of homemade cake and a cup of coffee, and after that, we were friends.

After a time, she noticed the bruises. She never commented on them. But we both knew that she knew my husband was beating me.

When I found out I was pregnant, I broke down and told her what was happening. How I needed to get out, but I didn't know how.

She knew I couldn't call the cops on Neil. And there was no way she could hide me there.

The only way was to disappear.

That was when she left the room and gave me the best gift I'd ever received. She gave me her granddaughter's identity card and birth certificate. She told me to take it. Change my name and disappear.

I finally had a way out.

She offered me money, too, but I couldn't take it.

I knew another way to get money anyway.

I hugged her tight. Thanked her.

And that was the start of how I was able to disappear.

I will thank Carrie Ford every day for the gift of her name.

Mrs. Ford and I said our good-byes yesterday. I'm going to miss her so much.

I walk quickly in the direction of the bus depot.

I'm jumping at every passing car and noise I hear, terrified that one of those cars is going to be Neil.

You're okay. He's in the city.

But what if one of his buddies is in a patrol car and sees me?

My fast walk becomes a jog.

Calm down. You're making yourself look more conspicuous.

I slow my jog back down to a fast walk.

Ten minutes later, without being seen, I reach the bus depot.

You're almost there. Nearly free.

Stopping outside the door to the bus depot, I pull the brim of my baseball cap down, shading my eyes, needing to cover my face. There are CCTV cameras inside the depot. Cameras that Neil will be able to get access to if he figures out how I left town and tries to find out which bus I left on. Also, I need to hide the red swelling on my cheek. It'd make me a little more memorable if he questioned the ticket cashiers, which is the last thing I want. Unfortunately, there isn't much that I can do about my split lip.

Through the glass door of the depot, I can see the electronic board detailing all of the upcoming bus departure times.

The next bus leaving is in fifteen minutes, going to a place called Canyon Lake in Texas.

Texas is hot.

I hate the heat. Being fair-skinned means I fry like chicken in the sun.

Neil knows this. So, he would never think that I would go to Texas.

It's perfect.

Keeping my head down, I take a deep breath, pull open the door, and walk inside the busy depot.

I walk quickly but calmly to an open counter. I purchase a one-way ticket to Canyon Lake, paying in cash.

Taking my ticket, I leave the depot and head for where the bus is waiting to take me far away from here.

Seeing a trash can, I stop.

I stare down at my left hand. My wedding ring.

A barrage of memories runs through my mind.

Our first date. The first time we had sex. Our wedding day.

The first time he hit me. The first time he raped me. The first time he choked me so badly that I passed out.

I pull my wedding ring off and drop it in the trash.

Then, I walk to the bus without a backward glance and climb on it. Trying to act normal, like I'm not running from my abusive husband and using the identification of a dead woman. I show the driver my ticket. He asks to see my ID card.

Swallowing nervously, I get it from my bag and hand it to him. He gives it a quick glance and hands it back to me.

And that's it.

I've done it.

I make my way down the aisle and sit down in a window seat, toward the back, putting my duffel at my feet.

And I let out a deep breath. My heart is racing in my chest.

I did it.

I'm on the bus that's going to take me to my freedom.

I keep expecting Neil to appear and drag me off the bus.

But he never does appear.

And the door closes on the bus, and it pulls out of the depot.

Taking me to my new life.

Carrie

I step off the bus into the bright sunshine and take in my new surroundings.

So, this is Canyon Lake.

My new home.

Our new home.

I press my hand to my flat stomach. "You hear that?" I whisper to the baby, leaning my head down. "We're home. We're safe."

The light breeze picks up my hair, a flash of red going across my gaze.

I brush away the strands, tucking it behind my ear.

I'm a redhead now. Vibrant red.

I dyed my hair in the restroom at the first of the many rest stops on the journey here. I bought an at-home hair dye from the store there along with a romance paperback and a burner phone.

The red is taking some getting used to after having blonde hair my whole life. But I do like it.

It makes my eye color pop, and the smattering of freckles on my nose look more prominent.

I look different. And different is exactly how I need to look.

I can't be Annie anymore. I have to be Carrie to survive.

I might still have the bruise on my face and the cut on my lip, but they'll be gone soon, and when they are, all traces of Annie will be gone, and I'll just be Carrie.

I move away from the bus, walking over to the sidewalk. I put my bag down for a moment. It's seriously warm here.

I know Texas is known for its heat, but I didn't think it would be this warm in November.

I look around, and other people don't seem bothered by the heat.

Either they're used to it or I'm a heat-phobe.

Or my body temperature has gone up a few notches since I became pregnant. Working back from my last period, I figure out that my baby is due in July sometime.

Jeez, if it's like this now, I'm going to be hugely pregnant in the hottest place in the US. I clearly didn't think through coming here well enough.

Well, I wasn't really thinking at all. Apart from choosing the first bus departing and Neil never thinking to look for me here in a million years.

Him not finding me here is worth suffering the heat through my pregnancy. I'll just invest in good air-conditioning and a portable fan.

On the subject of my due date, I haven't seen a doctor yet. Once I found out I was pregnant, everything had to move so quickly.

Registering with a doctor is on my list after getting a place to live. And, hopefully, I've already found the place.

On my long journey here, using my new phone, I started looking online at available rentals in Canyon Lake. It was slim pickings. There wasn't a lot to choose from. They were all either one-bed apartments or three-bed houses, and I need two bedrooms for the baby and me. I would rather not have to take a one-bed if possible, as it would mean having to move again when the baby started to grow.

So, it felt like fate when I stumbled across a two-bedroom, fully furnished house. The details said that it sat on a quiet residential street and that the house backed onto open forestland, which led through to the Guadalupe River.

There weren't any pictures of the house, but I'm not worried about that. It could be a shack, and I wouldn't care. So long as it's mine.

I called the number listed and spoke to the realtor, a pleasant-sounding woman called Marla. She said the house had literally just gone on the rental market, and that was why there weren't any pictures online yet.

That was when I knew it was meant to be.

For a moment, I felt like it was all too easy. Getting away from Neil. Finding this house.

But then I figured that I hadn't had it easy for most of my life and especially not the last seven years, so I was owed.

I asked Marla if I could view the house today, and she said that would be no problem. I did think it'd be best to be honest, so as not to waste my time or hers, and I told her that I didn't have references, but I could pay cash up-front, which she seemed more than happy with.

So, my appointment to meet her at the house is at one thirty. The bus was due to arrive here at one, which would give me a chance to get to the house. I pull out my phone to search for the address on Google Maps and see the time on my phone display—*1:27*.

Fudge knuckles.

I didn't realize the bus was even running late.

I quickly type the address into Google Maps to see how long it'll take me to walk there.

Fifteen minutes.

I fire off a quick text to the realtor, letting her know that I'm running a little late, and then, hooking my duffel higher on my shoulder, I start walking.

Fifteen minutes later, I'm walking down a beautiful tree-lined street. It's so peaceful down here. The only sound is from the birds.

The map tells me the house I'm looking for is near the end of the dead-end street.

A minute later, I spot the rental sign and the house that sits just beyond that.

It's love at first sight.

It's an old house, and I love old houses. It's a little weathered, like myself, but nothing a lick of paint won't fix.

It's single-story, which will be ideal for when the baby is here and crawling around—no stairs to worry about.

It has a front yard, and after a little gardening, which I enjoy doing, it will be great. I can imagine sitting out here in the front yard with the baby, maybe even chatting with neighbors as they pass.

I walk up the path toward the front door, and the door opens up just before I reach it.

"Miss Ford?" an attractive forty-something blonde lady greets me with a glossy-red-lipstick smile.

I see the moment her eyes catch sight of the now-black bruise on my cheek because her smile falters.

Shame curdles in my gut. I tilt my head down, letting my hair fall over my face, covering it. "Yes. But call me An—" I catch myself. "Carrie," I say clearly, scolding myself internally.

I really need to get used to calling myself Carrie.

Her smile comes back full force. "It's nice to meet you, Carrie." She reaches a hand out, and we shake hands. "I'm Marla. We spoke on the phone."

"Yes, of course."

"Would you like to come in and have a look around?" She gestures me inside to the small hallway and closes the door behind us. "Right then, follow me, and I'll give you the tour."

I follow her around the house, a smile on my face the whole time. I probably look like a crazy person, but I don't care. I'm just so happy to be here.

The house is perfect.

There's a large master that has its own bathroom, and the second bedroom, which will be the nursery, is also a good size and is right across the hall. And the main bathroom is right next door to it. The baby's room also looks out onto the back garden.

The house is fully furnished, which means I don't have to worry about furniture, only a crib for the nursery. And I just need to get some bedsheets for my bed and towels for the bathroom.

I have a really good feeling about this house. It feels … safe.

It's everything I've ever wanted.

A home.

I'm finally home.

"So, what do you think?" Marla asks me, stopping in the living room, back to where we started.

"I'll take it," I tell her without hesitation.

She smiles widely, showing me a full set of cosmetically enhanced pearly-white teeth. "Wonderful." She claps her hands together. "So, I will need at least six months rent up-front, with you not having any references."

"That's no problem," I tell her.

"Great. Well, I'll just go get the paperwork out of my car."

While she's gone, I count out the money that I'll need to cover six months rent.

Half an hour later, I've signed the lease, and I'm watching Marla as she pulls away in her shiny Audi.

I step back inside the house and close the door. Locking it behind me.

Then, I rest my forehead against the door and just breathe for a minute.

You did it, Annie. You got away from him. Your life starts now.

I take one last deep breath in before moving away from the door. I go and retrieve my duffel bag and then take it into the master bedroom with me.

I take out my clothes and toiletries and dump them on the bed. I take a few hundred dollars out and leave the rest of the money in there along with the ID card and birth certificate. I carry the bag over to the small walk-in-closet. I open up the largest drawer in the closet and stuff the duffel in there. I'll figure out a safer place to keep the money once I've familiarized myself with the house.

I peel my days-old clothes off, turn the shower on hot, and climb in, enjoying the feel of the almost burn on my skin. Washing away my past. The water runs pale red—the remnants of the dye in my hair that I didn't properly wash out in my rest-stop dye job.

I'm free.

Tears join the water, and I watch my past go down the drain.

I turn the shower off and grab the ratty old towel hanging on the rail.

I'll buy some new ones when I go to the store.

I dry off and brush my hair, leaving it down. I dress in jeans and a T-shirt. I'm going to need some clothes. Preferably shorts, tanks, and cotton dresses.

I go into the kitchen and make myself herbal tea, using a tea sachet that I got at one of the rest stops. I fill the kettle with water and turn it on, and then I locate the cups while it boils.

I make my tea, and carrying it out back, I stand on the porch. I rest my elbows on the railing.

I could do with a chair out here, so I could sit down and enjoy the solitude. But, for now, I'll stand and enjoy what I have.

It's so quiet. I've never known peace like it.

It's a soothing kind of silence. The kind that wraps you up and cocoons you.

It's perfect.

It's everything.

I take a sip of my tea, and then I hear Queen's "Bohemian Rhapsody" start to play from the neighboring house on my right.

I love this song. I don't even care that it's infiltrated my peace. If anything, it makes me smile.

My new neighbor has great taste in music.

Softly singing along to the lyrics, I glance over at my neighbor's place. I noticed the house earlier. It's hard not to. It's huge. It takes up most of the end of the street. It's a big, old colonial-style house. Without a doubt, it's the largest house on the street. It has one of those gorgeous wraparound porches, and the back part of the porch is visible from where I'm standing. I can see into the garden, too, and there's a pool out there. The garden is about twenty times the size of this one. There's a brick building, too. Probably a garage or work shed.

I wonder who lives there.

A house that size with a swimming pool, they're definitely wealthy. Maybe they've got kids. Young kids would be great because the baby would have someone to play with when it got a bit older.

Happiness warms my stomach at the thought that I could—no, that I *will* be here in years, watching my child grow, free of the past, and the baby will never know what my life was like before here.

I start humming along with Queen.

Then, I hear a screen door slam shut, and I bring my eyes to the sound.

There's a guy out on the back porch of the house. He's really tall from what I can tell. He has a head full of wavy, dark hair. I catch a glimpse of copper in it when he moves, the sunlight catching and highlighting the russet strands. It's shaved on the sides and long on the top. His chin is covered in what looks to be a good few days' worth of stubble.

Neil would never have stubble. He said it looked scruffy.

I like stubble and beards. I never told Neil that though. Opinions weren't something I was allowed to have.

One of my foster dads, Henry, had a beard. He was my favorite foster dad. A genuinely nice man. His beard was white though. Reminded me of Santa's beard.

He died though. He was old, to be fair. After he passed away, I continued living with Sandra, his wife. But then she followed him a year later.

I think her heart broke the day he died, and it never recovered.

I was moved to a new foster family.

So, yeah, beards give me a warm feeling inside.

From here, I can't tell how old my new neighbor is. I'd say, definitely under thirty. He has tattoos. Both arms are covered in them. His black T-shirt shows them off nicely.

Neil didn't like tattoos either.

He said tattoos and criminality went together hand in hand.

Neil still lived in the 1950s.

As Neil would say, my new neighbor looks like the kind of guy he puts in jail every day.

That means, he's probably nicer than my husband.

Sorry, my *ex-husband.*

Wow. That feels freeing, calling him that.

Not that I'll ever be able to divorce him. Not without alerting him to where I am, which I will never do. But I'm away from him, and that's all that matters.

I'm here, in my new home, starting my new life.

And my new neighbor is a walking version of everything that Neil doesn't like.

It makes me like him instantly.

My eyes move down to his hands, and I see a book in one and a glass of something in the other. He has what appears to be a cigar case tucked under his arm.

I watch as he puts the glass and cigar case down on the table. Then, he gets something out from one of his front pockets of his black jeans and tosses it onto the table—probably a lighter.

Then, without warning, he turns in my direction, catching me staring.

Fudgesicles.

I feel my face start to heat.

I'm going to have to say something; otherwise, I'm just going to look like a creeper.

I straighten up and lift my hand in greeting. "Hi." I smile.

He doesn't respond. Maybe he didn't hear me.

I speak louder this time, "I'm your new neighbor, An—" *Fudge.* "Carrie. My name is Carrie."

I get nothing.

He's just standing there, staring at me.

His eyes are dark and intense.

And hard.

Cold.

A chill slithers through me, all the warmth I was feeling a moment ago disappearing.

I shift on my bare feet. I don't know what to do. Do I just go back inside? But that would be rude.

But he's being rude, ignoring me.

Maybe he isn't actually ignoring me, and he really just can't hear me from all the way over there.

I decide to try one last time and yell over, "My name is Carrie. I just—"

The words die on my tongue when he abruptly turns around and stalks back inside his house.

The screen door slams so hard behind him that it bounces off the frame, making a loud cracking sound.

A few seconds later, the music stops playing, leaving me in total silence.

And this silence doesn't feel quite so welcoming.

Carrie

After my not-so-nice, awkward encounter with my rude neighbor, I decide to take a walk into town to find a grocery store and somewhere that sells bath towels and bed linens. I don't need to worry about buying a duvet with how warm I am at the moment, which I don't see changing anytime soon and which will only get worse the more pregnant I become.

So, I just need sheets, pillows, and pillowcases. And sunscreen. Because I'll fry like a piece of bacon if I don't wear it.

I should get some cover-up for my face, too.

Maybe that's why he was rude to me. Maybe he saw this bruise on my face and thought I was some kind of trouble. That I would bring trouble to the neighborhood.

Well, there's not much I can do about covering it up now. So, I do the only thing I can. I grab my hairbrush and part my hair over to the side, so it drapes over my eye and covers my cheek.

Using Google Maps, I start walking in the direction of where it says the closest grocery store is because my feet are my current mode of transport. Hopefully, I can get everything I need from there.

Maybe I should think about getting a car.

But that would mean spending more of Neil's dirty money than necessary.

No, thanks.

Get a job first. Then, maybe a car.

The walk to the supermarket is nice. Canyon Lake is a pretty place.

It's leafier than I would have expected for Texas.

As I near the town center, I spot a diner across the street. *Sadie's Diner*, the sign above the storefront says.

It's been a while since I last ate, so maybe I should grab some food here before going to the supermarket.

As I near the diner, I see a sign in the window that says they serve the best pies this side of Texas. I also see another sign in the window that makes my heart lift—*Help Wanted: Part-time waitress. Experience preferred but not essential. Smile is a must though. Apply within.*

Okay, so I'll grab some food here and a job, too, if I'm lucky.

I pull open the door and step inside the diner. Music is playing in the background. There are a few customers seated at the tables and booths.

Sweet Lord, it smells like heaven in here. Coffee scent fills the air, but it's the cherry-pie smell that captures my attention.

My stomach rumbles its enthusiasm.

Taking a seat on a stool at the counter, I try to think of the last time I ate out. And I can't remember.

We always ate at home. Neil really didn't like to eat out. He had a thing about different people touching his food.

I always cooked. Sometimes to his satisfaction. Sometimes not.

"Order up for table eight," a male voice calls from the kitchen behind the counter.

He appears a second later, putting two plates on the serving counter. He looks Latino. His hair is buzzed short. Angular, handsome face. Clean-shaven.

A waitress comes breezing past me and grabs the plates that the Latino guy, who I'm assuming is the cook, just put on the serving counter. She picks them up, smiling at me as she passes. "I'll be with you in a minute, hon."

"No rush," I tell her. Picking up a menu from the counter, I start to read it.

There's a smile on my face. And that's because I like it in here. It has a really warm, happy vibe to it.

The waitress appears back in front of me a few minutes later. "You ready to order?" she cheerily asks me.

I lift my head from the menu to look at her.

She has an order pad and pencil in her hand. Her name badge says *Sadie*. The diner is called Sadie's. I'm guessing she's the owner.

She's really pretty. About my height, five-six. Older than me. I'd say maybe early thirties. Light-brown hair, which is pinned up. A bright smile on her face.

That seems to dim when it flickers over my face.

The bruise.

Self-consciously, I tilt my head to the side, covering my cheek with my hair. The smile I was wearing just before, gone.

"Could I get a piece of cherry pie, please?" I was sold the second I smelled it when I walked in. "And a decaf tea, if possible."

"Sure. Anything with the pie—cream, ice cream?"

"Just the pie," I tell her.

"You got it." She smiles again. Not writing down my order. She puts her pad and pencil on the counter.

I watch as she moves around behind the counter, getting a plate, putting a piece of cherry pie on it for me, and putting it down in front of me along with fresh cutlery.

"Any sweetener or creamer for your tea?" she asks me as she grabs a cup and makes my tea, using the machine.

"No, thank you."

She puts a teapot, cup, and saucer down next to my pie. "You on vacation?" she congenially asks me.

I can tell she's trying not to look at my bruise, and I appreciate that, but honestly, in this moment, I feel tired of hiding it.

I lift my head, letting my hair fall back. "No, I just moved here," I tell her.

"We don't get many new people round here but plenty of tourists," she tells me.

"I can see why. It's a beautiful place."

"Yeah, it is. So, what brought you here? Family? I probably know them. It's hard not to know everybody in a town like this."

I shake my head, cutting a piece of pie. I put it in my mouth and chew, delaying my response. "No family. Just wanted a change of scenery."

"Oh. Sure." She nods, her eyes flickering to my mouth—the cut there—and back to my cheek before meeting my eyes. "It's a good place to move to. I came here ten years ago for a fresh start." She pauses, contemplating something.

I watch her expression. She looks like she's having some kind of internal argument. I see when she settles on it.

Then, she parts her lips and speaks, "Pardon me for saying this, but that's one helluva bruise you have there. I'm sure you've had it checked out, but—"

"It's fine." My hand instantly covers my cheek. The fork that I was holding clattering to the counter.

The good feeling in my chest starts to shrivel up.

"Look, you can tell me to mind my own business, but I was you ten years ago. I rolled up in town, covered in bruises—"

"I'm not covered in bruises. I just got hit in the face by a door. That's all. Nothing more. And you're right; you really should mind your own business," I snap.

It's not like me to be this assertive, but I'm upset that this woman took my good feeling from me. Just like my good feeling was stolen away by my jerk neighbor earlier.

Some people really can be sunshine-stealers.

And I don't want to be around those kind of people.

I stand, shoving my hand in my pocket, pulling out my money to pay for my food, so I can get the heck out of this place.

So much for my pie and the possibility of a job.

"Look, I'm sorry," she placates, putting her hands on the counter. "I'm not trying to interfere. I just know what it's like to be new in town with"—she gestures to her face—"while running from the person who gave them to you."

I bite the inside of my cheek. "It was a door."

"Okay"—she nods—"it was a door. I hear you. And I'm sorry that I upset you. The pie is on me. Please stay and finish it."

I pause for a moment, looking at her expression, the warmth in it, and I realize that she was only genuinely trying to be caring. And I also realize that I'm staring at a woman who went through something similar to what I've been through.

I slowly sit back down and pick up the fork, cutting off another piece of pie.

"Holler if you need anything," she tells me before walking away to tend to another customer who's approached the counter to pay his bill.

I eat my food and drink my tea in silence, just listening to the music, the sound of the pans cooking in the kitchen, and the low hum of chatter.

I'm just finishing up my tea when she reappears in front of me. "Can I get you anything else?" she asks.

"No, thanks."

"I am sorry about before," she says to me. "My being pushy."

"It's fine. I probably overreacted a little bit," I admit.

"No, you didn't. You were well within your right to say what you did."

Her words make me feel a little better.

"Can I just say ..." she continues. "And I'm only saying this with you being new to town and not knowing anyone, but decaf tea ... there's usually only one reason a woman round here drinks anything decaf, and that's because she's pregnant. Now, I'm not asking; I'm just saying, if you are, you're going to need a doctor, and the best around here is Dr. Mathers."

"Dr. Mathers," I repeat. "I'll give him a call. Thank you."

Her eyes go to my still-flat stomach. "So ... how far along are you? If you don't mind me asking."

I realize that she's the only other person, aside from Mrs. Ford, I have told about the baby.

I get the feeling she's actually not being nosy. She's caring. Which is why I don't mind answering. "I'm not sure exactly. But I'm not far along."

She offers a kind smile. "Well, Dr. Mathers will help you with that. And congratulations, by the way."

"Thank you." I slide off the stool, standing.

"Well, if you need anything ..." She pauses, waiting for me to tell her my name.

"Carrie," I fill in the blank for her.

"Carrie. I'm Sadie, which you've probably figured." She gestures to her name badge. "And you've also probably already figured that this is my place."

"It wouldn't take a genius."

I smile, and she laughs.

"Well, I just wanted to say, if you ever need anything—pie, decaf tea—you know where to find me."

"Actually, there is something I need …" I glance at the sign in the window before looking back to her. "I don't know how you feel about hiring pregnant women, but I really need a job."

"Have you waitressed before?" she asks.

I bite my lower lip. "No."

"When could you start?"

"Tomorrow," I suggest.

She thoughtfully purses her lips. "How would you feel about working the breakfast shift?"

"I'd feel great." And that's the truth.

"Okay. Be here tomorrow morning at six a.m. sharp, and I'll show you the ropes."

"I'm … hired?" I ask, daring to hope.

Her expression softens, and she smiles. "You're hired."

My own smile is bigger than this town. "Thank you so much, Sadie. I can't tell you how much I appreciate it."

"Work the breakfast shift first, and we'll see if you still feel that way," she jokes.

I laugh.

It feels light. I feel light.

"Okay"—I start for the door—"I'll see you bright and early tomorrow morning."

"Carrie," she softly calls my name, and I stop and turn around. She takes a step toward me, her voice lowering. "I just want to say … I'm really glad you got away from … the door."

The moment suddenly feels weighted with unspoken words. But also a kindred spirit. Like I'm finally talking to someone who understands.

Who knows what it's like to live the life I had.

Who gets why I still feel the need to lie and hide exactly where my bruises really came from.

The shame that still lives inside me.

I give a small smile, my hand pressing to my stomach. "Me, too," I say quietly. I'm about to turn away when something stops me, and I find myself saying, "Can I ask you something?"

"Sure." She smiles.

"Did the, um … did the … door you ran from, did it ever find you?"

"No," she confidently tells me. "My door never found me."

Carrie

I *have a job! An actual job!*

I would be skipping the whole way home if I wasn't weighed down by the obscene amount of groceries I was carrying.

But I have no one to blame but myself.

I got a little carried away at the store, which luckily also sold bedsheets and bath towels. But I also realized that I needed some pillows for the bed, so I bought two of those along with the essentials—bread, milk, eggs, oranges for fresh juice in the morning, pancake mix, and bacon.

So, I'm carrying a lot of stuff home. There are no local buses or taxis.

So, my feet it is.

I'm walking up the street, not too far from my house. There's no pavement on this part, so I'm walking in the middle of the road so that I'm visible to motorists. Not that any cars have passed me so far.

It's looking more and more likely that I'm going to need a car because walking groceries home all the time is not going to be easy, the more pregnant I get.

But, hopefully, I'll be able to get one soon when I start earning money from my new job.

I can't believe I have a job. I haven't worked since I was eighteen. After I left high school, I worked as a cashier at a local supermarket right before I met Neil. When I moved in with him, he had me quit my job.

Well, I'll never be quitting this job. The only way they'll get rid of me is if they sack me.

God, what if I'm really bad at the job and Sadie does sack me? I've never waitressed before. I mean, I know it's a case of taking down orders and getting food from the kitchen to the customer, but what if I can't remember who ordered what, and I mix things up?

No, it's going to be okay.

Sadie is going to show me what to do, and I'm going to figure it out just fine. Because I need this job.

The baby and I need this job.

I can do this, no prob—

Ah, nuts!

One of my plastic shopping bags has broken, and my food is currently all over the road.

The milk carton has split open and is pouring out onto the road. The oranges are rolling off in every direction, and I don't have a good feeling about the eggs.

I put my other shopping bags down and take a quick look at the egg carton, flipping it open.

Yep, they're all done for.

Double nuts!

I pick up the pancake mix and bacon, and then I start running around after the oranges, gathering them up.

I hear the roar of a car engine and lift my head to see a truck heading my way.

Hands full, I call out in a loud voice, "Hey! You need to stop. My stuff is in the street!"

But the truck doesn't stop, and I figure the driver couldn't hear me over the noise of the engine.

Tucking the food from both arms to one, I wave a hand to get the driver's attention.

But it doesn't seem to work.

If anything, the truck seems to have sped up. And it's getting closer and closer to the rest of my shopping items.

I move forward a step, dropping the food in my arms, and start waving them both in the air to get the driver's attention.

My new pillows, bedding, and towels are in those bags.

"Hey!" I repeat, yelling, hands waving. "You need to stop!"

But the truck doesn't stop, and I let out a cry of "No!" as the truck's big wheels run straight over my shopping bags.

"You mother-fudging son of a C-U-Next-Tuesday!" I yell at the back of the truck speeding away.

I can't believe this!

I let out a little yelp of upset when I see my now-squished shopping bags.

And, oh Christ, the truck went over the egg box, and the contents have splattered all over the shopping bags and my new bath towels.

I didn't get any laundry detergent, so I can't wash them yet, meaning I'll have to keep using the ratty old towel in the bathroom until I can.

Oh well, I've had worse things happen to me.

And the one saving grace is that my bed linens and pillows are covered in plastic wrap, which protected them. They might be a bit crushed, but they're still usable.

Going back, I gather up the oranges, pancake mix, and bacon. Then, I gingerly pick up the shopping bags.

The egg yolk drips off them.

Gross.

I start walking again.

I can't believe that driver. There is no way that he or she didn't at least see me. Fair enough if they didn't hear me, but I was literally jumping around, waving my hands in the air.

But whomever it was just chose to ignore me and ran straight over my stuff.

I round the corner and walk up the street toward my house.

I'm just about to turn up my path when I spot a truck sitting in my grumpy neighbor's driveway.

The truck that just ran over my stuff.

I know it's that truck because it was blue and had *Ford* in big silver letters on the front grill, which is the exact same truck currently sitting in his driveway.

It was him!

Oh my God! That guy is … he's a … well, he's a complete and utter asshat!

And, just as I think it, the asshat himself walks around from the back of the truck, carrying a bag of something—probably groceries—in his arms, which just annoys me even more.

He stops upon seeing me just standing here.

His eyes go down to the bags in my hand. Then, up to my face.

He frowns at me. His dark brows are like angry slashes above his hard eyes. "What the hell is your problem?" he barks at me. "Don't you know that it's fucking rude to stare?"

My mouth drops open at the sheer audacity of him.

He ran over my things and then has the brazenness to stand there and say those things to me.

The cheeky … son of a nutcracker!

I want to say something. But I don't know what.

I'm not good at confrontation.

But, if I was going to say something, I don't get the chance because he gives me one last look of disdain before he turns abruptly and walks inside his house, the door slamming loudly behind him.

Leaving me still standing here, mouth wide open in shock.

Twice in one day, he's done this to me.

Twice, he's been rude to me and then just walked away.

Gah! I really, really dislike this guy!

I stomp up my front pathway, let myself inside my house, dump my bags on the kitchen table, and let out a sound of frustration.

Ugh!

I swear to God, the next time he says something mean to me, I'm going to tell him exactly what I think of him.

Maybe.

I mean, I don't want to cause any trouble or bring any unnecessary attention to myself.

No! Stop being a coward.

You've spent the last seven years being belittled and hurt by a man.

No more.

So, the next time that guy speaks out of turn to me, he's getting the same right back.

River
Ten Years Old

"You got into another fight at school," Gran says the moment I walk in the door.

I'm guessing the school called her because she hasn't even looked at my face yet. I only got a busted-up lip though. The other kid came off worse.

I walk into the living room, where she is.

This is my gran's house. Well, my home, too. I live with her now.

Gran is sitting on her favorite armchair. She's smoking a cigar. She doesn't usually smoke them inside the house. Always out on the back porch. Things must be bad if she's smoking indoors.

I slip my backpack off and set it on the floor by the sofa. I take a seat.

She finally looks at me. "Are you all right?" she asks.

"Yeah." I nod. "Only my lip that got cut."

"You cleaned it up?"

I nod again.

She takes a puff of her cigar. The smoke filters in the air. Wafting into my nostrils.

I love the smell.

"You can't be fighting at school all the time, River."

I shrug. "The kid was an asshole. He said I was a freak." *And that my mom was a cop killer and that she should rot in jail.*

But she isn't a cop killer. I am. It should be me in prison, not her. But she wouldn't let me tell the truth.

She made me promise not to tell the truth about what had really happened that day in the kitchen. Not even to Grandma.

She said she'd failed me once. She wouldn't fail me this time.

I don't even know what she meant by that.

All I knew was, I didn't want them to take my mama away. But I didn't want to go to jail either. I was scared.

I'm still scared.

And angry. So damn angry all the time.

"Don't use that word," Gran tells me. "And you are not a freak." She leans forward to put her cigar out on the ashtray that sits on the coffee table. "The principal's threatening to expel you."

I shrug.

Like I care. I'd be happy to be out of that place. I hate it.

The kids are all assholes. The few friends that I used to have suddenly forgot my name when my mom got arrested.

Even the teachers ignore me.

I spend recess and lunchtime alone. Mostly, I just sit in the library and read.

I'm alone. But it's fine. Because I don't need anyone.

"Good," is my response to her words.

"River, your education is important. I know your grades are down after what happened, and that's expected, but the fighting has to stop. When those kids are giving you a hard time, you have to ignore them."

"Sure." I laugh, but I'm not feeling very funny right now. "I'll ignore them. So, when one of them punches me, I'm supposed to just walk away?"

"The boy today, did he hit you first?"

I kick the toe of my sneaker against the leg of the coffee table. "No."

She sighs. "Then, you walk away. But, if he hits you first, then you beat that boy's ass to the ground. You don't hit first, River. You hit second, and you hit harder. And I will back you the whole way with your principal. But you hit first, I got no defense for you."

I hide a smile. My gran can be kind of cool at times, but I don't want her to know I think that.

"And when they bad-mouth Mama? What am I supposed to do then, say nothing?"

The skin around her mouth tightens. "River"—she sighs again—"you can't stop what people say about your mama. And they're going to talk about what she did."

"They don't know anything!" I'm getting annoyed. I start to kick the table leg with more force.

"No, maybe they don't. They know what they hear in the news or from the gossip. But, as much as it pains me to say it, your mom is in prison because she killed someone."

"River, what have you done?"

My fists clench at my sides. My nails dig into my skin. I feel the moment the skin breaks.

"She shouldn't be in prison. And you won't even let me go see her."

"It's not me, River. You know this. Your mom doesn't want you to see her in that place."

"But she shouldn't be there!"

Another sigh. "I know you don't want to hear this—and I wish to God she wasn't there and that it hadn't happened—but she murdered him, River, and she has to pay for her crime."

"No, she didn't!" I yell, jumping up. The words are out of my mouth before I even realize.

Gran slowly stands up. Her eyes are staring at my face. "River?"

My body is shaking. I feel like I'm going to combust. There are all these words and noises in my head.

I dig my nails into my skin harder. I feel blood trickle down my palms. It normally calms me. But it isn't working this time.

"River …" she says my name firmer this time.

My eyes come to hers.

"What did you mean by that?"

"I-I …" I stammer. I haven't stammered in so long. "I-I … can't—"

"Talk to me," she snaps, her voice so harsh that it brings me to attention.

The words are out of my mouth before I can stop them. "It was me. I-I shot h-him."

Her face looks frozen. Her eyes are searching over my face like she's looking for something.

"Oh dear God," she whispers. Her old hands press to her face. She breathes in and out. Lowers her hands to her sides. "What happened?"

"I-I … c-can't …"

"Why did you shoot him? I don't understand. River, why would you do that? Answer me!"

She moves toward me in a quick movement, grabbing for my arm, and I stumble back.

"Don't touch me!" I cry.

She freezes. She's staring at me. Then, her expression crumbles. "Oh no. Oh God, no. River … did he … did he hurt you?"

"I c-can't. M-Mama said …"

"Oh God, River. I'm so sorry. But it's going to be okay now."

No, it's not. It's never going to be okay again.

"What did your mama tell you to do?"

I swallow. "To not tell anyone what really happened that day." *To not tell anyone what he did to me.*

"People won't understand, River. They'll treat you differently."

"And you haven't told anyone other than me?"

I shake my head.

"Okay. You don't speak this to another soul, you understand? You keep that promise to your mama. If you need to talk to someone, you talk to me."

I nod my head.

She reaches out to touch me but stops and holds her hands together in front of her. "No one's ever going to hurt you again, River. I swear to you."

I nod my head again.

"Do you have homework to do?" she suddenly asks me.

"No," I tell her.

"Good. We are going to carry on like everything is normal because, sometimes, that's the only way to get through things. And normality would mean punishment for getting into a fight at school."

"So, am I grounded?" Not that it would matter. It's not like I go anywhere, except to school.

She gives me a look, like she's just read the words in my mind.

"No, your punishment is to help me out in my workshop."

"Making that glass crap?"

My grandma does glassblowing. She has a workshop out back. She makes vases and shit and sells it to people.

She gives me a disapproving look. "Don't use that word. And it's not crap. It's art. And you, River, have way too much anger inside you. You need to learn how to handle that anger of yours, channel it, and the best way to do that is to work with something that's easily breakable."

Carrie

I'm sitting on my back porch on one of the Adirondack chairs I found for sale online for an absolute bargain. The two chairs came with a small table, which is where my achy feet are currently resting. The seller delivered them for free, which was a big help, as I still haven't invested in a car yet. So, I'm still walking everywhere. Honestly, I quite enjoy it, especially the walk to the diner every morning—where I've now officially been working for two weeks.

I love it.

The atmosphere in the diner is great.

Sadie is a brilliant boss, and she's also becoming a friend, I think. And Guy, who is the cook, seems like a nice person. I've only met one of the other waitresses, Shelley, as we have a brief shift crossover. She's a single mom, and she works when her kids are in school. She seems nice, too.

Folks in this town have been really welcoming and friendly. I'm enjoying meeting new people. It's wonderful, just being able to chat with them while I serve them without fear of retribution.

Not that I get a lot of time to stand around and chat with the customers because the diner is plenty busy from the moment the door opens. It's popular with locals and tourists.

I learned pretty quickly that Canyon Lake is a tourist town. People like to come here for the lake, those who enjoy water sports, and the warm weather.

I know the place is pretty as heck, but the continuing warmth is a nightmare for a heat-hating pregnant gal like myself.

It's supposed to be butt-freezing cold at this time of year. But, of course, it's not. I'm totally blaming global warming.

I mean, surely Texas must get cold at some point. Right?

I have at times questioned whether I made the right call in moving to Texas, but then I think about Neil and how this is the last place he'd think to look for me, and I know I did the right thing.

Even if it is eleven thirty and I'm as hot as balls, hence why I'm sitting outside with an iced tea, trying to cool down.

The electric fan I got for my room is doing nothing. I even tried taking a cool bath earlier. It worked just fine while I was in it. The moment I got out, I was uncomfortably warm again.

I cannot wait until I've earned enough money to afford to have air-conditioning fitted.

Leaning forward, I grab my iced tea from the table and take a sip, and then my eyes go straight back to the book I'm currently reading.

Sadie loaned it to me. She said it was amazing and that I had to read it, and she's not wrong. It's really good. It's about a tortured rock star and the girl he's in love with. *Le sigh*. If only real life were like books.

If it were, then I wouldn't be sitting here, pregnant and alone, on the run from an abusive husband.

I like to think there is real love out there.

Not for me though. This is the hand I was dealt. And I'm happy now. I have a baby on the way, and I couldn't be more excited about it.

I saw Dr. Mathers last week. He really is a great doctor, like Sadie said he was.

I had my first ever ultrasound while I was there, which was beyond anything I could've imagined. Seeing my baby on-screen brought emotions to my chest I hadn't even known I could feel. The baby doesn't look like a baby yet and is still only the size of a blueberry. That's what the website I'm following says; it charts the baby's weekly growth in comparison to fruit. But I'd never felt love and an overwhelming urge to protect like I felt in that moment, staring at the fuzzy black-and-white screen. Dr. Mathers gave me a printout of the ultrasound. It's taking pride of place on the mantel above the fireplace in the living room.

He also told me that I was six weeks pregnant, meaning I'm seven weeks now. My due date is the seventeenth of July, next year. And I cannot wait to meet my baby. Dr. Mathers said I could find out the gender of my baby at my next ultrasound if I would like. I'm not sure yet though. I do like the idea of knowing, so I can get organized. But I also like the idea of a surprise.

The sensor light comes on in my next-door neighbor's garden, catching my eye.

Guy from work told me my grumpy asshole neighbor is called River Wild.

Not that I was asking Guy about him. It was purely just happenstance. I was sitting at the counter on my first day with Sadie, and she was filling in my employee form as I provided her with the details, which honestly made me feel twitchy and kind of awful for having to lie to her about my name and date of birth.

But, anyway, I just recited my address to her, and Guy, who was standing nearby at the time, said, "Oh, you live next door to River."

And I confusedly said, "River?"

And Guy said, "Yeah, River Wild. Your new neighbor. Hot as Hades. Crazy as Kanye. And as mean as Regina."

And I said, "Regina?"

And he said, "George."

So, I said, "Oh, right. Yeah, I've met him—River." I didn't elaborate that, the first time I'd met him, he'd ignored me, and the second time was after he'd run over my groceries with his big, stupid truck, once again being a jerk.

Then, Guy said, "I went to school with him. The guy has serious—"

And the conversation was cut off when a timer went off in the kitchen, and Guy scooted off before finishing his sentence.

And, even though I was dying to glean more information from Guy about River, I didn't feel right in doing so. I don't want people asking questions about me, so me being nosy about him would have felt wrong.

I haven't spoken to River since he ran over my stuff—if you could call it speaking; it's more like him being a jerk to me. I have seen him a few times when he's been in the garden. I even saw him in the supermarket one time, and he point-blank ignored me. But I don't care. I don't want to be his friend.

I see movement over by his pool and wonder if it's him.

Lord, that pool.

What I wouldn't give to be able to jump in that cool water right now.

I'd honestly jump straight in there, wearing the pajama tank and shorts I have on, and I wouldn't care.

But it isn't River over by the pool. It appears to be a small animal.

Too big to be a squirrel. But too small to be a bear.

Are there any bears in Texas?

God, I hope not.

I can't see from here what it is.

I don't know why I'm so bothered, to be honest.

Letting curiosity get the better of me, I put my book down and get to my feet. I walk over to the railing to get a better look.

Oh, it's a dog.

I didn't know he had a dog.

I've never heard one barking or seen one in his garden before.

He probably keeps it cooped inside his gloomy house, the poor thing.

I think it's one of those shih tzu dogs. Cute. Looks a bit scruffy though.

I can't imagine grumpy River Wild with a cute little dog like that.

Honestly, I can't imagine him with any dog. Or any living, breathing thing, for that matter.

The dog wanders over to the pool edge and starts drinking from it.

"Oh, be careful, little dude. You don't want to fall in," I say, curling my fingers around the railing.

Dogs can swim, right? And should it even be drinking from the pool? The chlorine could make it sick.

River really shouldn't be letting his dog wander about the garden like this when he's got a pool. He should cover the pool or at least come outside with the dog while it does its thing.

And maybe give it fresh water, so it doesn't need to drink out of the pool.

I see the dog edge closer to the pool, my heart rate picking up a little, and the yell comes out of my mouth at the exact same time the dog falls into the pool.

"Oh no!"

I watch for a few seconds … and the dog isn't swimming.

I thought all dogs could swim?

Apparently not. Because this dog is struggling to keep its head above water.

"Fudging heck! I'm coming, little dude! Hold on!" I move quickly on bare feet, running down my porch steps and onto the grass.

I run across the garden, heading for the fence that separates our houses, right to the spot where I know there's a gap in the fence.

I saw the broken boards the other day when I was out here, digging up weeds.

Grabbing the boards, I shove them aside and squeeze myself through the tight gap. "I'm almost there, little dude!" I yell to the sound of the panicked barks coming from the pool. "Hold on!"

I race through River's big garden, through a flower bed—*sorry, flowers, but there's a dog's life at stake here*—and straight for the pool.

The poor dog is now in the middle of the pool, frantically trying to keep afloat.

Almost there.

A few seconds later, I reach the pool, and without another thought, I jump straight in.

Cool water rushes me as I go under.

Sweet Lord, that feels good.

I surface and quickly swim over to the dog.

"Hey, it's okay," I say in a calming voice as I reach out and take hold of the dog. Hugging it to my chest, I tread water. "I've got you. You're safe now."

The dog looks up at me with big doe eyes and then licks my face in thanks, I think.

"Well, you are very welcome." I laugh softly.

"What the fuck are you doing in my pool?" a voice booms, startling me.

Carrie

My head snaps up to find my grumpy-ass neighbor standing at the pool edge, glaring down at me. Big, tattooed arms folded over his huge chest, a white T-shirt straining over his biceps, faded jeans on his legs.

"And, with a"—he squints at the wet bundle in my arms—"fucking dog. What the hell are you doing in my pool with a dog?"

"You mean, *your* dog," I uncharacteristically snap as I start to swim, one-armed, toward him, keeping hold of the dog with my other arm. "That I just saved from drowning. You're welcome, by the way."

"I don't have a fucking dog," he snarls, bringing me to a stop close to the edge of the pool.

Hellfire, he's even bigger up close.

"Do you have to curse so much?" I say to him.

Those dark eyes glower down at me. "*Yes*, I *fucking* do."

Okay then.

"So, this dog isn't yours?"

"Nope." He lets the P pop.

I look down at the little cutie in my arms. "Well, whose dog is it?" I ponder.

"How the hell should I know?"

Ignoring his grumpiness, I ask, "Do you think it's a stray?"

"Why don't you ask me the more pertinent question?" His voice is a dark rumble, making my arms break out in goose bumps.

I look up at him. "Which is?"

"If I care. Which I don't, if you haven't already figured that out, Red."

Red?

Oh, my hair.

I roll my eyes. "How original," I scoff. Then, I move close to the pool steps. I put the dog down on the poolside and haul myself out of the water. I'm dripping everywhere.

And the dog has already moved and is now sniffing around River's feet, which are bare.

He has quite nice feet. Why I'm noticing that, I'll never know.

My eyes lift to see him scowling down at the dog, which gives me a chance to properly look at him for the first time.

He towers over me. I'd say he's about six-three at least. Way taller than me, and I stand at five-six. I still can't pin an age on him, but if I had to guess, I'd say twenty-eight or twenty-nine. He's better-looking closer up than I realized. I mean, I knew he was good-looking, but up close, he's impossibly handsome.

The kind of handsome that everyone notices. I can't imagine any woman or man not finding him attractive with his wavy dark copper hair, sharp jaw covered in stubble, dark eyes overhung by frowning eyebrows, long, dark lashes, high cheekbones, and perfectly straight nose.

He's beautiful.

Shame he's a total douche-canoe.

"Will you get this mutt the hell away from me?"

He gives the dog a shove with his foot. It's not a hard shove, but I still feel annoyed at him for pushing the dog away like that.

"Hey! Don't do that. You'll hurt her." I bend down, picking the dog up into my arms, holding it to my chest.

He cocks his head to the side, dark eyes appraising, arms still folded over his chest. "If it's not your dog, then how do you know it's a she?"

"Um … because she's cute and sweet, obviously."

The dog starts to wriggle in my arms, forcing me to put her down.

She immediately goes over to another flower bed where she cocks her leg up and has a pee.

Huh. I guess she is a he.

"And, now, your gender-confused dog is pissing on my flowers. Awesome," he grumbles.

I daren't tell him that I trod over a bunch of his precious flowers back there.

"Well, clearly, she's a boy dog—I mean, he's a boy dog!" I huff at him while I gather up my hair and wring out the excess water.

I'm soaked through.

My pajamas are plastered to my body, and … sweet Lord, I'm not wearing a bra!

As the realization hits me, I snap my gaze up to find River's eyes on me.

And he's not looking at my face.

Nope. His eyes are firmly fixed on my bra-free chest. I fold my arms over my boobs and loudly clear my throat.

He lifts his eyes to mine. All dark and moody.

He doesn't even have the decency to look embarrassed after being caught staring at my breasts.

Jerk.

"So … I guess I'll be on my way."

"And the dog?" The guy wears a perpetual frown on his face, but he still manages to frown on top of his frown.

Figure that one out.

I look over at the dog, who is now cutely growling at the grass. Or whatever is on the grass that's making him growl.

I walk over and pick him up. The growling ceases immediately, and he snuggles into my neck, like he's seeking comfort and contact.

For some reason, a lump forms in my throat. Must be pregnancy hormones playing me up. "I'll take him home with me and try to find out who he belongs to."

River gives a humorless laugh. "Trust me; that dog doesn't have an owner anymore. No collar and tag. He's skinny, and his fur is matted to hell. Someone got rid of him a while ago."

Now that I feel him in my arms, I register just how small he is, and I just thought his fur was matted up from the unexpected swim. But, now that River's pointed it out, I can see this dog is all alone. And my heart breaks in this moment.

I hold him a little tighter to me. "Why would anyone do that? Put a sweet, defenseless, little dog out onto the streets, all alone."

"Because people are selfish cunts."

I flinch at the harshness of his words.

He's staring at me. I look into his eyes. And what I see there surprises me.

It surprises me because I *know* that look. I used to see it in my own eyes every time I could bear to look in the mirror. I still see it now.

Like your soul is empty. Hollow.

The anger and pain and hurt have swallowed you up completely, and there's nothing left but emptiness.

He's felt pain. He knows what it's like.

He's like me.

I feel a jolt inside my chest and a sudden connection to him that I've never felt with anyone before in my life.

He blinks, and when his eyes reopen, they're back to hard and closed off. No emotion in them at all.

It makes me wonder if what I just saw was real. But I know it was. Because I *felt* it. As I feel my own hurt.

He's trying to shut me out. But it's too late. I've already seen him.

And he's right. People are selfish C-U-Next-Tuesdays. I married one after all.

But only some people, not all.

"You're right," I say to him. "Some people are selfish C-U-Next-Tuesdays, but—"

"C-U-Next-Tuesdays?" He barks out a laugh, cutting me off.

I roll my eyes again. Twice in the space of ten minutes. If I keep this up, I'm going to end up with a headache. "As I was saying," I haughtily continue on, "some people are selfish you-know-whats, but not all are. And I'm sure you can figure out what I meant by C-U-Next-Tuesday."

"Hate to burst your bubble, Red, but all people are selfish. And I got the weird acronym, all right. I've just never met anyone who went so out of their way to avoid saying the word *cunt*."

"I don't know why anyone would want to use it. It's a horrible word."

"I think it's one of the best and most versatile words in the English language. Same as *fuck* is. Funnily enough, fucking cunt is my favorite saying."

Ugh. If the jerk could smile, I know he'd be smirking right now.

"Seriously, do you have to be so crass?"

"Yes, Red, I do have to be so fucking crass."

Do not roll your eyes. Do not roll your eyes.

"And please stop calling me Red. My name is Carrie, which you know, of course, because I told you it—well, yelled it at you two weeks ago, from my porch, when you blatantly ignored me."

River doesn't say anything to that. Any normal person would at least be embarrassed at being called out, like I just called him out.

But he's not normal.

Of course he's not.

All I get from him is a devil-may-care shrug, and then he casually slips his hands into his jeans pockets, like he doesn't have a care in the world.

Jerk.

Deep breaths, Carrie. In and out.

"Right, well, we'll be off then," I state huffily, more than ready to get away from him and into some dry clothes. Then, I need to figure out what I'm going to do with my little buddy here.

I spin on my heel, ready to walk across his garden and back to mine through the gap in the fence, when his voice stops me.

"Where are you going?"

I look over my shoulder at him, giving him a stupid look. "Home. You know, the house next to yours."

Look at me, being all sassy. When did this happen?

I don't know. But I definitely like it.

"Funny. What you gonna do, Red? Scale the fence?"

I ignore the Red comment and say, "No, go through the gap in it."

He takes a step forward. "There's a gap?"

"Yep." I let the P pop, like he did before. "That's how I got in here in the first place."

"Fucking great," he huffs more to himself than me. "I'll be fixing that the first chance I get." He jerks a thumb over his shoulder. "There's a side gate there, Red. Use it."

It's my turn to frown at him. I turn slowly. "You know, the neighborly thing to do would be to let me go through your house instead of the side gate."

"Do I look neighborly to you?"

"No. You look like a grumpy asshole."

Oh my God! I can't believe I just said that.

I have to stop myself from slapping my hand over my mouth. Instead, I press my lips together, holding my breath, bracing myself. My body remembering what would happen if I ever spoke to Neil in this way.

But Neil's not here.

You're safe.

This guy might swear like a sailor, but he's not going to hurt you.

The dog restlessly shifts its warm little body against my chest. I force myself to relax.

I honestly don't know what's going on with me right now. It's so not like me to sass back like this.

"So, she does curse after all."

If I didn't know better, I would think there was a smirk on his lips.

The knowledge helps me to relax more.

I lift my chin, forging a strength I don't really feel. "I never said I didn't curse." *Liar.* "I said I didn't like the C-word."

"You mean *cunt.*"

I know he said it to get a rise out of me. But I'm not going to give him the satisfaction.

It's not like I never wanted to curse. It's that I wasn't allowed to.

Neil forbade it. And, if I ever made the mistake of cursing, I would pay for it.

"Sit at my feet, Annie."

Body trembling, I lowered myself to my knees in front of my husband and looked up at him, like I knew I was supposed to.

Emotionless, cold eyes stared down at me. "Women should not curse. Nor should they have opinions. They should be seen. Not heard. Women shouldn't work. They should stay home and take care of their husbands. And they should do everything their husbands tell them to. If they do not adhere to these rules, then the husbands have every right to punish them as they see fit. Recite the words back to me, Annie. Now."

I hold back the shudder my body wants to give at the memory echoing in my mind.

You're fine. You're safe.

I know all of these things, but I just want to go home now.

"Well … bye," I mumble as I walk past River, shaking the past off.

I'm pretty sure the little dog in my arms has fallen asleep against my shoulder. Bless his heart.

I get a whiff of what I think is the smell of cigar smoke as I pass by him. It does something funny to my stomach. A swoop and dive feeling. Weird. I hope the baby doesn't start craving the smell of cigar smoke.

Not healthy at all, my sweet baby.

"You should probably take the mutt to the vet." River's quiet, almost reluctant words reach me just before I get to the gate.

I stop and half-turn back to him. "You think so?"

"He's a stray who just took a dunk in my pool. So, I'd say, yeah, he needs to see a vet."

"Why do you care?" I raise my brow.

His expression shutters. "I don't. But I need to know if the mutt is carrying any diseases. It's been swimming in my pool after all."

"He's not a mutt. And he doesn't have any diseases." I hug the dog to me, and he tucks his face into my neck.

"Yeah, sure, Red. You keep telling yourself that. At the very least, the mutt has fleas, probably ticks."

Fleas? Ticks?

And, now, my skin's itching.

I scratch my arm. Then, my head.

Jesus H. Christ! This is all his fault, putting the fleas idea into my head.

"Won't the vet be closed?" I voice while scratching my neck. It must be nearing midnight by now.

"There's a twenty-four-hour clinic in town."

"Oh. Well, that would be good, but I don't have a car, and I really don't want to walk into town in the dark, so I'll have to take him in the morning."

And spend the night with the fleas and ticks. I scratch harder at the thought.

But I won't see this poor little dog out on the streets because of a few itchy bugs that he probably doesn't even have.

So, why am I even scratching?

Because of him putting the idea in my head!

I hear a loud, frustrated sigh come from River and watch as his hand rakes through his thick hair.

"For fuck's sake," he growls. "I'll take you to the clinic in my truck."

Wow.

The way he's going, you'd think I just asked him for a ride to the clinic.

It's on my tongue to tell him where to stick his ride, but I really should get the sweet little dog to the vet sooner rather than later.

So, I swallow my pride for the sake of my new doggie buddy and say, "That'd be great, thanks. I just need to run home and change into dry clothes. Can I leave the dog with you while I go? I'll only be a few minutes." I don't want to possibly bring fleas into my house before I've had a chance to get the dog treated at the vet.

"Of course. Take your time," he says sarcastically. "Actually, while you're at it, why don't you take a long, hot bath, wash your hair, and then get dressed, and I'll just stand out here with the flea-ridden mutt, waiting like a cunt?"

"Oh, that's so kind of you to offer, River." I smile wide, walking back to him. "But I don't want to leave you looking like a C-U-Next-Tuesday, so I'll just change my clothes and be back in two ticks." I hold the dog out to him, forcing him to take him from me. "Ticks—ha! Get it?"

I laugh, to which he growls.

I back up a few steps, grinning, enjoying the scowl framing his mouth, and then force myself to turn and walk away at a leisurely pace, back to my house to change.

River
Twelve Years Old

Gran has her record player on. Some band called The Flying Pickets. The song currently playing is called "Only You." Gran really does like some crap music. But, as songs go, this one is okay, I suppose.

We're in the workshop. Gran is over at the crucible. She's been going back and forth from there to the crushed glass she's using to create a vase she's been commissioned to make. She doesn't need me at the moment, so I'm finishing off the piece we made yesterday.

Using a grinding block, I'm buffing off the sharp edges on the bottom of the glass balloon. Well, it's a lampshade shaped like a balloon. It's varying shades of blue, going from light blue to midnight blue. It's for Mama. Blue is her favorite color. Not that she can have the lampshade in prison. But, when I make stuff for her, I take a photo of it and bring the picture to show her, as I now get to visit her every month after Gran convinced her that I needed to see her.

Mama likes our visits and the pictures a lot. She tells me that she has all the photos hanging on her wall. She tells me that she's happy that I'm doing glassblowing with Gran. She says I make her proud.

I know that's not true.

How could she be proud of me?

She's in that place because of me.

But, when she gets out of prison and we're together again, I'll make up for what I did.

Until then, I'll just keep making things for her and making her happy in the only way I can.

I glance at the shelf where all the things I've made for her are. It's starting to get quite full.

Gran starts singing along to the song while she works. She's a terrible singer.

I roll my eyes, but there's a smile on my lips.

The bell chimes in the workshop, telling us that someone is at the front door. Gran had the doorbell set up to ring in here, so she could hear when someone rang the bell because she's out in her workshop a lot.

We both are. I love working in here with her.

When she first made me start helping her, I thought I would hate it, but I actually really like doing it.

Because of the extreme heat involved in glassblowing, Gran won't let me do any work on my own, so my job is to do the blowing while Gran shapes. But the idea for the pieces come from me, and Gran helps me bring those to life. I sketch out what I want to make and show her the picture. I do enjoy the drawing. But creating it is the fun part. Glassblowing requires focus, meaning there's no time to think about how much I miss Mama or the reason she's in prison or how much I hate school and my life in general.

"I'll get the door," I tell Gran.

I carefully set down the glass balloon and grinding block on the workbench. I leave the workshop and head into the house.

As I move through the living room, I can see who is standing at the front door through the frosted glass window, and my pace falters.

A police officer.

My heart starts to race in my chest. Palms going clammy.

I curl my fingers into my hands and press my nails into my palms. The bite of pain helps a little.

The bell rings again.

The officer can see me through the glass, so there's no hiding.

I take a deep breath, bracing myself, and open the door.

"H-hello." My voice trembles. I hate that.

I force some spine into my back.

"River."

He knows me. I don't know him.

But then everyone knows who I am.

The child of the cop killer.

If only they knew the truth.

I wonder if he worked with my stepfather. If he was a friend of his.

Everyone was my stepfather's friend.

And that's because they didn't know the real him.

The officer's eyes regard me with distaste.

Like everyone's does in this godforsaken town.

I sometimes wish we could move away. But Gran won't leave. She's lived her whole life in this town. She was born in this house. Says she'll die here.

And she says we don't run from our problems. We face them.

But, if I could run, I would. Far, far away.

But I can't. So, here I stand.

I dig my feet into my sneakers, trying to ground myself. My hand trembles around the door that I'm holding on to.

"Is your grandmother home?" he asks.

I nod, pulse hammering in my suddenly dry throat.

"Well, can you go get her?"

I nod again. But I can't seem to move. I can't get my feet off the floor or my hand away from the door.

He frowns, lines drawn all over his face, and he steps forward, boots thudding against the wooden porch.

Boots thudding up the steps. He's home.

He leans down into my face. "Fuck is wrong with you, boy? You retarded or somethin'?"

Boy.

"You will do as I tell you, boy."

"No, he's not retarded." The whip-crack sound of my gran's voice is like a life raft from a nightmare. Her soft but strong hand lands on my shoulder, giving it a reassuring squeeze, and I relax a little. "And you might be the law in these parts, but don't ever talk to my grandson that way again."

The officer stares her down.

My gran might be small—I'm already taller than she is—but she's fierce.

She lifts her chin and stares right back at him.

"Whatever," he mutters. "I'm just here to deliver a message."

"Which is?" Gran says.

A smile passes over his face. And it's not a kind smile. He reaches his hand into his pocket and pulls out an official-looking envelope, but he doesn't hand it over. Instead, he begins speaking in a cold, calm voice, "Last night, there was a riot at the prison where your daughter was incarcerated. She was stabbed with a shank by another prisoner. She didn't make it. She's dead."

She's dead.

Dead.

No.

Gran's fingers tighten on my shoulder. The only sign that she heard what he just said.

He holds out the envelope to Gran. She takes it from him.

"Someone will be in touch about the body."

The body.

Then, he turns and walks away.

Dead.

Stabbed.

Body.

Mama.

No.

I hear someone screaming.

I don't realize it's me until Gran is pulling me into her arms, tightly holding me to her.

"No. No!" I push away from her, stumbling backward.

"River—"

"No! She's not … she's not … no!"

I turn and run through the house.

She can't be dead. She can't be.

No.

I'm back in the workshop.

The glass balloon is sitting where I left it.

She won't ever see it because she's dead.

She's dead because of me. Because of what I did.

I pick the balloon up and hurl it at the shelf where all the things I made her sit.

It hits the shelf with a resounding smash, all the other glass items smashing.

But it's not enough. The pain is still there in my chest. And it hurts.

I pick up one of the metal pipes we use for glassblowing, and I start to swing out, hitting anything I can.

The smashing of glass is all that can be heard. Along with the pounding of my heart.

And then there's nothing left to hit. My eyes are blurry, and my breaths are heavy. I drop the metal pipe to the floor with a loud clang in the echoing silence.

I clench my fists in and out.

Dead.

Mama's dead.

"River." Gran's soft voice comes from the doorway.

I turn my blurry eyes to her. "S-she's dead."

Her eyes dim. "Yes."

"S-she … I-I -k-killed her! I k-killed Mama!"

"No." Her voice is firm. She steps forward.

I back up, bumping into the workbench. "Y-yes! I-I k-killed her! S-she wouldn't have been there if I hadn't—"

"Stop!" Her voice comes out like a rumble of thunder.

I press my trembling lips together, holding all of my pain inside.

Gran walks over to me and gently wraps her hands around my upper arms. "You did not kill your mother," she speaks gently, but her voice breaks. She clears her throat. "I will not have you carrying that around with you. You blaming yourself is not what your mama would want. Not one thing that happened all those years ago was your fault. You hear me? You were just a child. You are *still* only a child."

I dip my chin, nodding, giving her the answer she wants.

But I don't mean it.

I know I killed Mama.

She was in prison because of me. Because of what I had done to him that day.

It should have been me in jail.

I should be dead.

I press my fingers into my palms. They're slick.

I look down. They're bleeding. Cut up from the glass.

I take in the state of the workshop. I've trashed it. Broken all of Gran's work.

"I-I'm sorry. I b-broke everything."

"You have nothing to be sorry for. It's just glass." She puts a hand under my chin and raises my eyes to her. "It can all be replaced."

But Mama can't be replaced.

I'm never going to see her again.

And I have no one to blame but myself.

A tear runs down my cheek.

I see Gran's eyes shimmer, and something deep inside me breaks.

Gran never cries. Not ever.

I've made her cry.

Because I killed her only child.

She must hate me.

I hate me.

"You stop those thoughts right now, River," she firmly says the words, like she can see straight inside my head. "I don't blame you. And I most certainly don't hate you. I love you."

But I don't feel worthy of her love.

Because I'm not worthy of anyone's love.

There is nothing good inside me.

Just blackness and broken parts that can never be repaired.

Carrie

It's one thirty in the morning, according to the clock on the dashboard in River's truck, and Selena Gomez's "Only You" is playing quietly from the radio while we drive back from the veterinary clinic.

Buddy—that's what I named the dog because they needed one to register him at the vet—is sitting in my lap, looking a lot better than he did when I took him there. The vet had the nurse give him a bath before he treated him for fleas. He said he didn't appear to have them but better to have the treatment than not. Apparently, the treatment keeps him free of fleas for a month, and then I'm to treat him again. He also gave him an injection, which the dog wasn't too happy about. Can't blame him really.

The vet assured me that, aside from being a little underweight, Buddy is just fine.

I bought some dog food from the vet and also a bunch of other things that Buddy will need.

So, now, I officially have a dog.

And he's the cutest dog ever.

I always thought it would be nice to have a dog. I couldn't have one while growing up in foster homes. And Neil hates dogs.

It makes me happy that I can give my baby this. A home and a dog.

Sounds so simple when I put it like that. But, sometimes, it's the simplest of things that matter most.

River reaches over and cuts the radio. I was enjoying the song, but I don't say anything.

River waited at the clinic the whole time I was in with Buddy. When I came out of the examination room, I was surprised to see him sitting there.

We hadn't talked about him giving me a ride home, and I figured I'd inconvenienced him enough by having him bring me out in the first place.

And I realize that I haven't thanked him either.

"Thank you for the ride to the vet and for waiting for us and giving us a ride home."

"Well, I couldn't exactly just leave you there," he grunts.

Yes, you could have. But I don't point that out.

Silence, and then, "So, you're keeping the mutt then."

"Don't call him that." I frown. "His name is Buddy. And of course I'm keeping him."

"You're an idiot."

"What?" I stare over at him, aghast. "I'm an idiot for keeping a harmless little dog who has nowhere to live? Well, if that determines an idiot, then I'll happily be one."

He glances at me, one of those angry brows raised. "You're an idiot for paying the prices you paid for all the shit you bought for the mutt," he says slowly. "You could've gotten all that shit from the supermarket for half the price."

"Oh. Well, the supermarket isn't open right now, and he needed these things."

"He needs a coat? Right now?" He glances over at my feet where the coat among Buddy's other things sit.

"Yes. He might get cold."

He looks at the temperature gauge in the car and then to me.

It's currently sixty-five degrees.

"Fine. He won't get cold right now. But he might get cold at some point."

"He has fur, Red. That's what it's there for. And you do realize that you live in *Texas.*"

"Okay, so he might not need the coat, but it's cute." It's pale blue with little pictures of doggie bones on it. "Anyway, it's always good to have things just in case of emergency. You know, in case it rains when I'm out walking him. It does rain in Texas."

"The coat is fleece."

Fudge. He's right.

"Fleece is waterproof." *Kind of. Okay, not at all.*

"Sure it is."

I can almost hear him rolling his eyes.

Such a smart-ass.

I refuse to admit he's right, so I bite my lip and stay quiet.

But River doesn't.

"I never told you my name." His words are low and quiet.

"Huh?"

"You called me River before, in my garden. I never told you my name."

No, you didn't. You were too busy ignoring me and being rude to me to share that piece of information about yourself.

But, yet again, I don't say what I'm thinking.

And, even though I've done nothing wrong, I feel like I've been caught with my hand in the cookie jar, and my face heats. I stare down at Buddy and stroke his soft fur. "I work at the diner in town—Sadie's Diner. The cook there, Guy, he heard that I was living next door to you, and he mentioned your name in passing. So, that's how I know it."

"In passing. Sure." He laughs without humor.

"Is it a problem that I know your name?"

He doesn't answer.

And it annoys me.

But I let my annoyance slide. I really don't want to get into an argument with the guy at one thirty in the morning.

He pulls his truck up outside my house and turns off the engine. That surprises me. I expected him to park on his drive, and I would walk over.

"Thanks again for the ride," I tell him. "Sorry to have kept you out so late."

He shrugs.

I take that as my cue to leave.

Holding on to Buddy, I open the passenger door and climb out of the truck. I'm about to reach back in to get Buddy's things from the floor of the truck when River appears out of nowhere. I didn't even realize he'd gotten out of the truck. He picks up Buddy's things and then shuts the passenger door.

"I got them," he says gruffly.

"Thank you," I whisper.

I walk to my front door, River trailing behind me.

I honestly don't get the guy. He acts like an asshole. Yet he drives me all the way into town to the vet at midnight and waits there with me for over an hour. Then, he drives me home. Parks outside my house. And is now carrying Buddy's things in for me.

That's not the act of an asshole.

Maybe River isn't the complete asshole that he seems to be.

Getting my key, I unlock my front door and walk inside. I left the lights on, so it wouldn't be dark, coming home.

I really don't like walking into a dark room.

Buddy gives a little wriggle in my arms, so I put him down to the floor.

"Welcome to your new home, Buddy." I watch him as he goes off, exploring the living room.

When I turn to River, I find him standing just inside the doorway, filling it out, watching me. Those dark brows of his are lowered over his eyes, concealing whatever is in them.

"Where do you want me to put this junk?" He lifts Buddy's things in gesture.

I ignore the junk comment and say, "On the coffee table will be fine, thanks."

I shut the door while River puts Buddy's things on the table.

He looks huge in my small living room.

After he puts the items down, he pauses, staring at the fireplace. Then, he turns abruptly. "Are you pregnant?" His eyes drop to my flat stomach.

Ah, he saw my ultrasound picture.

"Yes, I am. Seven weeks—that's why I'm not showing yet." I press my hand to my stomach.

"Where's the father?"

My lips part in surprise.

I stare at him—not wanting to answer, but unsure of what to say.

"I shouldn't have asked that. It's none of my business."

I fold my arms over my chest. "No, it's not."

Surprise flickers in his expression along with what I think is admiration. But I can't be sure with him.

"So, you're alone."

His words needle at me.

I narrow my gaze. "Clearly."

"Why didn't you say that you were pregnant?"

My brows furrow with confusion and annoyance. "I didn't know I had to announce it."

"Well, I wouldn't have let you carry that mutt around if I'd known you were pregnant." He throws his hands in the air, seeming irritated. Though I'm not really sure what he has to be irritated about.

"I'm pregnant, not ill. And please stop calling Buddy a mutt."

He grunts. "He looks like a mutt. An ugly little gremlin. Make sure you don't feed him after midnight."

"Did you just make a joke?" My lips spread into a smile even though he did just indirectly insult Buddy. "I didn't know you were capable of it."

His brows lower over his dark eyes. A shiver rakes down my spine.

"You'd be surprised at what I'm capable of."

I think his words are meant to scare me, but they don't.

This guy is all bark and no bite.

I've seen this from him tonight.

He heads for the front door.

He stops when I speak, "You know … I actually think you're a nice guy, not the jerk you like people to think you are."

The look he gives me could freeze the whole of Texas. Which would be quite nice in the current climate.

"I'm not nice, Red."

"If you say so," I say airily. "But I'll think what I think, and I think you're nice."

"I don't know how I'll ever get over it," he says dryly.

Then, he's out the front door, shutting it behind him, and I'm laughing to myself.

For the first time in a really long time, I'm actually laughing.

And the shocker is, it's because of my grumpy neighbor.

Carrie

Using the remote, I turn the TV off and stretch my body out. Buddy doesn't even move next to me. Little sleepyhead that he is.

I did a double shift tonight, as one of the waitresses called in sick, and after I finished work, I came home and took Buddy for a walk. Poor thing had been stuck inside all day while I worked. I stopped at the store and got a tub of mint chocolate chip ice cream, hot fudge topping, and marshmallows. The baby's craving these things. What can I do?

When we got home from our walk, *Scrooged* was just starting on TV. It's December now, so Christmas movies are in full swing. And I love Bill Murray movies. They always leave me with a good feeling.

So, I changed into my pajamas and got snuggled up on the sofa with Buddy and my ice cream concoction to watch the movie.

I watched. Buddy slept.

Thinking about Christmas, I glance around my living room.

I really need to get a Christmas tree. Weird that I haven't thought about it until now.

Neil always used to buy our tree and put it up. I was never allowed to decorate it. He said I would mess it up.

Well, guess what, Neil. I'm going to get a tree, and I'm going to decorate the heck out of it.

It's my day off tomorrow, so I'll head into town and do a little Christmas shopping.

There's a hardware store in town that sells and delivers Christmas trees. I saw them when I was in there last week, picking up a gardening trowel and fork set, so I could start on ridding the front garden of weeds.

I'll take Buddy for a walk into town in the morning and get a tree. I'll also pick up some decorations. Hopefully, they can do same-day delivery, and then I can spend the rest of my day decorating it. I might even grab some ingredients from the grocery store and bake some Christmas cookies.

I feel a tingle of excitement at the thought.

It's the little things that matter most to me. The things I never could do before.

Maybe I'll take some of the cookies to River. Another thank-you for his help with Buddy.

I give Buddy a gentle nudge with my hand, waking him.

"Come on, Bud. Toilet time."

I pick my bowl up to take to the kitchen and get up from the sofa. Buddy clambers down and sleepily follows me.

I place my bowl into the sink and then open the back door for him.

I step out onto the deck and watch him trot down the steps and onto the grass.

The panels on the fence are still broken. For all of River's complaining about them, he hasn't fixed them like he said he would.

So, I don't want to leave Buddy out alone in the garden in case he goes through the gap and into River's garden and ends up back in the pool.

It's been almost three weeks since I rescued Buddy out of River's pool. I haven't seen my neighbor around at all. If I were a paranoid person, I'd think he was avoiding me. But I'm not, so I don't.

It's not like I'm waiting around to see him.

I'm busy working at the diner and taking walks with Buddy. Life is good. Better than I could've ever imagined it would be.

I've also made a start at stripping the walls in the nursery, ready to prime it, so I can paint it.

I'm just not sure what color to go with.

I guess it depends on whether I decide to find out the sex of the baby when I have my next ultrasound.

But then I suppose it doesn't have to be a pink or blue room. It could be yellow or green or lilac or even white with colored accessories to brighten it up.

As I ponder the possibilities of paint colors, I watch Buddy over by the fence.

I wrap my arms around myself, shifting restlessly on my feet. "Hurry up, Bud," I say more to myself than him because what I've learned with Buddy is that he's a dog with his own mind.

He walks down the fence a little further. Stopping and sniffing before he finally takes a leak.

Hallelujah.

"Come on inside now, Bud." I clap my hands to get his attention. "Time for bed."

"No!" a voice cries out.

I freeze.

Buddy stops and turns back to the fence. A low growl emits from him.

"Don't you … fucking touch me!"

My heart drops through the floor at the words and the agony in them.

Is that River?

Buddy's growling increases.

"Buddy, come here." My voice is firm.

He looks at me and then back to the fence.

"Buddy."

Finally, he listens to me and comes back up the deck.

"Good boy." I reach down and pat him. I open the back door and usher him inside. "Wait here for me," I tell him before closing the door.

"Stop it, you sick fuck!" another agonized cry comes.

It's definitely coming from River's house.

What if he's in trouble? Or hurt? Or worse?

I have to go help him.

I look around for a weapon. My eyes land on the gardening fork and trowel that I left out here.

Fork or trowel?

What would do the most damage?

The fork is pointy. Meaning it's stabby. That'll do.

I grab it and head down the steps into my garden.

I walk quickly through my garden and slip through the gap in the fence, taking me into River's garden.

I quickly but quietly cross the garden, skirt around the pool, and go up to his house.

The upstairs window directly above me is open. That must be where he is. How I heard him from my place.

I call out his name.

No reply.

Maybe he's okay now. I mean, he hasn't made another sound in a—

"I'll do it! I swear!"

Looks like I'm going in.

Swallowing the fear I'm feeling, I take a deep breath.

You can do this. He needs your help.

Garden fork still in hand, I walk up to the back door. I try the handle—unlocked.

I guess, in Canyon Lake, people don't lock their doors.

I pause, hand on the handle. If I step inside, am I breaking and entering?

I really should call the police because, if he is in trouble, it's not like I can do much.

But the last thing I want to do is deal with the police, and it's not like I have a lot of trust in the police. Not that I think all cops are bad like Neil. But it's hard to trust them after I called his colleagues, asking for help, and they let me down so badly.

And it's not like I can just leave River in pain. Alone.

Guess it's just the garden fork and me.

"Don't touch me. I'll … ah, no! Fuck, it hurts." His cries sound painfully erotic.

My heart twists in my chest.

I open the door and step inside the house, leaving it open behind me in case I need a quick escape out of here.

My eyes adjust to the dark, but I still manage to catch my hip on the edge of a table.

"Fudge," I hiss.

I don't let the sting of pain slow me down.

I reach the stairs. Stopping at the bottom, I stare up at the darkness beyond.

Be brave.

Lifting the garden fork to chest height, I hold it with both hands, ready to stab or hit with it if necessary. I slowly step to walk up the wooden stairs on silent feet.

Another painful moan has me moving a little quicker, clutching the handle of the fork a little tighter.

I'm not thinking of myself in this moment. I'm thinking of him—another human being. Wanting to help him, the way I wish someone had been there to help me.

I reach the top where I stop and glance around, trying to figure out which room is his.

The noise was coming from the back window that was open, so that must be where he is.

And there's an open door at the far end of the hall.

Garden fork at the ready, I creep toward the door.

A floorboard creaks loudly in the silence, under my weight, and I freeze, holding my breath, listening for any sound or movement.

Nothing.

I inch forward, stepping lightly, not wanting to make any more noise.

I reach the open door. It's only open halfway, so I can't see fully into the room.

I can only see the open window.

An agonized moan comes from inside the room.

Fork poised and ready, lifting my foot, I carefully push the door open wider, using my big toe.

I see the end of the bed.

I step inside the room, the bed coming into view. And I see River in bed, his body strained and twisted, trapped deep inside of a nightmare.

I almost sigh in relief that he's not being murdered or beaten to death. Or worse.

Is there worse?

Yes, there is. I've lived it.

His legs kick restlessly at the sheet covering his lower half. Short gasps of breath hiss out from between his clenched teeth.

It feels wrong that I'm here. Witnessing this.

But, now that I'm here, I can't just leave him alone. Even if I did technically break into his house.

That he has nightmares doesn't surprise me. I saw the haunted look in his eyes that day.

I have nightmares sometimes, too.

I dream that Neil finds me. Takes me home. Hurts the baby …

I don't know what haunts River's dreams, but I know I can't leave him like this.

Lowering the fork, I step closer to the bed, standing at the end of it.

"River," I firmly say his name. "You're having a nightmare. You need to wake up."

He doesn't respond.

"River." I reach out and touch his sheet-covered foot.

Big mistake.

His eyes flick open, and he jolts out of bed.

His sudden movement startles me, and I step backward, somehow tripping over my own feet and landing on my ass.

And I quickly learn another thing about River.

He sleeps naked.

Carrie

"What the fuck are you doing in my bedroom?"

"Penis—River! Fudging heck!" I quickly clamber to my feet. "Sorry. I-I … I heard you yelling from outside. The door was unlocked—"

"And you thought that was an invitation to come straight on in?"

"I-I … thought you were being murdered or something. You were yelling. I was worried. I wanted to help."

I'm flustered. And the color of a tomato.

He's still naked. And just standing there.

Naked.

He hasn't seemed to register that he is naked. Or that his penis is totally erect right now.

That, or he doesn't care.

But I'm registering it.

And I'm trying to look away. I swear, I am.

But it's hard.

His penis. And my ability to look away.

Before now, I'd seen two men naked in my whole life.

But never one who looks like River does.

Compared to River, Neil would look pudgy. And Neil wasn't fat by any means of the word.

But River is ripped. Abs. And taut muscles covering his body and arms and legs. He's huge. *Everywhere.*

I don't have a lot of experience with penises. I'd only seen one other before Neil, and that was when I was sixteen and lost my virginity to a sixteen-year-old guy from school, who had no clue what he was doing. Except for the fact that he'd bet his friends he could get me to sleep with him. Clearly, he won that bet. Neil always hated the fact that I'd slept with someone before him. It was a reason he would use to start an argument when he had no other.

Neil's penis was about the same size as the first ass of a guy that I slept with, so I wasn't sure if they were normal-sized or big or what.

Compared to River's, they were definitely average-sized.

Maybe undersized.

Why am I still thinking about penises?

Because you're standing, staring at one.

I flick my eyes up to River's face. For once, he doesn't look angry.

His brows are lifted. A smug expression on his face.

He knows I've been looking at his penis.

Of course he knows. I was staring straight at it for ages.

When I meet his eyes, they are a stark contrast to the amusement on his face. They're burning with something I'm not willing to name right now.

My stomach dips.

I swallow roughly.

"What's that?" He lifts his chin in the direction of the gardening fork that's on the floor from when I fell on my ass.

"Oh." I pick it up. "It's my gardening fork."

"Well, that explains why it's on my floor."

"I dropped it when you startled me, and I fell."

"I startled you?" One of those humorless laughs of his. "*Riiight.*" He drags the word out. He lifts his tattooed arms from his sides and folds them over his chest.

Don't look down. Don't look down.

I force my eyes to stay on his face. I fidget on my feet. "I brought it with me. As a weapon. You know, in case I needed one."

His eyes go to the fork in my hand and then back up to my face. "What were you going to do, dig me to death?"

"Not you. Whoever was hurting you. And very funny." I roll my eyes.

"No, it's fucking not. You're pregnant, and you came in here, not knowing what you were walking into, with a shitty gardening fork as a weapon."

When he puts it like that, it does sound reckless.

"Okay, so I didn't exactly think it through."

"No shit, Sherlock. You're a fucking idiot, Red."

"Hey! That's … not nice! I came here to save your ass, you ass."

"And landed on your own."

He turns, picks up a pair of jeans slung across a chair, and pulls them on. I see a big tattoo framing his back, but I don't get to see what it is because he covers it up by pulling on a T-shirt.

Then, he flicks on the lamp on his nightstand and turns to face me.

I blink against the light. My eyes adjusting from the darkness.

"Nice pajamas. And do you mean that literally?"

"What?"

I look down.

Christ almighty.

Seriously, God?

Seriously?

You couldn't cut me a break just this once?

I'm wearing my new pajama set. I got them for a couple of dollars on sale. I bought a couple of sizes up, so they're baggy at the moment but not for long with my growing waistline. They're that soft, brushed cotton fabric. Comfort over fashion, right? And it's not like I ever expected anyone to see me in them.

But it's not the large size of them that he's referring to.

Oh no.

It's what's written on the top that has him smirking.

I Like Your Balls is written on the pajama top, and two Christmas baubles hang beneath the words.

Shoot me now.

It amused me at the time. It was one of the reasons I bought them.

I'm not feeling so amused right now though.

"You're hilarious," I mutter. "And, now, I'm going." I turn on my heel, walking quickly to the door.

"Aw, don't be embarrassed, Red. It's okay to like my balls." His laughter catches me as I pass through the door, leaving his room.

I can't even register the fact that it's the first time I've heard him laugh or that it's a nice, deep, husky sound.

Because I'm too embarrassed.

No, not embarrassed. Mortified.

I broke into his house with a garden fork in my hand. Scared the bejesus out of him and myself. Then, stared at his penis for a longer period of time than considered acceptable. Actually, I don't think it's acceptable to stare at anyone's penis. And, to top it all off, I'm wearing the most ridiculous pajamas ever. Pajamas that gave him the opportunity to ridicule me even more.

I'm such an idiot.

I practically run down the stairs and race back through the house the way I came in, weaving around his furniture, heading for the still-open back door.

"Mother-fudging nuts!" I yell, catching my foot on the same table I walked into earlier, stubbing my little toe. "That hurts!" I drop the fork and grab my foot with both hands. Tears sting my eyes.

Sweet Jesus, that really flipping hurts.

Light floods the room.

"Are you okay?"

Ugh, River. The mocker of all mockers.

I didn't even hear him coming. He's probably here to give me even more of a hard time.

"I'm fine."

"You don't look fine."

I let go of my foot and lower it to the floor.

I hold in a hiss of pain at the contact. My toe is throbbing.

"You're bleeding."

"What?" I look down, and sure enough, there's blood coming from my little toe. Blood is on my hands, too.

Fear clamps down over my chest.

"You always make a mess! Such a fucking mess! You useless fucking bitch!"

"Red?"

"I'm so sorry. I didn't mean to get blood on your floor. I'll clean it. I'll clean it now." My heart is pounding. I immediately lift my foot from the floor to prevent a further mess, and I turn my head, looking for the way to the kitchen to get something to clean it up with.

"Red, it's fine." His voice is softer. Like the way you'd talk to a spooked animal.

I stare at him.

An expression I don't like flickers in his eyes.

Pity.

I don't know exactly what's on my face that's making him look at me that way, but I can hazard a guess. I school my features to normal. That I can do. I'm well trained in it.

Calm down. He's not Neil. You're safe.

He walks closer to me. His movements slow, measured. "It's just a little blood, Red. Don't worry about it. Sit down. Let me take a look at your foot."

"I'm fine. Honestly. I'll just go." I really want to just get out of here.

I make to move, but his words stop me.

"Red, sit." His voice is firm but not harsh. More … concerned.

So, I give in. I hobble over to the sofa and sit down.

River follows and kneels at my feet. He lifts my foot with his hand, looking at my toe. "Just a little cut. I'll clean it up and put a Band-Aid on it, and you'll be fine."

"You don't have to."

His dark eyes meet with mine. "I know. But I'm still going to."

He gets to his feet. I watch him disappear out the door, into what I guess is the kitchen.

He's so confusing. One minute, he's being a jerk to me. Then, in a click of fingers, he's being nice.

I'm starting to think he might actually have split-personality disorder.

I can hear him rattling around. Cabinet doors opening and closing.

Then, he reappears with a first aid kit in hand.

He kneels back at my feet and opens the kit up. He takes my foot and rests it on his thigh. He takes an antiseptic wipe out of the kit. How do I know it's an antiseptic wipe, you ask? Well, I'm very familiar with the inside of first aid kits. The regular beatings and not being able to go to the hospital meant that I had to be.

"This will sting a bit," he says.

"I can handle pain."

He briefly glances up at me. The look in his eyes unreadable.

Then, eyes back down, he presses the wipe to my toe and gently cleans it up.

When he's done, he tosses the wipe back into the kit and gets a Band-Aid. He rips it open. But he doesn't put it on straightaway.

He takes hold of my foot and lifts it up. Then, he leans his face down and softly blows on my toe, drying the wet from the wipe.

Sweet Jesus.

I know I'm not supposed to feel anything. But I do.

Parts of me I didn't know existed start to sing.

I'm getting turned on from him blowing on my foot.

It confuses and surprises me.

Pregnancy hormones and seeing him naked have fuddled my brain.

"There, all done." He's lowering my foot to the floor.

I didn't even know he'd put the Band-Aid on; I was so distracted by what I was feeling. Or what I shouldn't be feeling.

I shoot to my feet. His dark eyes follow me up.

"Thanks," I blurt, a slight shake to my voice. "For fixing me up."

Thanks for fixing me up?

Christ on a cracker.

I sidestep him. "Well, bye then." I make a beeline for the still-open door that I came in through earlier.

"Where are you going?"

His deep voice catches my back, stopping me. I glance over my shoulder. He's standing now.

"Home."

"Your feet are bare."

I thought that was obvious. You know, since he was literally just blowing on my bare foot.

Don't think about it.

"Where are your shoes?"

I turn fully to face him. "I didn't come in with any. I was in a rush."

"Wear a pair of mine to go back in."

I glance down at his bare feet. They're huge. Just like his—

Annnd I'm bright red again.

"That's not necessary, and they wouldn't fit me anyway."

But, clearly, he's not listening to me because he's turning away and walking back into the kitchen, where he apparently keeps everything, and then he returns moments later with not one, but two pairs of shoes in his hands. Boots and sneakers.

He puts the sneakers by my feet. "Put them on."

Christ, he's bossy.

Ignoring his order—because I no longer take orders from men—I watch as he pulls the boots on his own feet, leaving the laces unfastened.

"Why do you need shoes?" I ask him.

Dark eyes lift to mine. "Because I don't walk the streets barefoot."

Huh.

"Put the sneakers on, Red."

I cross my arms over my chest. "I don't want to."

"You want to cut your foot open again? You're lucky you didn't on your way over here."

How would I cut my feet in our gardens? Unless he has broken glass scattered around his. Wouldn't surprise me.

"Fine." I sigh. Then, I slip my feet in his sneakers. They're massive, as expected. "I look like a clown."

"You do look ridiculous."

I scowl. "I never said I looked ridiculous. I said, I look like a clown."

"Same thing."

I don't even bother arguing.

"Well, thanks for the loan of the sneakers." Although I didn't actually want them.

I turn back to the door when his voice once again stops me.

"You have something against front doors? Or just my front door?"

I eye him over my shoulder. "Just going back the way I came."

"Ah, yeah. The gap in the fence. Never did get around to fixing that."

Why? I want to ask. But, of course, I don't.

He wouldn't tell me anyway.

I head through the door, grabbing the handle to close it behind me. But he's there, right behind me, in the doorway.

Letting go of the door, I step aside. "Are you going somewhere?" I ask.

His brow goes up, revealing his dark eye. "I'm walking you home."

"I live right there." I point at my house.

"And?"

"And I think I can make it there just fine."

"You think bad things don't happen to people, even in the shortest of distances?"

"No, I don't think that." *I know for a fact they do. I wasn't safe in my own home for seven long years.* But I also don't need a man looking out for me. I can take care of myself. "But I got over here just fine. So, I can make it back just as easy."

"Oh, yeah? With your trusty garden fork for protection?"

I realize then that I don't have the fork with me. It's still on the floor where I dropped it when I stubbed my toe. But I really don't want to go back in his house to get it. So, it can stay there.

"You're a real jerk sometimes," I tell him.

"I know. And yet, I'm still walking you home."

I sigh. "Suit yourself."

I stomp through his garden. It isn't easy, walking in shoes that are about five sizes too big for me.

"What size shoe do you wear?" I ask him.

"Thirteen." His voice comes behind me in the darkness.

Correction: seven sizes too big.

"I wear a size six."

"Thanks for that riveting piece of information. I'll sleep better tonight, knowing that." His tone is droll.

I want to point out that the reason I was in his house in the first place was because he wasn't sleeping well.

I push my way through the gap in the fence. Takes me longer than usual because his big, stupid shoes get in the way.

As I'm shoving my way through, the fence starts to shake.

When I make it back into my garden, I look up to see River climbing over the fence.

"What are you doing?" I ask him.

He stops midway and looks at me like I'm as dumb as bricks. "Climbing. The. Fence," he slowly says the words, like reciting them to a moron.

"I got that. I meant, why?"

He jumps down from the fence, landing easily on his feet. Way too graceful for a man of his size. As he stands before me, his dark eyes glitter down at me in the darkness.

"Because there was no way I'd fit through the gap."

"Oh."

"And, since someone doesn't like front doors or gates, it was my only option."

Hilarious.

I roll my eyes and then march across my grass, heading for the steps leading up to my back deck.

I stop at the bottom.

I slip my feet out of his sneakers, pick them up, and hold them out to him. He takes them from me.

"All the way to the back door," he tells me and then gestures for me to walk up the steps.

I sigh but don't bother arguing.

I reach my back door and open it. Light floods out onto the deck along with Buddy, who comes barreling out of the door, sniffing around my legs, making shuffling noises, like he's telling me he was worried.

"I'm okay, Bud." I reach down and stroke him.

He gazes up at me. Then, he seems to register River's presence, and his eyes dart to him. He eyes River for a good few seconds, like he's coming to some decision about him. Then, seeming to make his decision, he wags his tail and wanders over to sniff around his feet.

River ignores him.

That irritates me.

"You still have the mutt then."

That irritates me even more.

"Of course I still have *Buddy*." I highlight his name even though I know it's pointless. He'll call him whatever he wants.

Realizing he isn't getting anything from River, Buddy trots on back inside our house.

"Well … good night," I say.

"Why did you come to my house?"

I sigh again. I seem to do it a lot around this guy. "I already told you."

"I know what you said. What I meant was, why didn't you just call someone?"

"Like who?"

He shoves his hand through his thick hair. "The cops." His words are quieter. "If someone thought there was an intruder in a house, that something bad was happening … a person would normally call the cops. Not go in at their own risk. With a fucking gardening fork as their only weapon."

I can't tell him all the reasons I didn't call the police.

I lift my shoulders on the lie. "I guess … I didn't think."

His thick brows draw together. "No other reason?"

"What other reason would there be?"

He steps back out of the light of my doorway and into the dark of the night. "No reason."

He pushes his hands into his jeans pockets and walks toward the steps.

"Carrie." He stops me as I'm closing the door.

That's the first time he's ever said my name.

And it feels momentous for a reason I can't put my finger on.

I don't answer, as my voice seems to have been stolen, but I know he knows I'm listening.

"Thanks … for coming."

When no one else would.

He doesn't say those words out loud, but I somehow know that's what he means.

"You're welcome," I say to the darkness as he disappears into it.

Carrie

I don't expect to see River today. I can usually go days or weeks without seeing my neighbor. And, especially after last night's events, I figure it might be months before I see him next.

I still can't believe I broke into his house, thinking he was being attacked or something, and acted like a complete tool and embarrassed the heck out of myself and cut my toe open on his table, all with that garden fricking fork in my hand. Total doofus.

And I'm definitely not thinking about the fact that I saw him naked.

Very naked.

Nope, definitely not thinking about that right now.

Especially not when he's walking straight toward me because that would be creepy and out of the ordinary. Creepy, me thinking of him naked. Out of the ordinary, him coming over to speak to me.

Buddy and I pause on the sidewalk outside our house.

River comes to a stop in front of me. He's wearing a flannel shirt and jeans. The same boots on his feet as he had on last night. A beanie on his head, covering that thick hair of his.

It's cooler today—thankfully. I'm wearing a long, chunky dark green sweater over black leggings with some walking boots I picked up the other day on discount, and a black-and-white-checkered scarf is knotted around my neck, my hair down and doing its own thing.

"Red," he says in that low, dark voice of his.

"River." I smile at him.

He doesn't smile back. Or say anything else.

Just stands there, staring at me from beneath those lowered brows in that dark, brooding way of his. But I notice there's something else in his expression. I can see it in the set of his jaw and the tightness around his eyes. It looks like discomfort.

He's uncomfortable.

I didn't know he could feel the emotion.

This is a guy who had no problem standing stark naked in front of me last night. Or saying whatever is in his head. So, I have to wonder what has him feeling uncomfortable.

Maybe it's because he thanked you last night, a voice in my head says.

It could be that. I can't imagine River is used to thanking anyone for anything.

But he doesn't need to feel uncomfortable about that.

I want to ask him if that is it. Reassure him that he doesn't have to feel uncomfortable about it. But I'm not as straightforward as he is.

So, instead, I opt to ask what he wants—in a non-rude way, of course—when I notice my gardening fork in his hand.

"Is that mine?" I gesture to it.

He looks down at my gardening fork in his hand, like just remembering it's there. "Oh. Yeah." He clears his throat. "I found it on my living room floor. Thought you might need it. You know, for the next time you decide to do another breaking and entering."

"Funny." I take the gardening fork from him. "And I don't plan on doing any breaking and entering ever again."

"That so?"

"Yep."

"Shame. The highlight of my week was seeing those pajamas of yours."

For some reason, his words make me flush.

Maybe it's because you're thinking about the fact that, when you saw him, he wasn't wearing any pajamas.

I cough, clearing my throat, which turns into a bit of a choke when I breathe back my own spit.

"You okay?" he asks.

"Yep." I cough again, banging my hand to my chest to clear it.

I'm definitely not thinking about him naked at all. Nope.

"Is the baby okay?"

"What?"

"Your baby." His eyes go down to my stomach.

I'm still not showing. But then I am only ten weeks. I figure I'll pop anytime soon.

I instinctively press my hand to my stomach. "Oh, yes. All fine. No problems at all." So far, no morning sickness, and I think, if I were going to get it, I would've by now.

An awkward silence ensues between us. You know, the type where you have no idea what to say next but no idea how to end the conversation either.

And, for some inexplicable reason, I don't want the conversation to end just yet.

Weirdly, I do actually like talking with him. Well, verbally sparring with him. When I'm not making an ass out of myself in front of him, and he's not being a mean jerk to me.

But a part of me also wants him to do his River thing and just turn and walk away without another word.

Confusing, to say the least.

I guess one of us should say something. And it looks like that someone is going to be me.

"So, uh … thanks for bringing this back." I lift the fork in gesture. "I, um … I guess I'll see you around."

"You and the mutt going somewhere?" he asks, stopping me before I get a chance to leave.

I smile, ignoring the mutt comment. I know he only does it to get a rise out of me. And that oddly makes me happy, too.

I bite down on the smile and turn back to him. "Yes. Buddy and I are going to buy a Christmas tree."

"Where are you getting it from?"

"The hardware store in town."

"The trees are shit. They don't last a week."

"Oh." My built excitement at my Christmas tree shopping sinks down into the ground.

"You need to go to Thistleberry Farm. They have the best Christmas trees," he tells me.

That has me perking up a little. "Where is Thistleberry Farm?"

"New Braunfels."

"And where's New Braunfels?"

A smile touches the edge of his lips. Not a full-on smile, but still the first time that I've seen his mouth resemble anything close.

He did laugh last night. Not that I saw that. Only heard it. And it was at my expense.

I notice he has nice lips. Lower lip is slightly fuller than the top.

"It's a thirty-minute drive from here."

And my little shred of hope disappears. "Oh." Well, that's out then because I still haven't invested in a car. I really don't want to use the money I took from Neil. I want to pay for it with my earnings from the diner, and so far, I'm nowhere near getting one, especially not with the money I had to pay out for Buddy's vet bill. "Do they maybe deliver?" I guess I could call up and say what size tree I wanted. Then, I could pick up some decorations from town while I wait for it to come.

He shakes his head.

My lips turn down a little. "Oh. Well, never mind." I force myself to perk up. "A rubbish tree is better than no tree. Right?"

"Not really. It's just a waste of money."

Well, thanks for that, River.

So damn honest. It's annoying.

"Well, it's my only option. So, I'm going with it and making the best of it."

The look on his face … it's like he's looking at a brand-new species. Something he's never seen before.

"Why are you looking at me like that?" The words are out before I can stop them.

Surprise flickers across his countenance. But it's gone as quickly as it arrived.

"Because you're so fucking odd."

Well … okay. Guess I asked for that.

He shifts on his feet and shoves his hands in his jeans pockets. "Look … Red, I'm heading out to Thistleberry Farm later. I have something to drop off there. I can take you with me."

That brightens me up.

He's being nice again. Mean one second. Nice the next.

It's whiplash city with this guy.

And I do really want to take him up on his offer. But I don't want to impose. I've done that once already—the night he took me and Buddy to the vet. Well, twice, if you count last night. Although his truck wasn't involved in that. Just penises. Well, one penis—his—this garden fork, and my ridiculous pajamas.

Why am I thinking about it again?

Because, now, I'm looking at it again. Well, the bulge in his jeans.

Christ almighty.

Pregnancy hormones are wreaking havoc on me.

I blink my eyes away and up. "Are you sure?" I brush my hair behind my ear. "I don't want to put you to any trouble."

"Wouldn't offer if I wasn't." He's already backing away from me. "Look, take the mutt for his walk, and when you get back, we can head out to the farm. You can pick a tree out, and we'll bring it back in my truck." He turns on his heel and heads back to his house without waiting for my response.

I watch him walk away. Then, I look down at Buddy. "Well … that was unexpected." I laugh softly. "Come on, Bud. Let's get you walked, so I can go pick out our Christmas tree with the whiplash king."

Carrie

"How's your foot doing?"

"Oh. My toe. Yes, it's fine. Thanks again for fixing me up."

"I only put a Band-Aid on it."

And blew on it …

Sweet Lord in heaven.

I swallow down. "Yes, well, I appreciate it."

Silence.

"Did the blood clean up okay?" I ask.

"What?" His word is sharp, surprising me.

"My blood that I got on your floor. I'm hoping it didn't leave a stain."

"No. It cleaned up fine."

"Oh, good. I'm glad."

Silence again. The low hum of the engine and the whoosh of noise from passing cars are all that can be heard while River drives us to Thistleberry Farm.

"Do you mind if I put the radio on?" I ask him.

"Knock yourself out."

I reach over and press the On button, bringing the radio to life. "Last Christmas" by Wham! fills the car, and he groans.

"You don't like this song?" I ask him.

"Does anyone?"

Well, I do. But I keep that nugget of information to myself. Don't need to give him any more ammo to use against me.

I select another radio station.

The Pogues and Kirsty MacColl's "Fairytale of New York" is playing.

"I love this song," I tell River.

I know everyone is all about Mariah and the other upbeat Christmas songs, but for me, this tale of longing and melancholy is the best. I don't know what that says about me. Probably nothing good.

Neil always hated this song.

That's possibly one of the reasons I love it so much.

"*You* love this song?" He's skeptically looking at me.

"Yes. Why are you looking at me like that?"

"Like what?"

"Like you don't believe me."

"I'm just surprised. It's not the most well-known Christmas song in the US. And it has some offensive words in it. Just doesn't seem like your thing. I thought you'd be more of a 'All I Want for Christmas Is You' kind of girl."

Ugh.

"How do you know the song?" I challenge.

"It was my gran's favorite," he says low.

Was? Does that mean his gran is no longer with us?

"Oh. Well, first off, I'm hardly a girl. And, second, you don't know me well enough to make those kinds of assumptions. And, third, it is exactly my kind of song." Sad like me.

"True. I don't know you well. But I do know that you don't curse and that you complain—very loudly—when I do."

"I do curse. Just not excessively like you. You say the F-word every other word."

"Not every other word. At least every third word. And, yeah, I forgot you do curse." He mockingly taps his fingers to his forehead. "What was it? Oh, yeah. '*You mother-fudging son of a C-U-Next-Tuesday.*'" He mimics my voice—badly, might I add. "You're a total badass, Red," he adds drolly.

I flip him off.

Laughter bursts from him.

The sound is wonderful. Just like I heard last night. Deep and husky. But, this time, I'm seeing it, and his face is all lit up. His eyes bright with humor.

I feel a warmth in my chest. And like I just won something really special. I guess I did. Because I can't imagine laughter is easily earned from River.

But he's laughed twice with you—okay, at you—in two days.

And you know what? I'll take it.

"You're an idiot."

"So you keep saying."

I'm not offended this time because I'm starting to realize that, when River is doling out an insult, maybe it's not an insult at all.

"So, you did hear me then."

A quick glance. "When?"

"When you drove over my groceries. That's when I yelled that you were a mother-fudging son of a C-U-Next-Tuesday."

"Oh, yeah. That."

"Yes, *that.*"

"Well … I guess … it was a shitty thing to do."

A shitty thing to do? That's putting it mildly.

"Is that your version of an apology?"

He glances at me, brow raised. "Best you're gonna get."

"Hmm … I'll take it, I suppose. For now."

"For now?"

I know he's looking at me, but I don't look at him. Instead, I lean back in the seat, folding my arms over my chest, and say, "Yes. For now."

My face is impassive. But I'm smiling inside.

Standing up to River is … fun. The most fun I've had in ages.

River turns his truck onto a track leading straight to Thistleberry Farm. He pulls up outside the farm store, and my heart leaps with joy.

Christmas trees are everywhere. And the store is decorated with the most amazing decorations. And there is an inflatable Santa and snowman bobbing about and fake reindeer attached to a sleigh, filled with presents.

It looks awesome. I bet it looks even better at night when it's all lit up.

I wish I could see it at night.

River's already out of his truck. I climb out, too. He meets me around my side with a large box in his arms, which he got from the backseat.

"It's amazing," I say with awe.

He gives me a look. "It's a store."

"I meant, the decorations and the trees. I bet it looks really pretty at night when it's all lit up," I voice my earlier thoughts.

"You like all this Christmas stuff, huh?"

I stare up at him. "Doesn't everyone?"

He gives a shrug and shifts the box in his arms.

"You need a hand with that?" I ask him.

He gives me an amused look. "You're funny, Red. Come on; let's get this over with."

I follow him up the few steps to the store, stopping at the window when I spot the most beautiful glass tree ornaments. "Wow … look at these. They're gorgeous."

There are intricate decorations—little Santas, penguins, stacked gifts, Christmas trees, snowmen and snowwomen, and even a Mrs. Claus. A silver star-shaped glass ornament. A clear glass angel with a gold halo. Standard glass baubles filled with white glitter that looks like a storm, small white feathers, sprigs of Christmas trees, ones that look like glitter galaxies in colors in varying shades of blues and purples. And they're all made from glass and hand-painted. Or so the sign in the window says.

"It says they're made by a local artist." I tap my finger against the window. "I wonder how much they are. I would love to get some for my tree. Gosh, look at this one …"

I peer closer to the window. It's a glass train. The detail on it is intricate. For some reason, I feel a little choked up, looking at it. It looks like so much time and effort went into this one little, tiny Christmas tree ornament. The artist must really love what they do and have so much patience to create something so lovely and delicate.

"This is beautiful," I whisper. "I would love to get this for my tree."

"They're expensive. Especially that train. And, at this rate, you won't get a tree. They'll all be gone by the time I get you away from this window."

"Oh, hush, Christmas Grinch." I roll my eyes at him. "And how expensive are they?"

"The train is fifty dollars."

"How do you know?"

"It says so on the price tag." He lifts his chin in its direction.

Following with my eyes, I look back at the train and see a little brown price tag hanging from it. I missed it before. He's right. It's fifty dollars.

I can't afford that. Especially not for a tree ornament.

Sigh.

"Okay, let's go inside." I open the door for him because his hands are full and let him through before walking inside myself.

There are stacks of fresh produce. Homemade jams. Pickles.

My stomach rumbles.

I press my hand to it. I had breakfast not that long ago. But this baby is greedy. I'm going to be rolling around by the end of this pregnancy if the baby has anything to do with it.

River walks straight over to the counter, putting the box down on it, and is greeted by a woman in her seventies at least.

"River, always good to see you. What do you have for me today?" She nods down at the box.

I want to know, too. But River doesn't answer her question.

I move to stand beside him. The woman's eyes go to me.

"Hi." I smile.

"Hi."

"I'm Carrie, River's neighbor," I introduce myself because he clearly has no intention of doing so.

"It's nice to meet you, Carrie. I'm Ellie. I own this fine place."

"It's a wonderful store," I tell her. "I love the decorations you have up outside. And I was just admiring the glass tree ornaments in the window. Especially the train. It's beautiful."

"Yes, River is—"

"Here for a Christmas tree," he cuts her off. "Not me. Her." He jerks his thumb at me.

I stare at him. He's acting strange. Well, stranger than normal.

A smile touches Ellie's lips. Almost like a knowing smile.

"What kind of tree are you after?" she asks me.

"Are there different types?"

She smiles kindly at me. "Quite a few."

"Oh, I didn't know that. I've never bought a Christmas tree before." I feel a bit pathetic, making that admission.

"River knows the tree types. He used to come in every Christmas to pick one out with his mama. Such a beauty Mary was. Could've been a model on the runways, but then she … well, yes, and then, after Mary was gone, of course, he'd come in with his grandmother. But that stopped, when Greta passed. A real friend to me was Greta." She sighs sadly. "After she was gone, River stopped buying a Christmas tree. Maybe you can talk him into getting one again."

I guess that answers my question about Gran. She died.

But what happened to his mom?

My eyes move to River, and he's frozen still beside me. His face a mask. Body like a statue.

Concern fills me. "River," I quietly say his name.

"Oh, look at me, going on." Ellie blinks, seeming to realize that maybe she said a bit too much. "Old age getting the better of me. How about you and I sort through the things that you brought in for me, River, and I'll get Macy to help Carrie pick out a Christmas tree? Macy!" Ellie calls out.

"River." I touch his hand with mine.

He blinks, looking down at me, like he's remembering that I'm still here.

I see that vulnerability there in his eyes just for the briefest of moments, and then it's gone. His eyes are back to being closed off.

"You wanted me, Ellie?" A female voice cuts through the silence.

My eyes follow the sound of the voice to a woman, who looks to be around my age, maybe a few years younger. She's really pretty. Long, dark hair tied up into one of those messy buns that I've never been able to perfect. Wide brown eyes rimmed with long black lashes, set in a heart-shaped face. And an innocence about her that tells me she's only known good things in her life.

I envy that. But I'm glad for her.

"Yes. Can you help River's friend, Carrie, pick out a Christmas tree?" Ellie tells her as Macy approaches us. "She doesn't know what kind she wants, so if you could, explain the different types to her."

"Of course," she says. Her eyes pass straight over me and onto River. "Hi, River," she says with that tone in her voice that only a woman with a major crush would use.

I feel a few things in this moment. And confusion is definitely at the top of the list.

River, of course, ignores her.

It makes me feel bad for her. But it's also nice to know it's not just me he ignores. I was starting to wonder, as he was being so nice to Ellie. Well, as nice as River can be.

I give Macy a sympathetic look. A look of solidarity. Letting her know she's not alone in the rude and grouchy treatment from River. We are sisters together.

But … the look I get back from her is not one of sisterhood.

More like annoyance. And distaste.

Right. Okay then.

But still, he's being rude, and that's just not acceptable.

"River"—I nudge his arm with my elbow—"Macy said hi to you."

"I heard," he grunts.

"Aren't you going to say hello back?"

His eyes flick to mine. His expression screams, *Are you fudging kidding me?* Although I'm sure he's not thinking *fudging*. More like the F-word that ends in K.

I stare back at him, refusing to look away. "It's the polite thing to do," I say softly.

His brow lifts. "Have you met me?"

"Yes, quite a few times," I say dryly. "And, although I do know you're rude and impolite, I also know you can be nice when you want to be."

I know the word *nice* irks him.

He scowls. Eyes narrow. And he continues to stare.

So, I stare right back. Refusing to give in. And I smile. Widely.

It annoys him. I know this because he pinches the bridge of his nose. His eyes close. His jaw clenches. He huffs out a breath through his teeth.

His hand drops. He stares at me. "Hi, Macy," he grits out through that still-clenched jaw of his.

And I smile even wider. Not to be an ass. But because I'm proud of myself. I didn't back down to his intense stare, and trust me, the guy has got a stare that could refreeze the melted polar caps in the Antarctic.

That's a big thing for me. Not backing down.

A few months ago, I wouldn't have dared to speak to another person the way I just spoke to River.

And I managed to make a grumpy bear like River be nice to someone.

Go, me.

I pat him on the arm and turn to Ellie, whose eyes are pinging between me and River like we're a tennis match she's watching.

"Sorry about that, Ellie. So, I'll leave you guys to do your thing." I gesture to the box that's still sitting on the counter, unopened, River's hand now sitting protectively on the top of it. "I'll go outside with Macy and pick out my tree. Oh, and, Ellie, do you have any other tree ornaments than the ones you have in the window? I do love them a lot, but they're a little out of my price range."

Her warm eyes smile at me. "I have some right over there." She points in the direction of the far corner of the store. "I'll show you them when you come back in from picking your tree."

I give Ellie one last smile, and then I follow Macy outside, leaving River where he stands.

And I feel his eyes on me the whole way out.

Carrie

"She likes you," I say to River as he pulls upside my house and turns the engine off.

"Who?" He climbs out of the truck, not waiting for my response.

I climb out my side and meet him at the back of the truck, which he's opening to get my tree and decorations out.

I got some real nice tree ornaments at a great price. Not the glass ornaments. But still, really lovely. And a set of Christmas lights on discount.

"Macy," I tell him. The word feels a little sticky in my throat. I'm not sure why.

It's not because I'm interested in River. Of course I think River's handsome. His body is out of this world, as are other parts of his anatomy. But I have no interest in him in that way. I have zero interest in men in general. My focus is on my baby and Buddy and building us a great home and life. River is just a friend. If he's even that. I think, if you asked him, he'd say we weren't friends.

And Macy wasn't the friendliest of girls. But I think maybe she saw me with River and got the wrong idea about us. She was probably a little jealous. And River isn't the friendliest of guys. They'd be a perfect fit.

"She doesn't know me," he grunts as he drags the tree out of the back of the truck and hauls it onto his big shoulder.

I grab hold of the tree stand and box of ornaments, and I quickly follow after him to my front door.

"I don't mean she likes your personality," I tell him as I balance the box on the arm holding the tree stand while getting my keys out of my purse. I somehow manage it and unlock the front door, pushing it open. Buddy's there in an instant, jumping around with excitement at my arrival home. "Hey, Buddy boy. We'll have a fuss in a minute, just watch out while River carries the tree in," I tell Buddy as River navigates the tree through my front door and into my living room.

"You do realize that dog doesn't understand a fucking word you just said."

He called Buddy a dog. Definite upgrade from mutt.

I follow River in and put the box and stand down on the floor. I kneel on the floor, and Buddy climbs into my lap and starts licking my face.

"Yes, he does … don't you, you handsome boy?" I scratch Buddy behind his ears, the way I know he likes it.

River leans the tree against the wall and watches me with Buddy. He shakes his head.

"What?"

"Odd as fuck," he says.

"Grumpy as the Grinch," I tell him.

His eyes flash with humor.

I really do enjoy trading barbs with him. I have no idea what that says about our relationship. Not that we have a relationship. I'm not actually sure what we are, to be honest.

Then, I remember what I was saying about Macy. "Oh, so, yeah, as I was saying." I put Buddy to the floor and get to my feet. "Macy … I didn't mean she likes your personality. I meant that she likes *this*." I wave my hand up and down, gesturing to his body and face.

"Wow, Red. An insult and compliment in one. I'm impressed. And you do realize this tree is way too fucking big for this living room."

I stop and look at it leaning up against my wall. The top is bent over against the ceiling. Hmm … it looks quite big now that it's in here. I might've gotten a bit carried away when I was buying it. Maybe overestimated the height of the ceiling.

"Yeah." I sigh. "But it's only for a few weeks."

"Sure, a few weeks of not being able to sit in your living room because your big-ass Christmas tree has taken it over."

"Don't be dramatic. I can trim the top down, so it doesn't bend over against the ceiling."

He huffs out a laugh. "The top isn't your problem, Red. The problem will happen when I cut the rope off this tree, and it spreads right out and over your living room."

Oh. "Really?"

"Yes. Really."

I look at the tree, all packed into the rope and net covering it.

I think he's right.

"Fudge," I murmur.

"I think you mean, *fuck*."

"No, I definitely meant *fudge*." I press my finger to my lips, thinking. I come up with nothing. "What do you think I should do?"

"How the fuck should I know?"

"But you've had Christmas trees before."

He pauses and looks at me. "How come you've never had a tree before, if you're as into Christmas as you say you are?"

Ah.

"Well … I never said I haven't had one. I just"—I bite my lip—"never had any involvement in buying one or putting one up before."

He stares at me for a long moment. I entwine my fingers together in front of me.

"Trim it. Or toss it."

"I'm not tossing it out!" I say, aghast.

"Looks like you're trimming it then."

"Yeah." I sigh.

"You want me to cut the rope off for you?" he asks. "See what you're working with."

"Probably best. If I do, I might get buried beneath it."

He looks at me and then at the tree. "True. Pass me the stand."

I hand it over to him and watch as he fits the base of the tree into the stand, securing it. Then, he pushes the coffee table, so it's up against the sofa, trapping Buddy, who's on the sofa at the moment.

I go over and pick Buddy up, holding him in my arms, getting him out of the way.

River pulls a Swiss Army knife out of the pocket of his jeans. Flicks the knife out and starts to cut the rope on the tree.

I back up as the branches start falling free because … holy fudge knuckles. It's massive. It spreads out, covering half the sofa and coffee table. It's hanging over the television. Basically, it takes up half of the room.

Well … hells bells.

"Well … it's …" I helplessly gesture to it.

"The words you're looking for are *fucking ridiculous*. Actually, it reminds me of you."

"Ridiculous?" I frown.

"Pushy and invasive." He gives me a look.

Still frowning, I hug Buddy to my chest. "I'm not pushy and invasive." I'm the least nosy person I know.

"*Macy likes you.*" He imitates my voice, once again badly.

"You do realize I sound nothing like that?"

"Whiny and annoying?"

"Yes."

"You keep telling yourself that, Red."

"Jerk. And I was merely pointing out that Macy likes you. You know, just trying to be nice. You should try it sometime."

"News flash: I'm not nice. And I don't want to be nice. Some people like being assholes. I'm one of those people."

"The man doth protest too much, methinks." I tap my chin with my index finger. "You're nice, River. Deal with it."

He folds his knife up and puts it back in his pocket. "Okay, explain how I'm nice."

I falter a little. "Well … you're nice to me on occasion."

"No. I tolerate you on occasion."

I laugh at that. "You took me to get a tree. That was nice."

"No, it wasn't. I was going there anyway. I just took you with me because you're pregnant, and whether I'm an asshole or not, my gran would rise from her place of rest and come and kick my ass for leaving a pregnant woman to haul a Christmas tree around."

"Fair enough. And … I'm sorry about your gran."

"She was old." He shrugs. "And it was years ago."

"Well, I'm still sorry."

I want to ask about his mom, but I don't know how. So, instead, I skip right back to our conversation. "You were nice to Ellie when we were at the store."

"I was respectful. I was taught to respect my elders."

By his gran.

"Respect. Right." I nod. "You were nice to Macy—well, after I prompted you to be."

"Prompted? More like forced. And, if you think that was me being nice, then you need your head checked."

I smile wide. "Maybe I do."

"There's no maybe about it. Now, can we stop fucking around? It's wasting time and annoying me."

"Do you have somewhere to be?"

"No."

I tilt my head to the side, something occurring to me. "What do you do for a living?"

"This and that."

"Sounds vague."

"It is."

"I work at the diner."

He looks at me like I'm as thick as the Christmas tree. "Uh, I know. Because you already fucking told me."

"I'm a waitress there."

"Wow. Really? I'm shocked to learn this."

"I could have been the cook," I tell him.

"No, you couldn't because Guy is, and he still works there. Aside from a cook and waitress, there aren't any other jobs at the diner. So, let's cut to the chase and get to the point of this conversation."

"Well"—I lift my shoulders—"I just thought, if I told you what my job is, you might tell me yours."

"You thought wrong."

"Why?"

"Because it's none of your business."

"You're being rude, River."

"I was nice before, according to you."

"You were. And, now, you're being rude."

"I am rude. And mean. And an asshole."

"I can't argue with that."

"Good. So, stop fucking arguing with me now and go get me your pruning shears, so I can trim this damn tree for you."

"How do you know I have pruning shears?"

"Because I've seen you in the garden, trimming your bushes."

Laughter splutters out of me. "You do realize how that sounded, right?"

He gives me an innocent look. "I have no idea what you mean."

"Sure you don't." I roll my eyes. "And you do realize that, by offering to trim my tree—"

I snort and then clamp a hand over my mouth, and he laughs.

"You have a dirty mind, Red." He slowly shakes his head, holding my stare. "And did you just snort?"

"You laughed, too."

"But I didn't snort." His eyes darken with some unnamed emotion. "And I never claimed to be clean."

Well ... hells bells and Christmas tingle.

Something has tightened low in my belly, causing an ache to start between my legs. I press my thighs together and bite the inside of my cheek.

"You're being nice again," I say in a quieter voice.

"No. I'm offering to trim this tree because you're half as small as it is, and you're pregnant; therefore, you ain't going up any ladders."

I release a breath. "Yeah, you're right. That's not nice. That's called being kind and thoughtful."

"For fuck's sake," he groans.

"And I'm not that small, by the way."

Both brows rise in question. "Can you reach the top of the tree?"

"Well ... no."

"Go get the fucking shears, Red."

Sigh. "Fine."

I go and retrieve my pruning shears from the cabinet under the sink where I keep my gardening things and take them to River.

"You want anything to drink?" I ask him as I hand the shears over.

"Coffee. Black."

"Like your heart," I quip and then instantly regret it. "Ugh. Sorry, that was rude."

Especially after he took me to get the tree and is now helping me with it.

He stops and looks at me. "Don't be sorry. I've said worse things to you."

Has he though? He's said some jerky stuff but nothing as bad as that.

Turning away, I walk back into the kitchen, but guilt is prickling at me. I stop in the doorway and look back at him over my shoulder. "River …"

He doesn't look at me, but I know he's listening.

"I don't think your heart is black."

No response.

"River …"

"I heard you, Red. You don't think my heart is black."

"No, not that." I turn fully to face him. "I wanted to ask you something."

"Do I have to answer?"

"Only if you want to."

"I really don't."

"Okay."

"For fuck's sake." He sighs and turns to look at me. "What is it?"

I feel a bit stupid now. But I started this, so I have to forge on. I rub my hands together. "Well, I was just wondering … are we … friends?"

"Wait." He holds up a hand. "Have I just defied the laws of time and traveled back to grade school?"

"Funny."

"I know. And, no, Red, we aren't friends."

"Oh. Right." My heart dips. I bite my lower lip to stop it from turning down.

He sighs again. "I don't do friends, Carrie." His voice is lower now. "But, if I did, then you'd be the closest thing I have to one."

"Oh," I say again, brightening up. I'm biting back a smile now. Because, for River, I'd say that's as good as an admission that we are friends that I'm going to get.

I step into the kitchen and put the kettle on. While I wait for it to boil, I let Buddy outside to take a leak and watch him from the deck.

I call Buddy back in when the kettle boils, and he trots off into the living room. I make River's coffee and my tea and carry them back through.

I put his on the coffee table—the part that isn't covered in Christmas tree branches.

And I sit down on the floor, Buddy at my feet, and start unwrapping the protective paper and bubble wrap from the ornaments. Then, I get the lights out of the box, untangling them, ready for hanging.

Then, River's done trimming the tree. I help him gather up the trimmed branches and take them to the trash can outside.

We walk back in. He picks up his coffee, draining the cup. Puts it down and walks to the front door.

Guess he's leaving.

I follow him to the door.

"Thanks for everything today," I tell him. "I really appreciate it. I owe you big time."

"You don't owe me a thing, Red." And he's walking away, toward his house.

"Bye," I call after him.

The only response I receive is a lift of his hand.

That is progress in itself. Normally, he'd just ignore me completely.

I shut the door and go back inside. I bend down to pick the lights up from beside the box when something catches my eye on the inside of it. Something that wasn't there earlier.

The glass train.

I kneel beside the box. I reach inside and carefully pick it up. It's so beautiful. Even more so than I realized.

My eyes move to the front door River just left through.

Did he ...

Surely not ...

But it wasn't there before.

I know it wasn't. I unwrapped every single one of those ornaments.

And I definitely didn't buy it. And there's no way it could've gotten in there by accident.

I gently place the train back in the box and get to my feet.

"Be back in a minute, Bud." I pat him on the head before leaving my house.

I walk quickly over to River's house and ring the bell.

He swings open the door a few seconds later. I notice he hasn't even had a chance to take off his shoes.

Something catches me in this moment. I don't quite know what it is exactly. Maybe his kindness. Or the good heart he hides. Whatever it is, it takes my words right along with it.

"Carrie, what's up? Is the baby okay?" Worried eyes flick to my stomach and back up to my face.

"The baby's fine," I reassure him. "Just ... the train ... from the store ... the one I liked. It's in the box with the other ornaments, and it wasn't there before."

His face stays impassive. "Are you sure it wasn't there before?"

"Yes. I unwrapped each and every one of those ornaments, and it definitely wasn't there."

"Maybe you overlooked it."

"Even if I did, I didn't buy it. And there is no way it got in there by accident. Unless it came to life and choo-chooed its way into my box."

"Choo-chooed?" he echoes.

I can tell he's fighting a smile.

I glare at him. "Yes. Choo-chooed."

"You do realize that it's your shoe size that's six and not your age."

"Har-fudging-har."

Also, he remembered what size shoe I wear. That does surprise me. I didn't think he'd care to remember such a minute detail about me.

"Maybe Ellie gave it to you," he says.

"Why would she?"

"Because she's a good person. And you bought a tree from her and a shitload of tree decorations. Maybe it was a free gift."

It's my turn to lift a brow. "A fifty-dollar free gift?"

He folds his arms over his chest and lifts those big shoulders of his in a shrug. "She's a generous woman."

Mirroring him, I cross my arms over my own chest. "Even if it was a free gift … it would be weird that, out of all the ornaments hanging in that window, she would pick out the one I loved most to give to me as a free gift—which she didn't tell me about. That'd be one heck of a coincidence, don't you think?"

His lips purse. "Sure. But coincidences happen every day."

"Yeah … you're right. I should probably call Ellie up and check with her though and also thank her."

"I wouldn't."

"Why?" I'm fighting a smile.

His shoulders lift. "Well, it might embarrass her."

"Why?"

"Because she clearly gave you a gift and didn't want you to know it was from her."

"Uh-huh." I nod. "But it's also an expensive gift. One that I don't feel right about accepting."

He sighs. "It's just a fucking ornament, Red."

"River … did you buy me the ornament?"

"No. But, if I had and you were my almost friend, then I'd expect you to take the fucking ornament and not stand there, complaining about it."

"I'm not complaining."

Silence.

"River."

"What?"

"Thank you. For the train. It's beautiful."

He grunts, and I bite down on a smile.

I take a step back from the door. "So, there's a Christmas boat parade happening tomorrow night at the lake. Are you going?"

"No. I'd rather have my teeth pulled out with pliers than go to that shit-tastic waste of time and money."

"I'm going with Sadie and Guy. You know, my boss and colleague at the diner."

"How fun for you." His voice is as dry as the air.

"You should come with us."

"Teeth. Pliers."

"Awesome. So, I'll see you tomorrow night. We'll meet you there."

"Have you lost your hearing? Or are you actually as stupid as I accuse you of being?"

"Nope." I smile widely, showing all my teeth. "I'm just choosing to ignore you … you know, like you do to me." I turn on my heel and start to walk away. "It starts at seven thirty," I call over my shoulder.

"I'm not going," he calls out.

"Seven thirty, River," I reemphasize. "Don't be late."

"Jesus fucking Christ. Fucking annoying woman!" I hear him grumble from behind me, and then his front door slams shut.

My smile somehow gets even bigger, and I wear that smile the whole way into my house and for the rest of the day.

Carrie

I'm just on my way back from using the public restroom—because being pregnant requires frequent bathroom breaks—when I spot River loitering by a cluster of trees.

He came.

My insides light up.

I change direction and walk over to him. His eyes turn to me, like he sensed me, watching my approach.

He's wearing his beanie on his head, covering his hair. A black knitted sweater, faded black jeans, and boots. There's a slight chill to the air tonight. Hence why I'm wearing a knitted hat, coat, jeans, and boots.

I come to a stop in front of him. "You came." I smile.

"Yeah. Well, I didn't exactly have a choice, did I?"

He did. He could've just not come. But I don't point that out to him. Because I'm happy he's here.

He came tonight because he didn't want to let me down.

And that makes me happier than I can explain right now.

"You missed the parade though," I tell him, pushing my hands into my jacket pockets.

"Shame."

"I'm assuming that was on purpose?"

Amused eyes look down into mine. "You would assume right."

I laugh softly. "It was actually a very good parade."

"Now, I know that's a lie."

"Nuh-uh. I would never lie about something as important as a Christmas boat parade." I smile widely.

He chuckles. "You're an idiot, Red."

"Yeah, I know." I gently nudge his arm with my elbow. "Hey, why don't you come over and say hello to Sadie and Guy? They're sitting out by the lake. You went to school with Guy, right?"

"Yeah, I did. But I'd … rather not go over."

"Oh. Okay. Well, we can hang here for a while. Or take a walk? Whatever you want."

"A walk sounds good."

His eyes look different tonight. There's an unease to them that I've only seen once before—yesterday, when he came over to talk to me.

He was uncomfortable then. He's uncomfortable now.

"Awesome. Let me just run over and tell Sadie where I'm going."

Leaving River, I walk quickly back over to where Sadie and Guy are sitting in our chairs, sipping on warm cider.

"Hey." I tap the backs of their chairs, getting their attention. "I'm just gonna take a walk with River."

"River?" Guy asks.

"Yes. River."

"River Wild?" Guy cranes his neck to look around me. "He's here?"

"That's what I said. And stop staring at him." I move to block his vision.

"I just can't believe he's here. I've never seen him at any town function or … well, anything ever before. He's not exactly known for being sociable."

"Well, things change. Anyway, I just came to let you know where I was in case you wondered."

"I'm glad he came." Sadie smiles up at me.

I told her that I'd invited him. She seemed pleased about it at the time.

"You invited him?" Guy gives me an odd look.

"Yes," I say slowly so as not to be misunderstood.

"I can't believe you invited the town weirdo to the Christmas parade with us."

Guy barks out a laugh, and I don't like it.

He's acting like an ass.

"I don't see the big deal here. And River's not a weirdo." *Grumpy, honest to a fault, a bit of a jerk, but not a weirdo.*

"Well, he's not exactly normal."

"And what is normal?" I fire back at him.

"Not him; that's for sure. I knew you two were neighbors, but I didn't realize you were friends. Did you know this, Sadie?" He gives her an accusing look.

"I don't see the issue here. So what if I'm friends with him?"

"Because he's dangerous!" Guy exclaims.

"He is not dangerous." Sadie laughs.

"You can laugh, but how do you know he isn't? Crazy can be passed down genetically, you know."

"Stop talking shit, Guy," Sadie tells him.

"Can you please tell me what in the world you are going on about?" I ask them both.

Guy pins me with a knowing stare. "I'm talking about the fact that River's mom murdered a policeman. Shot him dead." He puts two fingers to his chest and mimics the firing of a gun with his thumb.

River's mom killed a cop.

"Guy!" Sadie chastises. "You really need to stop gossiping about people."

River's mom murdered a cop.

"It's not gossip when it's factual news," Guy says to Sadie. He looks back at me, a gleam in his eyes. "Everyone knows that River's mom murdered her cop husband, River's stepdad. Shot him dead in the kitchen, and River was there when it happened."

River was there?

"How old was River when it happened?" I find my voice to ask.

Guy looks up in thought. "Like, eight or nine, I think."

Jesus. He was just a kid.

"What happened to his mom?" I feel bad, asking these things while River is standing over there, waiting for me. But I also feel compelled to know.

"Charged with first-degree murder and got life in prison. She tried to say it was self-defense, but apparently, that was bullshit. The guy was unarmed, and she shot him with his own gun—his police-issued firearm. And she didn't have a scratch on her."

"Is she still in prison?" I'm quaking inside, and I'm not exactly sure why.

"Nope." He shakes his head. "She got shanked in prison."

"She got what?"

"Jesus, Guy, you really need to stop watching those damn prison shows," Sadie says to him. "River's mom was killed by another prisoner," she clarifies for me.

"Oh. Right."

She was killed. In prison.

Poor River.

I know his mom murdered someone—his stepdad—but she was still his mom, and he lost her in such awful circumstances. Her and his stepdad.

And I just can't believe that River's stepdad was a cop—that we have that connection. Not that it's a weird connection. Lots of people are police officers. My husband was one. River's stepdad was one. But the coincidence just feels too similar.

Not that I killed Neil. But there were times when I wanted to.

God, there were so many times when I imagined doing it. But I never did.

I wonder what happened to make his mom do that to her husband. What drove her to kill him like that?

Or maybe nothing drove her at all, except that she was just a bad person. There are plenty of those in the world.

I just can't imagine what River's been through and starting at such a young age.

No wonder he's so guarded.

I feel like my heart is doubling in size for him. For the pain he must have gone through as a child.

I'm standing here, not entirely sure what to do with this overload of information. It's not like I can go over there and pretend like I don't know this.

Yes, that's exactly what I can do.

If he wanted me to know, he would have told me.

And he's allowed his secrets. God knows I have mine.

If it were me, I wouldn't want him to come over and dredge my past up.

I definitely wouldn't.

No, I'll keep my thoughts to myself and just carry on like before. Like I know nothing about his mom or stepdad.

"Okay …" I take a step back. "Well, I won't be long."

"Take your time," Sadie says to me.

"Just be careful," Guy says. "Remember, there's murderous blood running through his veins. So, if he pulls out a gun, run like hell."

"Not funny, Guy." Sadie gives a disappointed shake of her head at him.

"What? It was just a joke!" Guy exclaims.

"It was the least funny joke I've ever heard," I say quietly before I turn on my heel and walk back toward River, who is standing exactly where I left him.

I'm kind of feeling bad that I got him to come tonight.

I thought it would be fun.

But he looks like he'd rather be anywhere but here.

"Ready?" I ask as I reach him.

We start walking further out, a small distance away from the hustle of people. I notice River keeps to my left, partially shielding himself from people. His shoulders are turned in. Like he's trying to make himself smaller, which is impossible because the man is huge.

I push my hands into my pockets and kick a small rock out of the way. "So, the baby's the size of a green olive at the moment," I tell him, measuring the size out with my finger and thumb. Not because he's ever asked or showed any interest in the development of my baby, but because of a want to say something, anything, and to get him talking. "And it weighs about three grams. I follow this website that charts the baby's growth in comparison to fruit."

"Fruit?"

"Yep."

"And you're currently pregnant with an olive."

"A baby olive."

"Olives are vile."

"I know, right?" I chuckle, and so does he.

"So, what size will the fruit baby be next week?"

"A fig."

"Also gross."

"True." I laugh again.

"So, when will the baby actually be the size of a decent fruit?"

"Hmm … well, it'll be apple-sized at fifteen weeks."

"Apples are okay as fruit goes. They taste better juiced though."

"Again, true."

"Are we actually having a fucking conversation about fruit right now?"

"Yep." I giggle.

"You're so odd."

"Hey! You were talking fruit, too."

"Humoring you, Red. I was humoring you."

"Sure you were." I roll my eyes.

All this talk of fruit has gotten me hungry—and also the smell of a vendor selling corn dogs. Not that it takes much nowadays to get me eating.

I start drifting in a bit, toward people and the corn-dog-selling vendor. "You hungry?" I ask him. "Because I could really go for a corn dog right now. My treat, for dragging you here?"

He gives me a look. "You're not buying me a corn dog, Red. I'll get them."

"You sure?"

Another look. "I'm sure. Wait here, and I'll be back in a minute."

I watch him walk over to the vendor, shoulders in, head down, avoiding eye contact with people.

Moving back a bit, I rest my butt against a large rock, half-sitting on it.

I've not even been sitting there a minute when a guy wanders over. He has short sandy-blond hair and a stocky frame; he's about six-foot I'd say, and he's handsome in a pretty-boy way.

He stops before me, a smile on his face, showing gleaming white teeth. "Hey. You work at the diner, right?"

"Yes."

"I'm Brad." He offers his hand to me.

I put my hand in his and shake it. The skin on his hand is soft. Like his hands have never seen a hard day's work before.

"Carrie." I pull my hand back.

"So, you're new to town?"

"Yes."

"We get a lot of tourists here but not many new residents. What brought you to Canyon Lake?" He moves to lean on the rock beside me.

Discomfort slithers through me. I shift up a bit. Something about this guy doesn't sit right with me. And I listen to my gut nowadays. It's always right.

"I fancied a change of scenery." I shrug.

He laughs. "You don't give much away, do you?"

I glance at him. His eyes are green. A nice color, but they're not kind eyes.

I shrug again.

He laughs again.

"Did you enjoy the parade?" he asks me.

"I did. I've never seen a Christmas boat parade before. It was fun to watch."

"So, are you here alone?" he asks, and I don't like the question.

"I came with friends," I firmly tell him.

There's a lull in the conversation, and I really wish he would just go. But he doesn't.

"So …" He scratches his chin. "I've seen you around town a few times and wanted to talk to you. I think you're a total knockout, Carrie, and I was wondering if you'd like to go out with me sometime."

Uh.

His direct approach kind of throws me for a moment. I'm about to turn down his offer, but I don't get a chance.

"No, she doesn't fucking want to go out with you."

My head turns at the sound of River, a face like thunder, sans corn dogs. Fire and ire burn in his eyes, and I'm getting the distinct impression River does not like Brad.

Brad stands and faces River. He lets out a laugh, and it's not a nice sound. "Well, this is the surprise of the century. What the fuck are you doing here? I thought you didn't leave that mausoleum you call a home."

And it looks like that feeling of dislike goes both ways.

"Come on; let's get you back to your friends," River says to me, ignoring Brad.

"Carrie doesn't want to go anywhere. Do you, Carrie? We were having a nice conversation before you showed up."

I open my mouth to speak, but River beats me to it.

"No, you were hitting on her, like you do with anything that has a pulse. Come on, Red."

"Red? Well, hold up now. This just got really interesting. Are you actually friends with the one-pump chump?" Brad says, lips twitching.

"You still filming people having sex without their knowledge?" River fires back at him.

What?

Brad laughs. "You never could take a joke."

"The only joke here is you."

"Well, now, that's just not nice. And I think it's only fair that the lovely Carrie here knows who she's spending her time with."

"Shut the fuck up, Brad," River snaps.

And that just makes Brad smile wider. An evil gleam in his eyes.

If I'm not mistaken, I'm guessing I already know what Brad is going to say.

I move and stand beside River.

"I already know who I'm spending my time with," I tell Brad.

"I'm not sure you do, sugar. You know, aside from being able to get it up long enough to satisfy a woman, he comes from bad blood. Do you know his mama murdered a cop in cold blood? Shot a good man to death in her kitchen while he stood there and watched her do it."

River freezes beside me.

"I don't think that's any of my business or yours." God knows how I manage to keep my voice steady.

"That's where you're wrong, sugar, because that man his mama murdered was my uncle. An honest, good, law-abiding man who deserved better than to be shot dead by some cheap whore who'd tricked him into marriage and taking on her fucked up kid."

I can feel River practically vibrating with rage next to me.

Brad is smirking like he's happy with the bomb he just dropped.

"Are you done?" I say quietly to Brad.

"I've not even started, sugar."

River turns so abruptly; his arm knocks into mine.

"River!" I call to him as I watch him stride away from us, heading for the mass of trees that leads into the woods at the back of our houses.

I look back at Brad with unconcealed disgust.

He stares back at me. "You're a fool if you're spending time with him," he says in a repugnant tone. "It won't be long before he snaps, just like his mama did, and whoever is in his way will end up like my uncle did."

"You don't know what you're talking about."

"That's where you're wrong."

But I'm already turning on my heel to go after River.

And it's him who's wrong. River isn't evil.

I know evil, and it's not in him. He's just a human being who's seen way too much in his lifetime, and he still carries all of that pain and hurt around with him.

River could've easily hit Brad just then, but he didn't.

He walked away.

"River!" I call out, rushing after him.

The man can sure move. I finally catch up with him just inside the first line of trees.

"River, will you just wait?" I gasp, out of breath.

He stops and turns to face me. His face a mask of anger and shame.

I hate that he feels that way. He has nothing to be ashamed about.

"River … what Brad said, it doesn't matter."

His lips curl with disdain. "Of course it fucking matters! What the hell is wrong with you? Wait … did you already know about my mom?" Accusing, defensive eyes stare down at me.

Crap.

I swallow, feeling like I've done something wrong. "Yes," I admit. "But I only found out tonight. Before our walk. Guy told me."

"Of course he did." He lets out a hollow laugh.

"River, your past is yours. It's none of my business."

"You don't even know what you're talking about," he says like he's not even listening to me. He stares down at the ground. "None of you do."

"River—"

"I fucking knew I shouldn't have come tonight." His eyes snap up to mine, wide and furious. "I knew something like this would happen. You shouldn't have pushed me about coming tonight, and I shouldn't have let you."

"I'm sorry," I say, feeling helpless.

"If you hadn't been talking to Brad, then I wouldn't have had to go over and deal with his crap. This is why I stay away from people, Red. To avoid shit like this!"

"I … I …" I hold out my hands. "Brad came over to me. What do you want me to do? Ignore him?"

His look is unwavering. "Yes."

"Why were you talking to him, Annie?"

"H-he started talking to me. I didn't know what to do. I didn't want to be rude."

He grabbed hold of my chin, and furious eyes stared into mine. I started to shake.

"You know you're not supposed to talk to other men."

"I-I know. I-I'm s-sorry."

"What were you talking to him about, Annie? Telling him what a bad husband I am to you? How you want to leave me?"

"N-no! I wasn't talking about you, Neil, I swear."

"Liar." Spittle hit my face. His other hand grabbed hold of my hair, yanking it tight, making my eyes water. "You were arranging to meet him, weren't you? You want to fuck him, don't you?"

"N-no. P-please, Neil."

"You're a lying, dirty whore! Well, if you want to be a fucking whore, then I'll treat you like one!"

I step back, shaking off the memory. My hands are trembling. I wrap my arms around myself, forcing strength into my spine. "I won't do that."

"Then, you're a fucking idiot. Brad is not someone you want to spend your time with."

"Funny. Because he just said the same thing about you," I say the words and immediately regret them when I see hurt flicker over his countenance. So brief that, if I hadn't been looking right at him, I would've missed it.

"He's right. I'm not someone you want to be around." His voice is filled with self-loathing, and that makes me sadder than I can explain.

"So, what are you telling me?" Melancholy starts to creep in around my heart because I already know what he's saying.

Hard, emotionless, defiant eyes stare back at me. "I'm telling you what you already know. We're not friends. We'll never be friends. So, stop fucking trying to push something that will never happen. I barely like you on a good day. I just fucking tolerate you because of the way you wander around, looking like a lost, lonely sheep. You just don't seem to get that you're not wanted."

I know his words are meant to wound and hurt. He's lashing out because he's pushing me away. But I won't be spoken to like this. I deserve better.

I lift my chin even though, inside, I feel gutted. "I get it," I say in a steady voice.

"Fucking finally."

"Okay"—I take a step back—"I guess I'll go. Have a nice life or not …"

Biting my trembling lip, I ignore the sting of tears I feel and turn and walk back out of the trees and into the light of people, leaving River standing there, alone in the darkness.

River
Sixteen Years Old

"What the fuck am I doing here?"

This is stupid. I shouldn't be here.

I don't do this. I don't come to parties.

Because you've never been invited to one before.

Standing outside the front door of the house, I can hear the music pumping loud behind it.

I'm at a party.

Well, almost.

Who would've thought it?

But, when Chloe Nelson, cheerleading stunner, invites you with the promise of something more—meaning sex—you turn up.

Chloe was dating Brad Thurlow, superstar football player. And the nephew of—

Nope. Not going there tonight.

I'm finally going to get laid. Pop my cherry.

With Chloe fucking Nelson.

And the bonus is getting back at Brad in the process.

I fucking hate that guy.

He's a dick of the highest order.

He is always doing shit to get at me at school. Fucking pranks, spreading rumors about me.

I mostly just ignore him. But it's still annoying.

And, as of four days ago, his girl—or ex-girl—and him broke up.

I checked around school to make sure it was true, not that I have actual friends to ask, but I listened around, and apparently, he dumped her. And, now, she's been texting me. Her parents are away, and she asked me to come to the party she's having at the big-ass mansion she lives in.

It's highly likely that she is using me to get back at Brad.

Do I give a fuck? Nope.

I'm about to stamp my V card with the hottest girl in school.

Not that I'll be telling her I'm still a virgin.

Chloe Nelson is gorgeous. Blonde-haired, blue-eyed, with a fan-fucking-tastic rack.

I've seen her in gym and at cheerleading practice, jumping around in those tight tops she wears, her tits bouncing around.

Shit. I'm getting hard, just thinking about it.

I rearrange my dick in my pants.

Okay, this is it. Get your ass inside, River.

But I don't move.

Because I'm a chickenshit.

I'm fucking nervous, okay?

I've never been to a party before. All the kids in school hate me. I honestly don't know why Chloe wants to be with me.

But I do want to lose my virginity, and she's the first girl who's shown a keen interest in making that happen.

Of course, I've hit first and second base with other girls.

We get a lot of tourists around here. Girls who know nothing about my past. Girls who wanna mess around with a local to pass the time.

But this is Chloe, and she knows who I am, yet she still seems to want me.

Come on, River. Man the fuck up and get yourself in there. You look like the freak they accuse you of being, standing out here on the doorstep.

I take hold of the door handle, turn it, and push open the door. The music is even louder in here. The party is in full swing. The house is packed with bodies.

No one even registers my appearance.

I've barely gotten three steps inside when Chloe appears in front of me. Her eyes are bright, cheeks flushed.

"You came!" She smiles up at me.

"Yep," I say. Full of words tonight I am.

"You want to mingle or," she reaches up on her tiptoes and speaks into my ear, "go upstairs for some privacy?"

I turn my eyes to hers. "Upstairs."

She grabs my hand and leads me past people and up the winding staircase to the second floor. I follow her down the hall and into what I'm guessing is her room. It's pink with a big four-poster bed, and there are pictures tacked to the walls—of her and her friends and still some of Brad.

She goes and sits on the edge of her bed. Then, she pats the spot beside her.

That's her bed.

Her bed.

My insides start to tremble. Queasiness eddies in my stomach.

Not now. For fuck's sake.

Pull yourself together, River.

Clenching my hands, I go over and sit down beside her.

"Your house is nice," I say, just for something to say.

"Yeah, it's okay, I guess."

I'm staring ahead at the wall in front of me like it has the answer to the meaning of life. My leg starts to jig with nerves.

"River?"

"Yeah?"

"Look at me."

I turn my face to hers. *God, she's so pretty.*

"Do you like me?"

"Sure I do."

Her tongue darts out to lick her bottom lip. I can't stop staring at it.

"I like you, too."

"You do?"

She laughs. It sounds awkward. I bring my eyes up to hers.

"Of course I do, silly. You wouldn't be here right now if I didn't."

True, but … I'm just surprised a girl like her would want a guy like me. All the kids at school think I'm a freak because of what my mom did …

What you did.

"You've barely spoken a handful of words to me up until a few days ago," I say to her, resting my hands on my thighs.

"Well, you know I was with Brad, and you know how he can be … but I've always thought you were hot." She starts to trace her fingertip over my hand, moving up my arm and onto my leg, moving up and up until she's running her fingernail over the zipper of my pants.

I swallow down hard.

She brings her lips close to my ear. "Do you want to … fuck me, River?" she whispers, and I nearly swallow my tongue.

Even though I had a pretty good idea that's what she wanted from me—from the tone of her messages and the way she brought me straight up here—hearing the way she casually just asked me to fuck blows my mind.

"Uh … y-yeah," I cough out the word, and she giggles.

Then, she kisses me.

Holy fuck. Her lips are so soft and plump.

I taste alcohol on her breath. I pull back. "How much have you had to drink?"

I don't want to take advantage of her.

"One beer." She holds up a finger. "I swear."

Her eyes look wide. Pupils dilated.

"Have you had … anything else?"

"Nope. Cross my heart." Using her finger, she draws an X over her chest, dragging my eyes downward to her tits.

She takes off her sweater and then her bra.

"Touch me, River."

So, I do.

And, God, she feels good. Warm and soft. Like nothing I've ever felt before.

I'm so fucking turned on; I feel like I might jizz in my pants. I have to think of mundane things to stop myself from coming.

Then, she's kissing me again, and clothes are being removed at the speed of lightning.

"Did you bring a condom?" she says against my lips.

"Yeah." I grab my pants from the floor and get the condom out of my pocket.

When I turn back, she's staring down at my cock, her mouth open.

"Is everything okay?" I ask her.

"Yeah … you're just big," she whispers. "I wasn't expecting you to be big."

Um … okay …

I look down at my cock. "Is that a problem?"

She shakes her head. "Get the condom on."

"Yes, ma'am."

My hands shake the whole time I put the rubber on, making it almost impossible. But I finally do it.

Chloe lies back on the bed. Every gorgeous inch of her. Her golden hair fanned out around her head.

"You're beautiful," I tell her. I feel like I might come just from looking at her lying here.

"Just fuck me, River," she says, sounding impatient.

Jesus, she's bossy. Not how I imagined a girl to be in bed, but what would I know? And I guess it's kind of hot, her telling me what to do.

God, this is it. I'm finally going to have sex with a girl.

I'm finally going to be normal. Like everyone else.

I climb over her, my body hovering over hers. My hips between her spread legs.

I'm hard. So hard, it's painful.

I hear a bang. It sounds like it's in her room.

My head snaps up. "What was that?"

"Nothing. Probably someone just looking for the bathroom." Her delicate hands curl around my face, bringing my eyes back to her. "I locked the door behind me. Don't worry. No one can get in." She lifts her mouth to mine, offering herself to me.

And I take her mouth, kissing her.

She wraps her legs around my waist.

I'm so worked up. I'm afraid I won't last long.

Please last. Please last.

"Do it, River. Put it in!" she orders.

"Fuck, okay, I'm doing it. God, you're so fucking hot. I can't believe I get to fuck you."

I push into her sweet fucking heaven … and—

Oh fuck, no …

But it's too late. I can't stop.

I drop my head onto her shoulder, my body shaking through the release.

"River."

"Yeah?"

"Did you just … come?"

"I'm so sorry," I mumble against her skin.

I'm so fucking embarrassed. No, I'm mortified.

"I'll make it up to you, Chloe, I swear."

I feel her body shaking beneath mine. It takes me a few moments to realize that she's laughing.

Heart pounding in my chest, I push up onto my hands, moving away from her.

"Did you get that?" she says.

"What?"

My head swings around, and I see Brad fucking Thurlow stepping out of her closet with his cell phone in his hand.

"Yep. Got it. All five seconds of it." He stares at me, laughing.

"What the fuck?" I jump off the bed and grab my jeans off the floor. I quickly pull them on along with my T-shirt, pushing my feet into my sneakers.

I hear a ping come from his phone.

"And, now, everyone else has it, too." He laughs again loudly, caustically.

"What the fuck did you do?"

My head is swiveling between him and Chloe.

"Did you send it already?" Chloe's voice is high-pitched and grating. "You said you'd make sure no one knew it was me!"

"Chill, babe. You can't tell it's you. You don't see your face, and he never said your name once. He could've been fucking his gran, for all anyone knows. Probably does, the freak."

"What the fuck did you do, Brad?" I growl, my hands clenching into fists at my sides.

Brad grins and holds his phone up, screen facing my way.

I can see my bare ass and the back of my head on-screen.

"Fuck, okay, I'm doing it. God, you're so fucking hot. I can't believe I get to fuck you," I hear myself say on the video.

A few seconds later, I'm watching myself come.

Misery crawls up my spine. I squeeze my eyes shut, trying to block it out. Shut everything out. Memories fighting to the surface, ones I fight so hard to keep locked away.

"River," I hear Chloe's voice on-screen.

I didn't notice the mocking tone when she first spoke. Probably because I was too overcome from coming. But I'm hearing it now.

"Yeah?"

"Did you just … come?"

"I'm so sorry."

The video ends, and Brad is doubled over with laughter.

"Dude, it was even better the second time around! It was like a fucking second, and you were blowing your load!"

"You fucking filmed me having sex with your ex-girlfriend?" I growl. My vision is going hazy with anger.

"Brad, you said we'd get back together if I did this for you."

My head turns to Chloe, stunned at what just came out of her mouth.

"Sure, babe. Sure."

"So, we're back together?"

"I said so, didn't I?" he snaps dismissively.

"What the fuck is wrong with you?" I bark at Brad. "You blackmailed her into doing this?" I swing around to look at Chloe. "Why would you do this? You can do better than this jerkwad."

"I love him," she whines, pouting.

"You heard the girl," Brad says smugly, answering for her. He puts his hand in his pocket and pulls out a little bag of white powder.

Cocaine.

"Here, babe, go do a line. You deserve it after that."

He tosses the bag to her, and she eagerly catches it. Scurrying away over to her dressing table, she tips the powder out and starts drawing out lines.

She's a cokehead.

I should've known.

I should've fucking known all of this was too good to be true.

Good things don't happen to me.

"You're fucked up. Both of you," I spit the words at him.

"Maybe I am. But I'll never be as fucked up as you. How was it, watching your mom blow my uncle away?"

"Fuck you." I stomp to the door.

"Look at it this way … I was doing you a favor. You got to fuck the hottest girl in school. I know it was only for a couple of seconds"—he laughs—"but it still counts. And, now, you won't be known just as the son of a cop killer. You'll also be known as the one-pump chump."

I turn back and storm toward him. He actually steps back, and that makes me laugh.

Fucking pussy.

I grab his phone from his hand, throw it on the floor, and stamp my foot on it.

"What the fuck?" he yells. "You'll pay for that, asshole! That was a brand-new phone! And, if you think that got rid of the video, think again. 'Cause I already sent it to everyone who goes to our school."

"What?"

"You heard me."

His expression is so arrogant and condescending. I want to hit him so bad.

I want to keep hitting him and never stop.

I turn my nails into my palms, pressing into the skin to ground myself. Stop myself from hitting him. I feel the skin break, blood seeping into my hands.

Walk away, River.

Walk. Away.

Releasing my fingers, I force myself to turn away from him and walk over to the door. I unlock it and yank it open, leaving my blood all over the handle, but like I fucking care.

Then, I'm out of there, speeding down the stairs and pushing through the mass of people, most already watching the video. I shut the front door on their laughter. Laughter about me. Aimed at me.

I jog quickly to my car. Getting inside it, I turn on the engine and peel out of there.

I'm so fucking dumb! I can't believe I fell for that.

They're all in there, laughing at me. Brad will be having a great fucking time, telling everyone about it.

Sick son of a bitch. Just like his uncle.

Hurt and pain well up inside me. Things long buried resurfacing.

"Fuck!" I roar, slamming my hand against the steering wheel. "I fucking hate people! I wish they would all just leave me alone!"

Never again will I be so stupid to trust a girl.

Never a-fucking-gain.

Carrie

I've got a car!

It's a fifteen-year-old Chevy Impala with too many miles on the odometer to count, but it's mine, and I got a great deal on it. It was selling for fifteen hundred bucks, but Ivan, who owns the local dealership, has been a regular at the diner since Sadie opened it, and he gave it to me for twelve hundred bucks. I'm not super flush with funds, but I've been saving up all my tips, and I've been picking up extra hours at the diner these past few months to pay for it, so no more walking for me. Yay!

I just picked the car up after my breakfast shift at the diner, and I was itching to take it out for a drive. So, I decided to take a drive out to Thistleberry Farm, which is where I'm heading now, to buy some of the fresh produce they sell. Healthy food for the baby, who is growing nicely.

I had my latest checkup and the twenty-week ultrasound yesterday.

I decided not to find out the gender at the ultrasound. I want the surprise at the birth. So, I've taken to calling the baby Olive since that conversation I had with River about the fruit—

And nope, not going there. River is a no-go topic for me nowadays.

I haven't seen him since that night. Not a glimpse. Not that I've been actively looking for him because I haven't been.

I refuse to even look in the direction of his house.

And I'm totally fine about it all now.

I was sad at first, but then I figured, I couldn't lose something that I never had, right? And, apparently, I never had his friendship.

Okay, so I might still be a little mad. But it's fine.

He's nothing to do with anything.

So, yeah, Olive is now the length of a small banana and coming along nicely. I have a decent-sized bump now, so I'm really showing, and I've had to invest in some maternity clothes to keep up with my ever-growing waistline. Thankfully, my diner uniform includes black pants, which I got a couple of maternity ones that have the stretchy waistband—so sexy. And my work shirt is provided by Sadie. She's ordered me in another shirt, a couple of sizes up, as the last one she got me, which I'm wearing now, is tight across my belly already.

I can't believe I'm twenty weeks, and it's March 1 already. Time is flying by. Christmas seems like an age ago.

I spent Christmas Day with Sadie and Buddy. Sadie cooked a turkey, and I helped with the rest. It was fun and happy. My first Christmas in a long time where I felt safe.

New Year's Eve I spent with Buddy. Sadie and Guy went out to some bars. They'd tried to talk me into going, but bars aren't really my thing. They'd said it was my last New Year before the baby came, my last New Year of freedom. But what they don't realize is, I have more freedom now than I ever have. And, honestly, I'd rather be home with Buddy.

I turn on the radio. My car fills with the sound of "River" by Leon Bridges.

Nope. Just nope.

I switch the radio off and travel the rest of the way in silence.

I arrive at Thistleberry Farm fifteen minutes later.

I park my car in one of the parking spots, grab my purse off the passenger seat, and head on into the store.

And I stop dead in my tracks.

River is standing behind the counter.

My heart does this weird shimmy in my chest at the sight of him.

I'm staring at him.

He's staring back at me. His face is a mask of surprise.

I think mine mirrors his.

I need to look away.

Turning away, I grab a basket and start moving through the store with no real direction other than to get as far away from him as possible.

What the fudge is he doing here? And why is he working behind the counter?

I really want to leave. But that would look weird, and if I just walked out, he'd know that I was bothered by seeing him.

Also, I came all this way for some fresh produce, and goddamn it, I'm getting my fresh produce!

As I move through the aisles, I start grabbing things off the shelves at random, dropping them in the basket.

When I stop and look down, I see I've got a jar of pickled green tomatoes, a jar of hot pickled radishes, a green pepper, a bunch of asparagus, a jar of applesauce, a tray of cherry tomatoes, a bag of pumpkin bread, and a jar of sweet potato butter.

Huh. Calm down there, Rachael Ray.

Well, I can't put the stuff back because I'll look like a complete tool, so I'll have to just buy it. And the pumpkin bread and sweet potato butter look yummy.

Calming down, I start actually looking at the items I'm getting, focusing on them and not in the direction of where I know River is still standing at the counter.

I hate that I'm so aware of him.

Ugh.

I stop by the gala apples and look down at them, picking out ones that look the best, dropping them into my basket.

I feel movement to my right. Followed by the scent of cigar smoke.

River.

"Red."

The sound of his voice is like welcome rain on a hot day. I hate that, too. I hate the way it intensifies the ache in my chest.

Why is he talking to me?

He made it perfectly clear that talking to me was the last thing he wanted to do.

So, I do the only thing I can do.

I walk away from him.

I hear him mutter, "Fuck."

I walk to the far side of the store until there's nowhere else to go, and I find myself standing among glass ornaments on display.

Momentarily forgetting River and the hurt I feel, I look at the shimmering glass items on the shelves.

Vases of all different colors, shapes, and sizes. There's one that looks like a hanging basket, complete with a handle. So pretty.

There's a bright red glass apple. It makes me think of *Snow White and the Seven Dwarfs.*

And Grumpy, the giant dwarf, is right over there.

My eyes follow over to some balloons hanging down from the ceiling.

They're made from glass. They have a light inside them.

Oh, they're a light shade.

So beautiful.

I especially love the blue one. It's iridescent.

"Amazing, aren't they?" A voice comes from behind me.

I turn to see Macy standing there.

"Yes."

"Oh, I remember you. You're River's neighbor, right? Carol."

"Carrie."

"Carrie. Of course." She moves closer to the balloons, looking up at them. "He's really talented, isn't he?"

It takes me a second to catch her meaning. "Oh, the artist? Yes. Very."

She brings her eyes to mine. "You mean, River?"

"What?"

"River. He's the artist. He makes these. All of these." She lifts her hand in the direction of the ornaments.

River makes these glass ornaments?

That brash, callous man over there makes these beautiful, delicate items.

Why didn't he tell me?

"Oh. Didn't you know?" she says, looking pleased at the fact that she knew something about River that I didn't.

I swallow and shake my head. "No. He never told me." I curse my voice for sounding so weak.

"How strange." She flicks her long hair over her shoulder. "I wonder why he never said anything. But then he isn't a big talker. Except with me, of course. We talk *a lot.* All the time in fact. We spend hours just chatting about nothing really."

Okay, Macy, don't oversell it. I'm not a threat to you when it comes to River.

The guy doesn't want to be my friend, let alone anything else.

Not that I do either.

"That's … nice for you." I hold back the eye roll I really want to do. I'm about to walk away from her when something occurs to me. "Did River make the Christmas ornaments you sold here last December?"

"Of course. We only sell his art here."

The train. He made that.

He knew I loved it, and he gave it to me and never once said that he'd created it. He didn't even want me to know he was the one who had given it to me.

Why?

He doesn't seem to have a problem with Macy knowing. So, why me?

Probably because he thought I'd use it as something else to talk to him about. And he wouldn't want that. Because he barely liked me on a good day, right?

Ugh. Why am I even bothered by this?

I'm not. I'm not bothered at all.

"Well … nice seeing you again"—*not*—"but I need to get my shopping finished."

"Of course." She moves out of my way as I turn.

Her eyes drop to my belly.

"Oh. I didn't know you were pregnant." She sounds genuinely surprised. Like my pregnancy has some bearing on her life.

"Yes." I place my hand over my bump. "Five months."

"Well … congratulations."

I've never heard a more disingenuous congratulations in my life.

"Thank you."

"River never mentioned you were married."

Is this woman for real?

You don't have to be married to have a baby, Macy. It's not the 1950s.

Christ, she and Neil would be perfect for each other.

Then, I immediately hate myself for that thought. Because she doesn't deserve someone like Neil. No one does.

"I'm not married." My ring finger twitches with the lie. "And I don't have a boyfriend either." Might as well clear that up as well.

"Oh." Her eyes move down to my bump again and then back up to my face. I don't like the look in her eyes. "I see."

No, Macy, you really don't.

She casts a glance over to where River is. He's back standing at the counter, pen in his hand, staring down, as he writes something onto a sheet of paper.

"I don't have a kid, so I wouldn't know, but I hear that being a single mom is really hard," she says, voice lowered, so only I can hear. "And it would totally make sense if you were looking for a daddy for your baby … but, well, River isn't your guy. He's … *unavailable*, if you know what I mean." The look she gives me makes me know exactly what she means.

I ignore the painful twist in my chest at the knowledge.

He doesn't want to be my friend. But he has no problem being super besties with benefits with Macy. Or whatever they are.

Fine. I don't need his friendship anyway. I never did.

I have Olive and Buddy, Sadie, and Guy, even though he can be a total gossip at times. But I have them, and I don't need anyone else.

"Well, that's great for you guys. And don't worry; the last thing I'm looking for is a father for my baby. And, even if I were, River wouldn't even make the list."

"Oh, good. I'm so glad we understand each other." She gives me a congenial smile, but there's nothing nice about her. "I'll leave you to your shopping—unless there's anything else you need help with?"

Anything else? I never asked for your help in the first place.

"Nope. I'm good." I smile widely. I don't want her to know she's affected me in any way. And one thing I am good at is hiding my true feelings.

"Fabulous. Well, *ciao* for now." She gives me a finger wave, and with a flick of her hair, she sashays off.

Ciao *for now?*

Ugh.

Fudge off, you C-U-Next-Tuesday muffin.

I'm so done here.

I want to go home and eat the contents of my shopping basket even if I know for a fact that a vast majority of this food will give me heartburn for days.

Ugh. Why did River have to be here?

He's totally crapped on my day.

I was super happy with my new car, and now, him and his *ciao*-for-now Macy have spoiled it.

Angrily, I march over and dump my basket on the counter, not once looking at River.

"Red."

I cast my eyes in his direction but don't look directly at him. Like the sun.

"Don't call me that," I snap. "My name is Carrie."

"Okay. Carrie." His voice sounds quieter than normal. Less confident.

Good.

"Is this everything?"

"Yep."

"I'll ring it up for you then."

"You do that."

I turn my head to the side. Staring out the window, I fold my arms over my chest, resting them on the top of my bump, while he rings me up.

It feels like he's taking forever.

I start tapping my foot with impatience.

I can see him putting my things into a paper bag for me. Almost done, and then I'm out of here.

"That'll be thirty-seven forty, Re—Carrie."

I dig my wallet out of my bag and pull out forty dollars, holding the bills to him.

I still haven't looked at his face this whole time.

I'm currently staring at his chest.

He takes the money from my outstretched hand.

The brush of his fingers against mine surprises me. As does the flare of heat that shoots up my arm.

Pregnancy hormones. Just pregnancy hormones.

Nothing to do with him because he's a big, stupid, mean jerk.

I hear him ring the money up and take my change out of the cash register.

"Here's your change."

I hold my palm out while he counts the money into it.

I don't even bother putting the money back in my wallet. I drop it straight into my purse.

I grab the grocery bag off the counter and make for the door.

"Carrie." His insistent tone makes me stop.

I finally look at his face for the first time since I stepped in here.

His eyes are searching my face. He looks … lost.

The ache starts up in my chest again.

I cast a blanket over my feelings and smooth my face to impassive.

"What?" I ask with just the right amount of impatience. Proud of myself for being so strong.

"Just …" He shakes his head. "Your receipt." He holds it up. "Do you want it?"

"Nope. Put it in the trash." *You know, the same place you put our friendship—or non-friendship.*

Then, I walk out of there, chin held high, and I don't let it drop until I'm back in the safety of my car.

Carrie

The bang of River's front door catches my attention.

The sight of Macy leaving his house does nothing to improve my mood. The mood I've been in since yesterday, after seeing River at the store.

I guess Macy's doing house visits now.

Makes sense if they're together.

I ignore the pinch in my chest that I feel. It's just … I know River's a complete and utter tool. But he does have a good heart deep down in there somewhere. And I'm just not sure about Macy. I think she's … self-motivated and conniving.

Not that it's any of my business.

I watch her lithely body slide into a little red Ford that's parked behind his truck on his driveway. I don't lithely slide anywhere nowadays with my ever-growing bump.

I hear her engine come on, and I quickly turn my attention back to the trunk of my car, so I don't have to acknowledge her as she drives by.

I know I'm being childish. I'm just really not in the mood for Macy today.

I'm tired and cranky.

I was up most of the night with heartburn from the food I ate yesterday, as I'd predicted I would be. Didn't stop me from eating it though, did it? The diner was super busy this morning. I barely had time to stop. And then, after my shift at the diner finished, I went straight to the hardware store to pick up the paint I'd ordered because they'd called to let me know it was in. I'd finally decided on a color—Vanilla Frost. It's a neutral color. I thought I'd keep the walls a fresh, plain color. I'm going to get some wall decals with cute animals and put them up and then brighten it up with accessories. Also, while I was at the hardware store, I got some sheets to protect the floor, paint rollers, and brushes. Figured I'd start on the painting this afternoon.

The sound of Macy's car driving past allows me to move.

I lift one of the paint cans out of the trunk of my car and feel a sharp ache in my back.

"Ouch!" I press my free hand to my back, against the ache.

"Carrie, are you okay?"

I turn, startled, to see River moving quickly toward me.

He takes the paint can from my hand, allowing me to press both hands to my back to stretch it out. He puts the paint can back in the trunk of my car.

"Let's get you inside. You need to sit down."

"I'm fine," I snap. "It's just a bit of a backache. It's to be expected with pregnancy."

"Sure. And carrying paint cans isn't exactly going to help."

"Just exactly what business is it of yours?" I bite, finally looking up at him.

He blanches, but his expression quickly recovers. "It's not." His voice is low. "But I, uh …" He shifts on his feet. If I didn't know better, I'd think he was nervous. "You just … you have to think of the baby."

"Are you saying I'm not thinking of my baby? That I'm somehow putting my baby's health at risk?"

His brows draw together. "That's not what I'm saying at all."

My hands go to my hips. Then, I remember that they don't fit there anymore, so I cross them over my expanding chest. "Then, what are you saying?"

"Just …" He takes a measured breath and then blows it out, equally as controlled. "Just that you shouldn't be carrying around cans of paint."

"Well, I don't have anyone else to do it." I shrug. "So, my options are limited to … well, me."

"I can help you."

"Huh?" I stop and give him a confused look. "Why would you? We're not friends."

"We're, um, neighbors. Neighbors help each other."

"True." I nod. "But you made it perfectly clear that you wanted nothing to do with me, period. So, why would you want to be neighborly and help me?"

"Because you're pregnant?" It sounds more like a question than an answer.

"I've been pregnant for five months now, and I've managed just fine on my own for all that time."

"Not all the time."

"No?" My eyes widen with annoyance.

He shakes his head. "Your Christmas tree. You needed help with that."

"I didn't *need* help. You offered it, and I accepted, thinking we were friends. But, the next day, I learned that wasn't the case. You just fudging tolerated me, right?"

He winces.

"I brought you a tomato." He shoves his hand into his jacket pocket and pulls out a large tomato, holding it in his outstretched palm to me.

"A tomato?" I slowly say the words to make sure I got that right.

I see the tips of his ears redden.

"An heirloom tomato. That's how big the fruit baby is now, right? The size of an heirloom tomato."

Oh.

An ache flickers in my chest. "How do you know that?" I say quietly.

He lifts his shoulders, giving an awkward shrug. "I saw it on the fruit baby website."

"Why were you looking at that?" I lift my eyes to his.

Another shrug, one shoulder this time.

"I didn't know you knew how far along I was."

"I don't exactly." His words are quieter. "I just remembered the olive conversation and figured it out from there."

I remember the olive conversation, too. That was the night that you threw our friendship away.

The tomato is just sitting there in his outstretched hand. I think this is his way of extending an apology—an olive branch so to say, no pun intended. But it's just not enough.

He hurt my feelings.

"Well, you miscalculated. I'm a little further along. The baby's the size of a small banana now."

His expression falls. "Oh," he murmurs in a voice even quieter than before.

Guilt clogs my throat even though I have nothing to feel guilty for.

"Guess it was stupid to bring you a tomato anyway," he mumbles.

Not stupid. Actually sweet. But it doesn't change anything.

"Why did you bring me the tomato?"

Expressionless eyes flicker to mine. "Because the baby …" He stops, sighs, and shakes his head. "I don't know."

"I think you do." I'm surprised by my assertiveness.

I shouldn't have to give him a push, but I know River is the type of person who needs one.

"I … um …" He shifts on his feet. Thrusts a hand through his hair. Sighs. Stops and looks at me. "I'm sorry." The words rush out of him. "I was a fucking asshole that night. I was angry with Brad. I took it out on you, and I shouldn't have. These last few months have been …" He looks up to the sky like he's searching for the words there. "Dull."

"Dull?"

He looks down at me, eyes guarded. "Yes. Dull. I've missed, uh … disagreeing with you. When you aren't around, life is just … dull."

Oh.

I think that's the nicest thing anyone has ever said to me.

"Thank you … for apologizing," I tell him because I know how hard that must have been for him to do.

I see the relief flicker in his eyes.

He shoves his hands into his jacket pockets. "So, can we, uh, go back to the way we were before?"

And, now, I feel bad for what I'm about to say.

"I don't know. I don't think so." I shake my head.

His eyes search mine. "Why not?"

"Because I don't trust you not to hurt my feelings again."

"Oh. Right."

Yeah. Oh.

He lifts his chin, a determined look on his face. "Well, trust is earned, right?"

"Yes," I say cautiously.

"So, let me earn it back. Your trust."

What am I supposed to say to that?

"Give me one reason why I should."

"Because you're my best friend, Red," he says softly, eyes sweeping the floor beneath our feet. "My only friend."

And, fudge, I'm going to cry.

Tears prick the backs of my eyes. I bite the inside of my cheek to keep them at bay.

When I feel like I can speak without blubbering, I say, "Okay."

Hopeful eyes lift to mine. "Okay?"

"Yes. But, if you hurt my feelings like that again, you're out."

"Got it." He gives a sharp nod.

"But I'm not your only friend, River. You have Ellie and Macy."

He gives me a funny look. "Ellie was my gran's friend, and she's a business acquaintance. And Macy's not my friend."

"No?"

"No."

"But I just saw her leaving your place."

Some light, unnamed emotion takes up residence in his eyes. "After I locked up last night, I brought home the stockroom key with me by accident. She came to pick it up on her way into the store."

"Oh. So, she's not your girlfriend?"

His brows draw together. "No, Red," he says slowly, holding my eyes. "She's not my girlfriend. She's not *my* anything."

Well played, Macy. Well played.

She sure had me convinced.

I realize I'm still staring into his eyes, so I look away. "How come you were working at the store?"

"Ellie was unwell. I was helping out."

"I hope nothing serious."

"She had a fall, sprained her ankle. I was helping out until she was back on her feet."

"Was?"

"She called last night, said she was getting back to work today. That's when I realized I had the store key. She asked Macy to come collect it from me."

I nod, and it's my turn to shift on my feet. "I probably should confess something."

"What?"

I don't miss the note of wariness in his voice.

I look into his eyes again. "I know you made the Christmas train ornament."

"Oh," he says.

"Macy told me at the store yesterday. I was looking at your vase and those gorgeous glass balloons, and she said you were the artist. Why didn't you tell me they were yours?"

"I don't tell anyone."

"Macy knows."

He frowns. "She works at the store, and she knows better than to tell people."

"Why keep it a secret? You're incredibly talented, River."

"Because I want to sell them, and people around here wouldn't buy them if they knew I'd created them."

It's my turn to say, "Oh." Because I know exactly what he's not saying. They wouldn't buy the art because of what his mom did all those years ago. "Well, they're idiots. Your art is beautiful."

He shrugs dismissively. I can tell he's embarrassed by my compliment.

"Do you sell them elsewhere, aside from Thistleberry Farm?" I ask him.

"I sell to a few stores in the city—San Antonio," he clarifies.

He turns his face to the side, staring at my car. I know this conversation is over. Well, about that subject anyway.

"You bought a car," he says in a rough-sounding voice.

"I did." I smile.

His eyes move to the trunk and the paint cans sitting inside. "You're painting?"

"Yep. I'm decorating the baby's room."

He finally looks at me. "You want some help?"

I smile inside. "I'd love some help."

He reaches in the trunk and grabs the rollers, trays, and cans of paint. "You okay with the rest?" he asks.

I look down at the pack of paintbrushes and floor sheets. "I think I can just about manage," I say dryly.

He follows me to my front door. I unlock it and let us inside. I put my stuff down and crouch down to fuss over Buddy.

"Where's the baby's room?" he asks, lifting up the paint cans.

"Down the hall, door on the right," I tell him, rising to my feet. "You want a coffee?" I ask, walking toward the kitchen before he disappears down the hall.

"Sure."

I turn the kettle on and let Buddy out, watching him putter around the garden and do his business.

I call him inside when the kettle boils. I make River's coffee and a decaf tea for myself and carry them through to the baby's room.

I see River has also brought through the paintbrushes and sheets that I left in the living room. He's already opened the pack of sheets and is laying the last one down.

I cross the room and hand his coffee to him.

"Thanks." He takes it and has a sip. "You've already primed it?" he asks.

"Yep." I nod, taking a sip of my tea.

"You did a good job."

"Thanks." My eyes smile at him. I swallow another sip of my tea and put it on the windowsill.

"Do you have any stepladders?" he asks me. "If not, I have some—"

"Oh!" My hand goes to my stomach, my eyes looking down at my bump.

Was that …

"What's wrong?" River puts his coffee down on the windowsill next to mine and approaches me.

"Nothing's wrong. I think … the baby just … kicked."

"Has it kicked before?"

I shake my head. I can feel tears welling in my eyes. I don't even know why I'm getting emotional. "No, that's the first time," I whisper.

He smiles, moving even closer, and I feel some unnamed emotion expand in my chest.

I stare up into his eyes. "I mean, it could've been wind or—not!" I laugh at the feel of another kick. A strong, healthy kick.

"The baby's kicking right now?" he asks.

"Olive," I say. "I nicknamed the baby Olive."

"Oh," he whispers.

That feeling expands further.

"Can I … would it be okay if I …"

I reach out, take hold of his hand, and press it to my bump.

I hear his breath hitch and see his Adam's apple bob on a swallow.

That feeling in my chest spreads out, casting out of me and over him, like a net wrapping around the both of us.

River's eyes are focused on where his hand rests.

And, when Olive kicks again, he laughs. His eyes widen and brighten with awe. "Hi, Olive," he says to my bump. "I'm River. Your neighbor."

He sounds so formal; I want to laugh. A small chuckle escapes me.

His gaze comes up to mine. "What?" He's smiling.

I chuckle again, shaking my head. "Nothing. You just make me laugh."

He seems to like that from the look on his face.

Olive kicks again, drawing his eyes back to my bump.

"God, it's fucking amazing, Red." He shakes his head. "You have a baby inside of you right now."

"Five months now," I deadpan.

His eyes come back to mine. "You know what I mean. Of course, I knew you were pregnant, but it wasn't ..."

He's struggling to find the right word, so I offer one up. "Real."

"Yeah." His eyes flicker down and then come back to mine to stay. "It wasn't real. Until now."

His eyes are still staring into mine, and I'm looking right back into those dark depths of his.

I feel it—the exact moment something shifts between us. Like it snaps and then clicks into place. I know he feels it, too.

I don't quite know exactly what it is or what it means, but I just know that it matters.

It matters a lot.

Carrie

I hum along to the lyrics of "I Found" by Amber Run, which is playing from my phone, while I fit the mobile onto the baby's crib.

It's adorable. I ordered it from a store online. It has clouds and stars hanging from it. And hanging in the middle is a crescent moon, and an elephant is sleeping on it.

The delivery box was waiting on my doorstep for me when I got home, so of course, I had to fit the mobile to the crib straightaway.

The nursery is almost done. The walls are fresh with the color I picked out. On the wall directly above the crib, there is a black-and-gold decal sticker that says, *Dream Big, Little One*, with stars and a crescent moon surrounding them. Olive's crib is a brown wooden sleigh crib. The cream bedding with little gold stars is on the mattress. The crib bumper fitted to the crib. Matching chest of drawers and the changing table sit nicely around the room. Baby clothes hang in the closet and are folded up in the drawers. I have a rocking chair over by the window, so I can feed Olive during the night.

River pulled up the old carpet and sanded and varnished down the floorboards. It looks amazing. I got a fluffy white rug for the floor, which Buddy has taken a liking to sleeping on.

River's been such a big help in getting the room ready these past few weeks. I don't think I could've done it without him. But, of course, I won't admit that.

I'm an independent woman nowadays.

River has become incredibly important to me.

He's my friend. Probably my best friend.

But it also feels like things have shifted between us. There's a slow, shimmering attraction there. I feel it. I think he does, too. Or maybe I'm just imagining it, and it's all on my part.

Either way, I have no intention of acting upon it.

I would never do anything to risk our friendship.

I'd say we have a unique friendship though.

It's like we know everything about each other and absolutely nothing at all.

We know the basic facts. The likes and dislikes.

But we don't know the big stuff.

He doesn't know about Neil. Or my life before Carrie. When I was still Annie Coombs.

I don't really know anything of his past.

I know about his mom. And that he lived with his gran in the house that he still lives in now.

But I also know there's more from his past that I don't know.

His eyes are that of a survivor.

He has seen things and knows things he never should've.

And I don't just mean the murder of his stepfather.

I mean the reason his stepfather was murdered.

There was a reason River's mom shot her husband that day. And something tells me that reason was River.

Or I could be way off.

But I'm not going to ask him. And he won't ask me about my past.

It's an unspoken agreement between us. Because neither of us wants to discuss our pasts by bringing up the other's.

We want to leave them just there. In the past.

"Red?"

The sound of River's voice has me turning my head.

"Baby's room," I call to him.

I listen to the sound of his boots against the floor as he makes his way toward me.

Tightening the last plastic fitting to the crib, I stand back to admire the mobile.

"The mobile came," he says, entering the room. "Looks good."

"Doesn't it?" I smile, turning to him.

He has a box in his hands, and a small brown paper bag sits on the top of it.

"What's in the box?" I ask.

I'm pretty sure I already know what's in the paper bag. River has taken to bringing me fruit every week for the day the baby hits that size. This week is a large mango.

"A gift." He crosses the room and puts the box down on the changing table.

I follow him over there, standing beside him. I stare down at the box. My heart starts to pound an erratic beat, like it always does when I'm this physically close to him.

He hands me the paper bag. I reach inside and pull out a mango.

I smile up at him. "You want to share?" I ask him, knowing what his answer will be.

His nose wrinkles up. "No. And I still can't believe you eat the fruit babies that I bring you. It's fucking gross, Red."

I laugh out loud, holding the piece of fruit up. "It's a mango. Not an actual baby. And I'm not just going to let a perfectly good piece of fruit go to waste."

"You let the spaghetti squash go to waste last week."

"Yeah, but that was *gross*." Honestly, I only eat the fruit to wind him up. I think it's adorable how it freaks him out. "You're cute. You know that?" I tell him, bumping his hip with mine.

"I'm not fucking cute," he grumbles. "Bunnies are cute. Puppies and kittens are cute. I most definitely am not."

No. You're beautiful. Inside and out.

"True. You're more like a bear. But a cute, fluffy bear, one that will rip someone's head off if they get too close to you."

"Better. Marginally," he mutters, frown lines marring his brow. "And are you gonna open the fucking gift anytime today?"

"Am I supposed to? You never said it was for me. You just said it was a gift." I smile sweetly up at him.

"Smart-ass." His eyes smile down at me. "Of course it's for you. Now, will you just open it? Oh, and FYI, Red, it's not edible."

"Hilarious." I pull open the top of the box and stare down into it.

Oh my God.

"You made this?" I ask even though I know he did. It has his artistic touch all over it.

"It's a light fixture," he tells me, like he needs to explain. "For the baby. But, if you don't like it, it's fine. I won't be offended."

"Not like it?" I drag my eyes from the light fixture and stare up at him. "I love it, River. So much. Thank you."

The tips of his ears are red. That's his tell when he's nervous or embarrassed.

"Do you want me to put it up now?"

"Yes," I say eagerly.

I wait while he goes and gets a screwdriver. I watch as he takes down the old hanging light fixture and then carefully gets his from the box and fits it to the wires before screwing it to the ceiling.

"Should I turn it on?" he asks.

I nod, staring up at it.

He flicks the switch on, and it comes to life. Not that it wasn't already alive with the mix of colors. There must be forty different glass balloons, all varying sizes, hanging on thin wires from the metal fitting, where the lights gleam down on them, alighting the multiple colors. There are numerous shades of reds, greens, yellows, oranges, and blues.

It's the most amazing thing I've ever seen.

He steps closer to me. "Is it okay?" he asks with an uncertainty that I've come to know from him.

For all his brash and bravado, River is also incredibly insecure and shy.

I turn my face to his. "It's perfect. Olive is going to love it. I love it." I press my hand to my chest.

He smiles, and it's blinding. My heart swells, feeling like it's tripled in size.

River and I rarely touch each other. I don't know if it's a conscious thing on either of our parts, but it's just not something we do.

Neither of us are tactile people. But I want him to know just how much this means to me. That he took the time to make this for Olive.

So, I reach up on my tiptoes and press a kiss to his cheek. I wrap my arms around his shoulders. "Thank you so much, River," I whisper close to his ear. "It's the best gift I've ever received."

He doesn't hug me back. I feel a shudder run through his body. Not knowing what it means, I release him and step back.

"Sorry, I just—"

"No," he says low.

His hand reaches out and catches hold of mine.

Our eyes meet. For once, his aren't guarded. I can see right into them, and they're telling me everything I haven't been sure about.

I can feel his hand trembling as he lifts mine and places it against his chest. Over his heart.

I flatten my palm. I can feel his heart pounding beneath his solid chest.

"You make it do that," he roughly tells me.

My stomach flutters, and whether it's the baby or him making it do so, I can't tell. But it's definitely him that has my heart fighting to catch pace with his.

His hand leaves mine. He gently runs his knuckles down my cheek. His thumb traces a path over my lips. My breath hitches.

I swallow down.

The tenderness of his touch … the intensity of the moment is almost overwhelming.

Almost.

"Red," he whispers, lowering his face to mine.

A kiss to my forehead. The barest of touches. His stubble brushes over my skin. It's softer than I thought it would be.

I close my eyes.

His lips press gently to my temple.

To my cheek.

My jaw.

His nose grazes mine.

I feel his warm breath against my lips.

"Carrie."

I open my eyes. He's staring straight into mine. Those dark depths of his are wide open to me in a way they've never been before.

Then, he closes them.

And presses his mouth to mine.

The softest of touches.

His lips brush over mine.

Once. Twice.

I sigh, parting my lips.

His tongue runs along the seam.

I curl my fingers in his shirt.

"Jesus, Carrie," he groans.

I feel that groan everywhere.

He cradles my face in those big, talented hands of his and fits his mouth over mine.

My toes curl into the rug beneath my feet.

He kisses me hard and soft, all at the same time.

He kisses me like it's all he's ever wanted.

He touches me with reverence.

Like it matters.

Like *I* matter.

Then, Olive decides to start kicking. And I mean, kicks hard. River feels it.

He chuckles against my lips. "Feisty, like her mama."

"Her?" I question.

"Definitely."

His hand slides into my hair, bringing my head to rest against his chest. I wrap my arms around his waist.

"Carrie …" he says in a quiet voice, filled with something that instantly squashes my good feeling.

"Don't …" I say quietly. "Don't spoil the moment."

So, he doesn't.

He doesn't say another word.

Carrie

River is driving us into the city, so I can go shopping for a stroller. I could have come alone, but he said he'd like to come with me. I think he worries about me driving the more pregnant I get.

I'm seven months pregnant now. Olive is the size of a cabbage. I made a slaw with the one River brought me. He, of course, refused to eat it.

He's so weird.

It's been seven weeks since River kissed me. And nothing.

He hasn't talked about it or made any move to do the same.

And neither have I.

But I still go to sleep every night with the feel of his lips on mine.

I'm not sure why he hasn't kissed me again. I can still feel the attraction there between us, and it's only gotten stronger since the kiss.

It's hard to keep my feelings in check at times when I'm around him as much as I am and as hormonal as I currently am.

But he's choosing to ignore what's happening between us. Or not, as the case might be. That means I'm doing the same.

I think it's because I'm pregnant. Why he hasn't kissed me again.

And I can understand that.

I'm carrying another man's child. A man who River has no clue about.

Of course he doesn't want to get into any form of romantic entanglement with me.

Because it's not just me he'd be getting tangled up with.

It'd be the baby as well.

No, it's better that we're just friends.

I need to focus on becoming a mom, which is fast approaching. Hence the stroller shopping.

"You okay, Red?" River's deep voice carries across the inside of the truck. "You're quiet over there. And you're never quiet."

I smile at him. "Just a little tired. The diner was busy today."

"The diner's always busy. You shouldn't be working up to the birth."

"I only get six weeks paid maternity leave, so that's all I can afford to take." And that's really good because most places don't pay maternity leave at all, but thankfully, I have an awesome boss. "And I want to spend those six weeks with the baby before I have to go back to work." And put Olive in daycare. But I'm choosing not to think about that just yet.

River huffs but says nothing more on the subject.

He parks the car into a parking spot close to the baby store, and we both climb out of his truck.

I have a fairly good idea of what I want after looking at strollers online, so we shouldn't be in here too long. I know how much men dislike shopping, and I figure River is no different.

Once the stroller is purchased, I'll ask River if he fancies getting dinner out. I'm hungry, and I could really go for pizza right now.

River holds the door to the store open for me, and I walk inside.

Holy strollers! There are loads of them.

"Please tell me you know exactly which stroller you want," River says close to my ear.

I hold back the shiver I feel.

I meet his eyes. "I have a pretty good idea."

"Thank God."

He exhales, and I laugh softly.

"I want the travel system one," I tell him as we walk over to the strollers. "You can buy the car seat to go with them. It clips into the stroller. And they're really lightweight."

"Travel system with car seat. Gotcha. This way." River points to the sign that says *Travel System Strollers.*

We walk over to them. He walks at my slow, waddling pace and places his hand on my lower back, guiding me.

Every sense and nerve ending in my body is focused on that one single place where his hand is touching.

"Okay, so any specific brand you want?" he asks, moving away to look at a red stroller, his hand leaving my back.

I'm not disappointed at all.

Okay, well, just a little disappointed.

"There was one that I saw online. The Nuna. It has gray fabric—found it." I clap my hands in delight. It looks just as good as it did online. "It's really nice." Expensive. But totally worth it. "What do you think?"

No response.

"River?" I lift my gaze from the stroller to him to find his eyes fixed in the opposite direction of me. "River," I say his name firmer, but he still doesn't seem to hear me, and he's not exactly far away.

I look in the direction of where he's looking. All I can see are people looking at strollers.

"River!" I holler his name to get his attention, and it works.

His eyes flick to mine. "What?" he snaps, taking me back a step.

My eyes widen in surprise. "I was talking to you."

"And?"

He's acting like an ass. It's been a while since he's behaved like this around me.

"*And* you were ignoring me. What were you looking at?"

"Nothing."

"Didn't seem like nothing," I challenge.

His body is all rigid. Tight with tension. And his hands are clenched at his sides.

Something, or someone, has got him spooked.

And I don't like it. It's worrying me.

I look over my shoulder in that direction, trying to see what's got him so agitated.

"Did you see someone? From your … past maybe?" I ask quietly.

Considering I know nothing about his past, it's a pretty broad question. But I don't want to say nothing. I want him to know I care. That I'm here.

"Stop prying into my business," he says low and harsh. "Which you know exactly fucking zero about. And buy the fucking stroller, which is what you came here to do."

Jerk.

Tears sting my eyes.

I hate pregnancy hormones. They make me cry way more easily than I normally would.

Biting the inside of my cheek to keep the tears at bay, I turn back to the stroller, not really in the mood for shopping anymore.

So long as it keeps Olive safe, that's all that matters.

I see a store worker passing by and wave to catch his attention.

"Can I help you?" he asks, approaching me with a kind smile.

At least someone's being kind at the moment.

Unlike the big horse's ass standing behind me.

"Yes. I'd like to take this stroller." I pat it with my hand.

"Of course. I'll have one brought up to the cash register for you."

"Thank you." I walk away, heading for the cash registers, not even bothering to look if River is following me or not.

I pay for the stroller. River carries it out to his truck and puts it in the trunk.

We get in the truck, and he pulls out into traffic.

He seems to be in a world of his own. On edge even.

The drive home is masked in silence, filled only by the radio playing. I keep my face buried in my phone, playing a game on it. Feeling simultaneously annoyed, upset, and confused by his behavior.

River isn't exactly a stranger to mood swings. But this mood swing came from out of nowhere.

He pulls up outside my house. He's out of the truck and getting the stroller out of the trunk before I even have my seat belt off.

I head straight for my front door, unlocking it.

Buddy is there to greet me like always.

"Hey, Bud." I blow him a kiss.

Bending down to pet him isn't an option at the moment with the size of this belly I'm carrying around. I honestly don't think I'd get back up again if I attempted to bend down.

"Where do you want this?" River's gruff voice comes behind me.

I jolt at the sound of him after having his silence for the last hour.

"Olive's room, please."

I waddle to the sofa, lowering myself onto it, and kick off my shoes. Buddy hops up onto the sofa and snuggles in beside me. I start stroking his fur.

I hear the sound of River's boots thumping down the hall. Even though he's acting like an ass at the moment, we do have dinner together almost every night, and I am starving.

So, I ask, "Do you want to order in tonight or—"

The sound of my front door slamming shut has my words halting.

I spin my head around to the closed door.

Did he just leave?

I push up off the sofa, which takes some doing nowadays, and waddle over to the window just in time to see River's truck turning in the street and peeling out of there.

River

I'm sitting in my truck across the street and a little way down from the house I'm watching.

Watching and waiting for its occupant to come home.

Taking my box of cigars from the center console, I take a cigar out, cut the end off using my cutter, and light up.

On a deep inhale, I drag the smoke into me.

My gran used to smoke cigars. Every night after dinner, she would sit on the porch out back, smoke a cigar, and have a glass of whiskey.

I love the smell of cigars. It reminds me of my gran. Of home. Of the one place where I knew I was safe.

That's why I still live in that fucking house. Why I couldn't bring myself to move after Gran died.

Because it's the only place I've ever felt truly secure after that sick bastard of a stepdad killed every safe feeling I ever had.

He took everything from me.

Except for Gran. And that house.

He could never take that.

Sexual predators care for only one thing—themselves and their sick, fucked up wants.

They don't care about the destruction they leave in their wake.

They're fucking monsters.

And don't ever be fooled into thinking you know what one of those sick fucks looks like.

They're not the image of old, dirty, greasy, seedy-looking men that we once believed to be true.

They are men and women of any age, any look, and any job. They can be the server at your local deli or the man who fixes your car. They can be the doctor you've visited for years. The person you trust to educate your child. Your dentist. The kid who bags your groceries. Or the middle-aged woman you take that Zumba class with.

They can be your best friend, aunt, uncle, mom, dad, or fucking stepdad.

They are and can be anyone.

They look just like you and I do.

Monsters in plain clothing.

I always think of them like the characters from Roald Dahl's book *The Witches.*

Regular-looking people until the masks come off.

The current sick fuck that I'm waiting on used to be a teacher. A kindergarten teacher.

But, you might say, surely, before hiring, the school does background checks with the Criminal Justice Information Services to ensure they have no criminal record.

Of course they do. But all that means is, they either haven't offended yet or they haven't been caught.

And that motherfucker was the latter.

Parents entrusted their children with this monster in plain clothes.

He took that trust and used it to his advantage to get what he wanted. In turn, ruining the lives of two young boys and their families.

He created more of me.

Boys who will grow into men with more pain and resentment than they know what to do with.

I hope those boys can move on. Live a full life. Love and be loved.

That's not in the cards for me.

I'm a barely functioning human being.

This keeps me going. What I'm doing now, it gives me purpose. And, the glass art that Gran taught me to do, that helps keep my mind calm.

And Red. She's a balm to the open wounds I have.

Something I didn't even know I needed.

Just being around her brings a calming peace to me.

Even when we're disagreeing.

Life without her now would be … hard.

She's going to wonder why I just checked out on her.

I'll go see her tomorrow morning. Make up some bullshit excuse. She doesn't need to know about this. She doesn't need to know anything more about me. Her knowing about my mom is more than I wanted her to know.

But, surprisingly, it didn't change things.

Well, I did. I fucked it up for a while. And I'm lucky as hell that she gave me another chance.

I just … I like the way she looks at me. The way she treats me. Like I'm normal.

I don't want anything to ever change that.

But, when I saw him in the store earlier … the store filled with kids and their parents … I wanted to walk over to him and rip his dead heart out of his chest.

The only reason I didn't was because I was with Red.

He didn't see me though.

But he will very soon.

I made my presence known to him when he got out of jail two months ago.

He'd only served a sickening two years before he was put back out on the streets.

And that was where I came in.

I approached him and told him I'd be keeping tabs on him. Warned him to keep his nose clean.

Clearly, he didn't take heed.

Stupid cunt.

So, I'm back here to remind him what will happen if I ever see him near kids.

I can feel anger coursing through my veins. I take a long pull on my cigar, curling my fingers into the palm of my other hand, digging my nails into the skin until I feel it break. The little trickle of blood calms me some.

The burner cell I keep in my truck rings.

I know who it is. Marcus. The only person who has this number.

I'm part of a group called The Avengers of Injustice.

Marcus is the head of the group. He founded it. He's also a Marvel nerd, hence the group name.

When I was nineteen, I discovered them purely by chance while browsing social media.

They're what some might call a vigilante group.

To me, we're the antitoxin before the disease.

Watching the videos they had posted, showing them entrapping and catching sexual predators before they even got a chance to hurt anyone, gave me a feeling that I'd never felt before … like, if I could do this, then I could make a difference. I could stop bad things from happening.

I remember how my hand shook as I typed out a message to the group via the social media page.

An hour later, a man called Marcus North wrote me back.

He asked how I would like to help. I told them entrapment wasn't something I was interested in doing.

Neither was being videoed while confronting these sick fuckers and putting it out on social media. But helping them was. Stopping the problem before more started was.

Marcus asked if we could talk offline.

Curious, I agreed.

I called the number he had given me.

That was when Marcus told me that there was a job that I could do for them.

But it was an off-the-books kind of job. Then, he explained it.

Without hesitation, I told him I was in.

And my life finally had meaning.

I had purpose.

So, I became an enforcer.

I keep down those who won't stop.

Those who won't listen.

I make sure they listen.

I do what needs to be done.

I'm a big man. I can be a scary motherfucker when needed. But, if you asked Red, she'd say I was nice. I'm not nice. Only to her.

I know what it's like to be a terrified kid subjected to horrific things at the hands of one of those sick fucks.

I'm the right kind of man for the job.

The social media aspect of the group, they do the bait-trapping—posing as children online to trap the predators, arranging a meetup, and then turning up with their cameras and filming them before posting it online. And the namers and shamers post the details on local predators in their areas. They have no clue about the enforcers.

Not everyone would agree with what I do. We currently have thirty enforcers across the country. None of us know who the others are. It's better that way. But more will join and become enforcers. Because of sick fuckers like my stepdad and the men and women we keep track of, there are more people like me in the world than I care to think about.

Marcus knows who I am.

But we never use our real names.

I'm Enforcer Nine. Or E9, as Marcus refers to me as.

Marcus has recruited twenty-one more enforcers since I joined them.

Twenty-one more fucked up people just like me because of sick fuckers like the one I'm waiting on.

I snatch up my cell from the passenger seat, answering it.

"Has he shown yet?" Marcus's gravelly voice travels down the line.

I called him straight after I got Red home safely to let him know what I was doing. I always check in with Marcus when I'm onto one of these sick fuckers.

Marcus North is in his mid-thirties. Unmarried. No kids. And he's as messed up as I am. He started the group when he was in his early twenties. A coping mechanism, I would guess. Not that he's ever spoken of his past to me. Like I never have to him.

But it's easy enough to recognize a person carrying the same weight as you.

I see it in Red, too. And that scares the fucking shit out of me.

"No," I tell him, stubbing out my cigar on my cigar box. I put it back in the box to finish later.

"You're definitely sure it was him?"

"One hundred percent."

I don't forget their faces. Every one of these sick fuckers' faces is burned into my mind. Just like my stepfather is and always will be.

Marcus sighs. "He's going to be a problem; you know that."

"I know."

A shadowy figure approaches the house, hands stuffed in his pockets.

"He's here. Gotta go."

"Do what's necessary. Check back in when it's done."

I toss my cell onto the passenger seat. Grab my ball cap, pull it low over my eyes. Then, I pause, looking at my cigar cutter. I pick it up and slip it into my pocket.

I get out of my truck and cross the street, walking quickly, blending into the shadows. My large strides easily eating up the space between me and him.

My heart pounds in my chest. Adrenaline coursing through my veins. Ready. So fucking ready for this.

I move around the house. Slipping down the side, I let myself into the garden through the back gate.

I tread soundlessly over the pathway leading around to the back door.

The kitchen is in darkness.

I try the door. Locked.

It takes me less than thirty seconds to have it open.

I soundlessly slip inside the house, closing the door behind me.

I can hear the television on in the adjacent living room.

I hear the toilet flush. He's in the downstairs bathroom.

I head in that direction on silent feet. For a big man, I can move quietly when I want to.

Years of trying to be invisible in the house around my stepdad when I was a kid.

Not that it ever made a difference.

I know the basic layout of this prick's house. Marcus sent me the floor plan via email while I was sitting outside, waiting.

The bathroom door is open.

He's standing in front of the sink, washing his hands. His head is down.

I can see myself in the mirror above his head.

I try not to look at myself.

I wait for him to lift his eyes and see me.

His head rises, and he blanches.

"Remember me?" I smile evilly at him in the mirror.

He moves quickly, grabbing the door to shut it.

I'm quicker.

I force the door back open.

He stumbles back against the counter. "I haven't done anything!" he cries.

I cock my head to the side. "You sure about that?"

"I haven't! I swear!"

I recite the store name where I saw him.

Fear fills his face.

Righteousness covers mine.

"Told you I'd be watching." I turn and close the bathroom door behind me, locking it. "And you didn't listen. So, it's time for you and I to have the second part of our little chat."

"No! No!" the weak, pathetic, sick little fucker chants, sliding along the counter. "Yes, I was in there! But I didn't do anything. I promise! I was only looking. I didn't touch anyone, I swear!"

Only looking.

"It's your fault, River. You make me do this. You're so beautiful. I can't help myself. Be quiet now. It will only hurt for a minute."

I squeezed my eyes shut tight.

I'm not here. I'm somewhere else. Someplace safe.

Just don't look, River. Don't open your eyes. It'll be over soon.

Bile rises in my throat. I swallow it down.

I grab the sick bastard by his fat, meaty hand, dragging him to me.

He's crying now.

And I feel nothing.

I bend down to his height, lowering my face to his. He's crying harder now. His face is white with fear.

Fucking pussy.

He can give it, but he can't take it.

I smile. It's a twisted kind of smile. I'd like to say it was an act. But it's not. Because I know I'm going to enjoy this.

"Don't worry," I tell him, getting the cigar cutter from my pocket. I tighten my hold on his hand, singling out his little fat finger. "This will only hurt for a minute."

Unlike the lifetime of pain that you gave to those two boys, I think as I slide the cutter over the tip of his finger.

Carrie

I can't sleep. I'm all weirded out by River's behavior earlier. And, honestly, I'm worried about him. I even tried calling his cell to check on him, but of course, he didn't answer, and I didn't bother to leave a message.

Plus, Olive doesn't seem to be in the mood to sleep either. She's restless. Constantly on the move tonight.

And, now, even I'm calling Olive a *she* now. It's all River's fault.

I'm just sitting on the sofa with Buddy lying fast asleep beside me, snoring. I'm staring at the TV without really watching it, my mind elsewhere—on River.

Not even the sight of David Boreanaz in the *Buffy the Vampire Slayer* rerun I'm watching can take my mind off of River.

It's frustrating. And annoying.

I'm not even thinking about the fact that I have to be in the diner for the breakfast shift in six hours.

Sigh.

I hear the low roar of a car driving past my house.

River.

I clamber up off the sofa, and for the second time this evening, I'm looking out the window for him.

I see his truck pulling into his driveway and him climbing out and heading inside his house.

Well, he's alive at least.

Although he might not be when I'm finished with him.

Usually, I never question River on anything to do with his life because I don't want him prying into my life, but for some reason tonight, I'm sick of the secrets.

I want to know what happened in the store tonight.

I want to know why he dumped me off here and drove off like his ass was on fire.

I want to know where he's been for all these hours.

And I want to know these things because I care about him.

I'm pulling my cardigan on over my pajama top and sliding my feet into my sneakers before I can change my mind about going over there.

"Back soon," I tell Buddy when he lifts his head from the sofa to see where I'm going.

I let myself out of my front door and walk the short distance over to River's house.

I don't even bother to knock. I just walk straight in. I'm that fired up.

He's not in the living room. I see the light on in the kitchen, so I head in there.

I see him standing at the sink, his back to me.

"You forget how to knock, Red?"

He heard me come in. Well, I wasn't exactly being quiet.

"Oh, give me a break," I fire back, in no mood to spar with him right now. "You never knock at my house anymore. You just walk straight in if the door's unlocked.

And, if you don't want me coming in your house, then lock the fudging door."

He glances back at me over his shoulder.

The look on his face jolts me. His eyes look … darkly primitive. Almost sexual. His face looks flushed. His skin is glowing, like he's just done some physical exertion. And his hair is disheveled, like he's been repeatedly running his hands through it.

Or maybe someone else has.

I add up all the aspects of his appearance and don't like the outcome that I come up with.

Has he been with a woman?

My chest pinches painfully.

I swallow down.

"Where have you been?" My quiet voice sounds loud in the silence of his kitchen.

He turns his face back to the sink and turns the faucet off. He reaches for a towel and dries his hands.

Then, he turns to face me.

I immediately spot the blood, and all thoughts of him and another woman vanish.

"Oh my God!" I exclaim, moving toward him. "Are you hurt? What happened?"

He frowns. Then, he glances down at his white T-shirt. At the marks of blood on it.

His eyes lift back to mine, and I don't like what I see in them.

All those things I just added up, I got wrong. Very wrong.

Add in the blood, and you've got a whole different scenario.

A violent scenario.

Sense and experience have me moving back a step.

His frown deepens at that.

"Nothing happened. I'm fine." He reaches back and pulls the T-shirt over his head. He bundles it up into a ball and throws it in the trash can.

He moves toward me. Instinctively, I step aside, giving him a wide berth.

"Don't do that," he says low, stopping before me.

"Do what?" My voice is a whisper.

"Act like you're afraid of me."

"Maybe I am right now."

Dark eyes burn into mine. "You know I'd never hurt you."

"Do I?"

His lips tighten, forming lines around his mouth. "I thought you did. Clearly, I was wrong."

"What am I supposed to think? You acted weird at the store. Dropped me home and then disappeared off in your truck without a word. Then, showed back up after midnight, washing what I can only assume was blood off your hands, getting that from the fact that it was all over your shirt."

"You should think that, in all the time you've known me, I've never once hurt you."

"Only my feelings, right, River? Not physically, so that makes it okay."

He sighs. "You know I was sorry for that."

"Yeah, I know. And I know that your actions stemmed from what'd happened in your past. But I don't know everything about your past. So, therefore, I don't know what else you're capable of."

I would never have thought this of him before now. But, after this, I'm thinking it.

"That's low, Red."

I lift my chin. "No. It's the truth. You want me to trust that you would never physically hurt me? Then, tell me where you went tonight. Where did the blood come from? Or *who* did it come from?"

His eyes darken to black, brows lowering. "Why did you move here, Carrie? Who's the father of your baby?"

My mouth slams shut. I wrap my arms over my chest, trying to ward off the chill I feel inside.

"Just what I thought." He lets out a humorless laugh. "I don't know shit about you, Carrie. And I don't ask shit about you. So, don't fucking come in here, into my house, demanding to know where I've been and what I've been doing when you're not willing to give up anything on yourself. We don't talk about the big stuff. That's how this thing works between you and me." He gestures a finger between us.

I take another step back, ready to turn and walk out of here.

Then, I change my mind.

And move forward a step.

"You're right. I'm asking you to tell me things about yourself that you've probably never told anyone. And, all the while, you don't know a single thing about me. Not one thing. And it's stupid. Because we should know each other. I want to know you because I care about you, River. So, here it is. This is me, laid bare." I spread my hands out.

"I was married for seven years. I'm still married. And my husband—the police detective—" I see River's eyes flash with an emotion that I know links back to his stepdad. "Yep, that's right; I'm married to a cop. Who I can never divorce because I can't risk him finding out where I am; if he does, he *will* kill me. Without a doubt. Because behind the good cop facade he wears for the rest of the world is a sick, violent sadist, who, for almost every day of the seven years I was with him, beat and raped me to the point of unconsciousness." I swallow against the memories prickling at my skin.

"And, when I found out I was pregnant, I ran. I stole his dirty cop money. Got a new identity. Changed the color of my hair. Climbed onto that bus that brought me here and became Carrie Ford. So, that's why I won't be around violence, River. Because I lived it. And I risked my life to escape it. Because I *will* give my child a better life than the life I had, no matter the cost to me. I won't be around violence again in any way, shape, or form. I will not have my child's life tainted by it.

"So, you see, this is why I'm asking you where you were tonight and where the blood came from. And I will ask again one last time ..." I pull in a fortifying breath. "Where were you tonight, River?"

I wait.

Heart in my throat. Chest pounding. Blood roaring in my ears.

But his answer never comes.

So, I do the only thing I can.

I walk out of there, and I don't look back.

Carrie

I don't sit around, feeling sorry for myself. That's not who I am anymore.

When I left my miserable life behind, I made the conscious decision not to be unhappy ever again. I had already spent enough years of my life being sad.

So, I chose to be optimistic. To be happy.

I wouldn't ever be truly sad ever again. Not even when the bad memories creep into my dreams at night and turn them into nightmares would I feel sorrow. I just shut them into a box and lock it up tight.

Because those memories are not my life anymore.

I'm no longer Annie.

I'm Carrie.

And Carrie is happy. She is strong and brave. She is everything I ever wanted to be.

But, right now, I don't feel any of those things.

And I'm most definitely not happy.

I told River everything. I trusted him with my deepest, darkest secrets, and he said nothing.

Nothing.

So, yeah, my heart hurts.

And, since I walked out of his house over an hour ago, I've done nothing but lie on my sofa—on my side, of course, because, if I lay on my back, I'd probably never get up again—and eat chocolate-covered pretzels while listening to sad music. Even Buddy couldn't take my self-pity party and trotted off into my bedroom.

Lord Huron's "The Night We Met" just finished up, and Kesha's "Praying" has started up when I hear the rap on the door.

It's a quiet knock but loud enough for me to hear.

I know it's River. Because no one else would be knocking on my door after one in the morning.

But I'm not answering the door. And I'm definitely not letting him in.

I put another chocolate pretzel in my mouth and chew slowly.

"Red, it's me." His deep voice comes through the door.

"I know. That's why I'm not answering the door," I call back.

"Carrie … I just … I need to talk to you. You're safe with me. I promise. I would never hurt you. But, if you don't feel safe with me, which I totally understand, then text Sadie and tell her that I'm here."

I push myself to sit upright. It takes some effort. Then, I stand and walk over to the door. "And why would I do that?" I ask.

"So, if I did anything to you, the cops would know that it was me who hurt you."

"I'd rather not take the risk. Thanks."

"Please, Carrie." I hear his head thump against the door. "I just … fuck, I just need to see you. What you told me—"

"Forget what I said."

"I can't. I can't get the images out of my head. Of him hurting you." He sounds like he's in physical pain. "I just need to know you're okay."

I wrap my arms around myself. "I'm fine."

I take another step to the door until I'm up close to it. I can hear him breathing on the other side.

"I'm not," he says quietly.

I don't know if he means for me to hear him or not. But it's those words that have me reaching for the door and unlocking it.

I pull the door open a bit and look at him through the crack.

He looks terrible.

I can smell cigar smoke on him. It weakens my resolve a little bit more.

"Hey," he says softly.

I catch the smell of alcohol on his breath.

And I don't like it one bit.

"You've been drinking."

"What? Shit. Yes, but I'm not drunk. I had one whiskey. I always have one with my cigar before bed. You know that."

That's true. I do know that.

"Okay," I say. "So, why aren't you in bed now?"

"Red …" His dark brows draw together. "There was no way I was sleeping tonight. And, by the looks of it, you either."

I shake my head.

"You should rest though. For Olive's sake."

"She's not sleeping right now, so …" I shrug my shoulders.

"She's on the move?" he asks, staring down at my bump.

"Yep," I answer quietly.

He lifts his eyes back to mine. There's a pleading look to them. "Can I come in? There are things I need to say to you … things I need to tell you, and I don't want to say them out here. But I will if that's what you want. If that's what will make you feel more comfortable."

I think for a few seconds. Then, I step back. Widening the door, I let him in.

"Thank you," he says quietly as I close the door behind him.

I walk over to the sofa and lower myself to sit down. He comes and sits down beside me, angling his body toward mine, so I do the same.

There's a moment of silence where he's just staring at my face, his eyes roaming like he's looking for something.

"Why are you staring at me like that?" I ask self-consciously.

"You're beautiful, Carrie. I've never told you that before, and I should have because it's the truth. I thought it the moment I saw you. And every single time after that, even when I was being an ass to you."

My lips part in surprise. "Why are you telling me this now?"

"Because you want us to be truthful with each other. And that's the truth. I think you're beautiful. The most beautiful woman I've ever seen. You're good and pure and honest. And I wanted to start with that because the rest of the things I have to tell you are not good or pure or honest. They're dark and black and fucked up."

"Okay." I swallow, preparing myself for whatever is about to come out of his mouth.

"Okay," he echoes, shifting in his seat. "I'm not sure exactly where to start."

"The beginning is usually a good place."

He lets out a breath and shakes his head. "No. I'll start at the end and work my way back to the beginning."

His fingers are flexing in and out in agitation.

"River … you don't have to do this if it's too much."

His eyes come to mine. They're filled with determination.

"You stood there, in my kitchen, and told me things that I can only imagine were incredibly painful for you to say. You're brave, Red. And you make me want to be brave, too." He rubs the back of his neck with his hand. "No one outside of my mama and Gran has cared about me in the way you do. I want to be worthy of that."

"You are," I tell him. Reaching out, I take hold of his hand and squeeze it.

He stares down at our hands. "No, I'm not. But I want to be." He lifts his eyes to mine. The emotion in them is almost overwhelming. "I … I care about you, too, you know."

I swallow down my feelings that are threatening to turn to tears. *Damn pregnancy hormones.*

Afraid to speak, I just nod.

He lifts my hand to his mouth and presses the sweetest of kisses to it. Then, he lays my hand back in my lap, letting go.

He takes a deep breath and starts to talk, "At the store earlier, I saw a man who I know is a convicted sex offender."

I stiffen at his words.

"He went to prison for two years for the molestation of two young boys at the school where he was a teacher."

The molestation of two young boys.

"I know this because I make it my job to know. I'm part of an organization who bait-trap and expose pedophiles. We also keep track of recently released sex offenders, too. That's where I … focus my efforts."

"And by focus your efforts, you mean …"

He glances at me. "I do what's necessary to make sure they don't hurt another child."

I take in a sharp breath. "And to what extent do you go to ensure that?"

"Are you asking if I killed him?"

I pull my lower lip into my mouth, not sure if I want to know the answer to this question. But I nod despite myself.

"The answer is no. But, after I dropped you home, I went to his house. I waited for him. And … I hurt him. I'd warned him. Told him what would come if he was seen in the vicinity of children. He hadn't listened. So, I followed through. But, if it came to it … between a child being hurt and killing one of those sick fuckers, I wouldn't hesitate, Carrie."

I think of the child I'm carrying inside me and know that there isn't anything I wouldn't do to protect her. But would I go to that extent for other people's children like he is?

And I honestly don't know the answer to that question.

"So, you're a vigilante, who is part of a group working to protect children from pedophiles." I need to say it out loud, so it's clear in my head.

"I don't think of myself as a vigilante. I'm more like … the antitoxin before the disease."

"But you can't possibly stop every bad thing that happens," I say softly.

"No, I can't. But I can stop more than if I sat back and did nothing. And, if I can save just one kid from enduring the horrors of that kind of abuse, then it's worth it."

"Don't you worry about getting in trouble with the … law?"

He laughs. It's a hollow sound. I can understand why.

"No. What's the worst thing they can do to me?"

"Put you in prison," I whisper.

"Trust me, Red; that wouldn't be the worst thing that's happened to me."

I worry my lip with my teeth.

"You're wondering why I do this," he says in a low voice. "Why I would want to help stop other people's children from being hurt."

"Yes," I say quietly.

The silence is long. My heart thuds hard with every second I wait.

His voice is agonizingly, painfully low when he says, "Because I was one of those kids, Carrie. I was hurt by someone who was supposed to care for me."

God, no.

My throat thickens with tears. I swallow roughly.

I knew something bad had happened to him. The thought that it had been this passed through my mind … but to hear him say it …

It's hard to hear. It hurts me more than I ever thought possible.

The tears fill my eyes. I'm afraid to look at him because, if I do, I know they'll flow freely.

"W-was it … your stepdad?" My voice trembles.

"Yes." His voice is like ice.

I take a controlled breath to steady my voice. "Is that why your mom killed him? Did she find out that he was hurting you, and she shot him?" I know that I would do the same if it were my child.

He lets out a ragged breath, and I finally lift my eyes to his. The tears I was holding back overflow and run down my face.

He slowly shakes his head. "No, Carrie. That's why *I* killed him."

Carrie

"*What?*" I shift back in my seat.

He killed his stepdad.

I don't know what he sees on my face, but whatever it is, it makes his pale.

"Shit. Carrie, I'm not going to hurt you." He holds his hands up, like he's surrendering.

"What?" I stutter, realization quickly dawning on me. "Oh God, no. I know you won't hurt me."

If he was going to hurt me, then he would have by now. And a man who hunts down sex offenders to protect children is not a man I need to be afraid of.

I move closer to him to reassure him that my reaction was not one out of fear.

"I'm not scared of you. I'm just …" *Stunned. Lost for words.* "I don't know what I am. Shocked, I guess. It's a lot of information to take in, in one go." I'm blinking furiously, trying to clear my mind and gather my thoughts. "But you were just a child when he … when you …"

He exhales a breath and nods, eyes fixed on the wall ahead. "I was eight when I killed him. It … the abuse had been going on for a long time prior to that. Things were … getting worse. I couldn't tell my mom what was happening because he said he would kill her if I did, and then I'd be left with him. Just me and him."

Tears refill my eyes and trickle down my cheeks. I brush them away with my wrist.

"He was a police officer. People in this town respected him. I knew that, if I did say something … no one would believe me. I was … trapped.

"It was a Sunday. It was always a fucking Sunday. She was at her book club. I was alone at home with him. He called me into the kitchen. I knew what was going to happen. What always happened when she wasn't there." He rubs his hands over his face, pushing his fingers up and through his hair.

"He left his gun out on the kitchen counter. He never did that. And I honestly don't know what made me pick up the gun that day. But I did. I pointed it at him. He laughed in my face. Then, he got mad. He came at me, and then I shot him. And I kept pulling the trigger until the gun was empty. I don't know how much time passed … it seemed like none at all, and then Mama was home, and she saw what I'd done. She made me tell her what had happened. So, I did. I told her the ugly truth. She cried. Then, she picked up the phone and called the police. While we waited for them to come, she told me to agree with everything that she said. That it was her who had killed him. They'd fought. He'd attacked her, and she'd grabbed his gun and shot him in self-defense. I didn't want to lie. I didn't want her to go to prison."

His eyes, red with emotion, flick to mine, telling me without words that he needs me to believe that. If not anything else, he needs me to believe that.

"She died in that place, and it was because of me."

His head lowers. I scoot closer to him and grab hold of his hand.

"No. She was your mom, and she was protecting you in the only way she could because she loved you, River. Nothing that happened on that day or in the time leading up to it was your fault."

I squeeze his hand, and he lifts his eyes to mine. They're wet with tears, and my heart squeezes painfully.

"You were a child, River. A little boy."

"I should have said something. Told the truth. But I didn't. I did as she'd told me, and I stayed quiet. I never told the truth, and she went into that hellhole and never came out."

"And what good would have come of it if you had told the truth?"

"She would be here … and I wouldn't."

"Don't talk like that," I say sharply.

I'm frustrated because he can't see how amazing he is. I don't think I fully saw it until now.

"I'm not good, Carrie." He stares down at his hands that are stretched out on his thighs. "There's a darkness inside of me."

"No. There's a survivor inside of you, doing what he needs to. You're a good person, River. In here, where it counts." I press my hand to his chest, over his heart. "You can tell me what you want, but I know what I see. And I see a good man."

"I enjoy it, Red. Hurting them." He turns dark eyes up to mine. "You need to know that about me. Know who I really am."

I swallow down.

I move my hand down from his chest to his forearm and give it a squeeze. I don't want to stop touching him in case he thinks it's because I believe what he's saying. That I think he's bad.

It's very important that he realizes that I don't. And that I'm not afraid of him.

"And I won't lie and say that what you do … how you … deal with these sickos doesn't freak me out a bit because it does. But I didn't live your life. Who's to say I wouldn't feel the same if I were you? Trust me; there were nights when I would lie in bed and dream about killing Neil, my ex," I explain, realizing that's the first time I've told River his name. "It would help me get through the really bad days."

"But that's the difference between you and me. I would've killed him." He fixes his eyes on mine. "I want to kill him for hurting you. I got satisfaction tonight when I hurt that sick fuck. I like knowing that I've meted out some form of punishment to them … let them know just an iota of the pain they brought about to an innocent child. That does not make me a good man."

The way he says it, so calm and cold, it's like he wants me to be afraid of him.

He wants to push me away. He wants me to tell him to leave.

Because he can handle that. He can handle the bad.

It's the good that he's terrified of.

"You're not going to scare me away, River."

I take his face in my hands, lifting his face to mine. His cheeks are damp. I wipe them dry with my thumbs.

"I know bad. And you are not it. You can be a total douche-canoe at times." I give him a watery smile. "But you do that to keep people away. I get that. You had your trust and innocence stolen from you at a young age. You had to … fight to survive. You could've given up, but you didn't. And you still haven't. You're out there, fighting the good fight, trying to save other children from the suffering you endured. You might not do it in a way that people agree with. Violence is not something I agree with; I hate it. But, if anyone ever hurt Olive …" I close my eyes on a blink, exhaling a breath. "She's not even here yet, but I know without a doubt that I would kill them with my bare hands without a second thought. Everyone is capable of violence, River. Even me, who endured it. Sometimes, animals—no, not animals because Buddy is an animal, and he's awesome. No, pure evil, like my ex-husband and your stepfather and those sick mother-fudgers you … deal with … they only understand their own language. And, if you can save just one child, then … I get it. I really do."

He's looking at me with such a rawness; it's stripping away everything I thought I knew and believed.

I never would have thought that I could care for someone who lived with violence as part of their daily life.

But River is showing me that there isn't just black and white.

There's gray in all its varying shades.

There are people like Neil and River's stepdad who take their own pleasure in hurting people who don't deserve it. They're sadistic, sick C-U-Next-Tuesdays.

And then there are people like River, who have lived the pain and suffering that those sadistic, sick C-U-Next-Tuesdays doled out … and the law, the justice system, has failed them, so they fight fire with fire.

The Bible says an eye for eye.

Maybe God knew that not everyone could be dealt with the same.

There are those you can punish using the justice system.

And then there are those who live outside the law. Those who are so purely evil that sitting them in a jail cell is not going to make an iota of difference.

So, you speak to them in the only way they know.

I guess that's why some states still have corporal punishment.

"You don't see me … differently now?" he says barely above a whisper. "Knowing everything."

"Do you see me differently after what I told you about my ex?"

"Of course not." He empathetically shakes his head.

"Then, you have your answer. The only thing I see is more of you. All of you. And I like every part."

He lets out a breath that sounds so relief-filled that it makes my chest ache.

Turning to me, he cups his hand around the back of my head and leans his forehead against mine. I close my eyes and breathe him in.

"Thank you," he whispers.

"For what?"

"For being here. For being you."

A tear runs from the corner of my eye.

He tugs me closer to him and lies back against the sofa, bringing me with him. My bump rests against his hard stomach. I lay my head on his chest, just listening to the steady beat of his heart.

His fingers start to run through my hair. I suddenly feel exhausted.

"What color is your hair naturally?" he asks.

I tilt my face up to look at him. "Blonde."

He holds some strands of my hair up, rubbing it between his fingers. "I can't imagine you as a blonde." He looks into my eyes. "I like the red."

"Yeah, I do, too," I say, lowering my face back down.

I snuggle in closer. He wraps his arms around my waist and strokes his fingers over my bump.

"What was your name before you changed it?"

"Annie."

"Carrie suits you better."

"I think so."

He's silent a moment. "Carrie … I want you to know that I …"

He stops, and I hold my breath, waiting for what he's going to say.

"You will always be safe with me. You and Olive. I will never let anyone hurt either of you."

I place my hand over his heart. "I know. I trust you, River Wild."

He exhales softly and presses a gentle kiss to the top of my head.

"I trust you, too, Red."

Carrie

"Oof, that mother-trucking hurts." I pause on my way back from the bathroom—because you know, that's where I spend a good portion of my life nowadays—and grab hold of the sofa, bending forward ever so slightly while I wait for the pain to subside.

I've been feeling off all day. I keep getting these tightening pains in my stomach. They feel like period cramps. They started this morning while I was at work. But they weren't as strong as they are now.

I think it's Braxton Hicks.

I read about it on the pregnancy website I follow. It's really common around this time. The body preparing for labor.

I've got another two weeks before my due date.

I just hope that I won't have another two weeks of these cramping pains.

I can't believe I'm so close to the end of my pregnancy.

And River has been here for every part of it.

After our confessions to one another, we've definitely grown closer. Things changed between us that night. An understanding that wasn't there before.

But, oddly, things are still the same, too.

River does what he needs to do. I don't ask him about it or question him.

Not because I don't care. But because I do.

He's used to being alone. He needs time to get used to having me to share things with. And he will—when he's ready.

And it's not like I'm his girlfriend.

I'm not really sure what we are.

All I know is that we spend all of our free time together.

He sometimes holds my hand when we sit together, watching TV, and he rubs my feet when they're swollen and aching from being at the diner. He comforts me when I get emotional at the Adopt a Shelter Pet advertisements. And he brings me whatever food I happen to be craving that day. There's no consistency in my cravings.

He cares for me. And I care for him.

But there's no … physical intimacy between us.

Basically, there's still no kissing between us.

I think the attraction is still there.

Well, it definitely is on my part.

Maybe not his anymore. If it ever was.

And who would blame him? I'm currently the size of a house, and in this Texas climate, I spend most of my time sweating like a pig while wearing skirts with elastic waists. The new thing is to have milk leaking from my breasts, which was not in the least embarrassing when it happened to me while River and I were at the supermarket last week.

A glamorous lady these things do not make.

Not that I've ever been glamorous.

But whatever.

I hear my front door open. And I'm still standing here, holding on to the sofa, bent over as far as I can actually bend, which isn't very far, eyes on the floor.

"Red?"

"Yep."

"You okay there?"

I lift my head. "Uh-huh, just a stomach cramp."

"You sure?"

"Yeah. It's just Braxton Hicks."

"Oh, the fake labor pains."

I'm staring at him, surprised. "How do you know what Braxton Hicks is?"

The tips of his ears go red. He's now looking anywhere but at me. "I might have read about it in a pregnancy book."

My brows go up. I'm smiling on the inside. "When did you read a pregnancy book?"

"Recently. Anyway, I brought you something—"

His words cut off at the sound of a splash of water.

"Carrie"—his eyes are staring at my feet—"did you just, uh … pee yourself?"

I follow his eyes down to the puddle of water at my feet.

"No." I shake my head.

"Did your water just break?"

I lift my eyes to his. "Uh, I think so." I nod dumbly.

"So, I guess now is not the time to tell you I brought you some leeks?" He pulls them out of the brown paper bag he was holding behind his back.

I stare at them. Then, I burst out laughing.

"It's leek week! And I just leaked!"

River is staring at me like I've lost my mind.

"You don't get it?" I frown. "Olive is a leek this week, and I just … *leaked* water." I point down at the amniotic fluid on the floor.

"Oh, I got it all right. I'm just waiting for *you* to get it."

"Huh?" I tip my head in confusion.

"That you're in labor, Red. And, instead of standing here, cracking shit jokes, we should probably be getting you to the hospital."

Oh.

Jesus H. Christ.

"Hells bells!" I yell. "I'm in labor, River! I'm in labor!" I grab his arms, shaking them, panic filling me. "But it's too early! I have another two weeks to go!"

"Not according to that puddle on the floor. Looks like Olive is ready to make an entrance."

"Oh crap. I'm having a baby." The panic starts to slow to actual realization. "I'm having a baby. An actual real-life baby." I know my eyes are as wide as saucers right now.

"Really? I had no idea."

"Not funny."

"Hey, you were the one joking a minute ago."

"I'm also the one about to birth a baby."

"Well, hopefully not before I get you to the hospital. Where's your hospital bag?"

"In the trunk of my car."

"Okay. I'll grab it out of there, and we'll go."

"Why?"

"Because I'm not driving your shit-mobile to the hospital."

"Hey! Just for that, you're taking me to the hospital in my car."

"Fuck's sake, Red."

"Let's go. Bye, Buddy." I wave to him, sprawled out on the sofa. "Crap. Buddy! Who's going to take care of him while I'm at the hospital?"

"He'll be fine for now. I'll come back once you're settled in at the hospital. It takes ages for babies to be born, right? So, I'll get you to the hospital, come back here, get him sorted, and then go back to the hospital. It's all good,

Red. Buddy probably won't even realize you're gone; he sleeps that much."

"You called him Buddy." That's the first time he's called him Buddy. I feel tears well in my eyes. I'm being stupid.

River sighs. I can almost see the mental eye roll coming from him. "Well, that's his fucking name, isn't it?"

"Yep."

"Red, are you crying?"

"No. Let's go." I discreetly run my fingers under my eyes, drying away my stupid tears.

River slips my shoes onto my feet and opens the front door for me. With his arm around my back, he guides me out of my house, locking up for me.

He helps me into the passenger seat of my car, and then he's in the driver's seat, pushing the chair back to make room for his long legs. Key in ignition, he turns on the engine.

"Christus Santa Rosa Hospital, right?" he checks.

The man does pay attention.

"Yes," I answer, breathing through what I believe is a contraction.

Same as what I've been having all day.

And I thought it was just Braxton Hicks.

Idiot that I am.

"Ow!" I cry. Cradling my bump, I lean forward.

"You okay?"

I feel his hand on my back, rubbing.

"No. It hurts." Tears well in my eyes as I breathe through it until it passes, River rubbing my back the whole time.

Once the pain ebbs, I lean back, resting my head against the seat, breathing heavily.

"Okay?" he checks.

I turn my face to him. "I'm scared," I admit quietly.

His expression softens. "Don't be. I've got you. I'm going to be with you every step of the way."

"Okay. But can you do the pain part? I'm not so keen on that." I offer a weak smile.

Lifting my hand to his mouth, he kisses it. "Red, if I could take all of your pain away, I would do it in a heartbeat."

Good Lord, this man …

He doesn't offer sweet words often, but when he does, they mother-fudging slay me.

He puts my hand down onto his thigh. "When it hurts, squeeze my leg as hard as you need to. Well, okay, not *too* hard because I bruise like a fucking banana." His teeth flash white at me before he puts the car into drive and pulls away from my house.

Destination: hospital.

Carrie

We're fifteen minutes into the thirty-minute drive to the hospital when my car starts making a sputtering, chugging noise. The car comes to a slow, rolling stop at the side of the road.

"Uh, what's happening?" I wheeze out, mid-contraction pain.

I've been trying to keep track, but they seem to be coming thick and fast. And they're getting more and more painful.

I'm going to need all the drugs when I get to the hospital.

"I don't know." River turns the ignition again, and nothing happens. "Wait here."

He flicks the hazards on and climbs out of the car. He lifts the hood, and I see a crapload of smoke billow out of it.

I wind my window down and stick my head out of it. "What's going on?"

"I'm no mechanic, but I'd say your shit car has broken down," River grunts from under the hood.

"Hey! Don't be hating on the Impala."

His head appears around the hood. "Seriously? You're in labor, your car broke down—our only current way to get you to the hospital—and you're upset because I'm calling your car shit?"

Ugh. Fudgesicles. He's right.

"I fucking knew we should have gone in my truck. But, oh no, we had to go in your car."

"I didn't know it was going to break down!" I yell at him.

He slams the hood down. "Well, this is just fucking great."

I open the door and ungracefully clamber out of my car. "I don't know what you're annoyed about. I'm the one in la—bor—argh!"

I pitch forward, grabbing hold of the car door. River's at my side in an instant.

"They're getting worse," River says.

"No kidding," I bite.

"Be nice, Red."

"Fudge off. I've currently got a baby playing Twister with my uterus, so I think it warrants me being a bee-yatch."

"You mean, bitch."

I give him an evil glare. The jerk just smiles.

I breathe deeply through my nose, letting the breath out of my mouth, riding the contraction out. River rubs my lower back. It helps.

"Let's get you back in the car," he tells me.

"Why? It's not exactly going anywhere." And neither are we. Panic starts to circle in my chest. "What are we going to do?" My voice has dropped to a whisper.

River looks around. The road is deserted. No cars have passed since we broke down.

"Someone will come soon."

"And what are we going to do, hitch a ride?"

"You're being bitchy again, Red."

"Didn't we already have this discussion? Lady in labor means a pass to be bitchy."

A grin spreads across his face. "You just said bitch."

"No, I didn't."

"Did."

"Did—argh! Christ on a fudging bike!" I clutch my tightening stomach, panting out breaths.

"Jesus, Carrie. We need to get you back in the car."

I let him gently maneuver me onto the backseat. He leaves the door open.

"I'm gonna call an ambulance," he tells me.

"Good. And tell them to hurry because I think Olive's getting impatient, and I really don't want to give birth on the side of the road!"

I hear River talking to emergency services, and then he's back, crouching at the side of the car.

"How're you doing?"

I give him a look. "My car is broken. It's hot as Lucifer, and I have no air-conditioning. Oh yeah, I'm in labor! How do you think I'm freaking doing?"

"Fuck, I love it when you're angry, Red. It's so hot."

"Fudge off." I scowl at him, not in the mood for his teasing.

Another contraction hits.

"Sweet fudging Jesus! It hurts!" Tears prick my eyes.

I grab hold of River's forearm, which is the closest thing available to me, and squeeze hard. He covers my hand with his, holding me, and rubs my leg.

"Breathe deep, Carrie," he encourages softly. "In through the nose, out through the mouth."

"I-I think Olive's coming, River. I keep feeling like I need to push."

"What?" he gasps.

It would be comical right now, the look on his face, if my baby wasn't trying to currently climb out of my body, like the alien does in the film *Alien*.

"No, she can't come now! The ambulance isn't here!"

"Well, it's not like I've got a lot of say in the matter!"

"Can't you just hold her in?"

I stare at him blankly. "Are you fudging serious right now? Hold her in?"

"Yeah, like when you need a shit and there's no bathroom around."

"Olive is not a piece of poop!" I yell. "And, no, I can't freaking hold her in—FUDGE!" I scream at the top of my lungs at the hit of another contraction. "Jesus Lord! She's coming!"

"Holy fuck!" He pulls at his hair. "Shit, what do I do?"

"I don't know! I'm not a doctor!"

"News flash: neither am I!"

"Stop yelling at me!" I shout.

"Christ. The baby's really coming now?"

I stare at him, panting, sweat-soaked hair sticking to my face. "Yes, River, the baby is really coming."

"Okay. I'm calling 911 again. See if this ambulance is any closer to getting here."

He's just got his cell out when I hear the wail of a siren.

"The ambulance is here," River states the obvious, looking as relieved as a man who just got a last-minute pardon before going to the electric chair.

The ambulance pulls up behind my car.

"Hey, what have we got here today?"

"A baby." River jabs a finger in my direction, sounding flustered. "Red's in labor. Her water broke. And she's two weeks early. We were on our way to the hospital when her shitty car broke down."

"Okay." A lady crouches down next to me, putting a medical bag down beside herself. "Hey, honey. My name is Hope. I'm a paramedic, and I'm here to help you."

"I'm Carrie," I tell her through a pant.

"Well, it's nice to meet you, Carrie. So, you're in labor. Thirty-eight weeks—is that right?"

"Yes."

"Contractions are how far apart?"

"It's hard, keeping track. They're coming real fast though. And I feel like I need to push."

"Okay. And your water broke?"

Biting my lip, I nod.

"When did that happen?"

"About thirty minutes ago."

"Okay. Would you mind if I just have a feel of your stomach?"

"Go ahead."

I sit while she presses and pushes at my stomach. I wince when it hurts.

"I'm sorry," she says in a soothing voice. "It hurts, huh?"

"Like you wouldn't believe."

"I've got two of my own. Boys. So, I know where you're at right now. Okay, Carrie, do you think you can move for me? I need to get you in the ambulance."

"No." I shake my head. "I can't. I feel like, if I stand up, the baby's just gonna come out."

"Okay. So, that means, I'm going to have to examine you here. I need to see how dilated you are."

"Examine her here?" River pipes up. "Can't you just take her to the hospital?"

She shakes her head. "If I'm right—and I usually am—there is no time to get to the hospital. This baby is ready to come out now."

"The fuck?" River gasps.

I'm at the point where I don't even care anymore. I just want the pain to stop, and I'll do anything to make that happen.

"Right, Carrie, I need to move you back a bit, so we can get you lying down on the seat."

"Okay."

"Dad, I need you to go around to the other side of the car and go behind Carrie. With your arms under her armpits, help guide her back as seamlessly as possible."

Dad. She thinks River is Olive's dad.

I meet River's eyes in this moment. I can't tell what he's thinking. I wait for him to correct her. But he doesn't.

And neither do I.

River comes to the other side of the car and opens the door behind me. He helps me move into a flat position. But he doesn't move away. He stays there, kneeling on the floor beside the car. His head by mine. His hand stroking the hair off my face.

"Carrie, you're wearing a skirt, which makes my job easier. But I'm going to need to remove your panties, so I can see what's going on down there. Is that okay?"

"Yes," I tell her.

I'm lying on the backseat of my car on the side of the road. My skirt is up and over my bent knees. My panties are gone. And a stranger-to-me woman is currently examining my vagina.

Dignity, meet trash can.

"Okay." Hope lifts her head from down below and looks at me. "Looks like we're delivering your baby here."

"What?" River and I say at the same time.

I shouldn't be surprised. I had a strong feeling this was going to be the case.

The need to push my baby out is getting stronger.

"You're fully dilated, and the baby is ready to come."

Sweet Lord in heaven.

I'm giving birth in the back of my car.

So not how I envisaged this moment happening.

"I just need to grab some things from the back of the ambulance. I'll be back in two ticks."

I blow out a breath. Tears trickle from the corners of my eyes. "I can't believe this is happening," I say to River.

"It's not ideal," he says, still brushing my hair back from my face. "But it does mean that we're going to get to meet Olive sooner rather than later. And that's good, right?"

I lift my eyes to him. Looking at his face upside down. He's even handsome from this angle.

"Yeah, it's good."

"Right, I'm back." Hope reappears at my feet. "Let's get to delivering this baby." She claps her latex-covered hands together.

She's feeling a lot more enthusiastic about this than I am. But then she's not the one pushing out a baby right now.

"Dad, can you sit in behind Mom and offer her some support? It'll help when it's time to push."

"Sure."

Hope helps me sit forward while River climbs in the car behind me. He shuts the door and leans his back against it. I lean my back against his solid chest.

Hope knew what she was talking about when she said it would help. Because being close to him right now is helping already.

"Do we know what we're having?" Hope asks me.

"A baby," River says next to my ear, and I honestly don't know if he's being serious or not.

"She meant the sex of the baby." I roll my eyes at him. "And, no, I didn't find out the sex," I tell Hope.

"A surprise. I love surprises." She beams.

"I do, too, but not the kind of surprises when they think squeezing your uterus like a grapefruit in a vise is fun!" I grit the words out as another wave of pain hits.

"Another contraction?" Hope asks.

"Y-e-s," I pant out.

Holy God, I think I'm dying. It hurts like no pain I've ever felt before.

"Do you still feel like you need to push?" Hope asks me.

I nod.

"Okay, well, you just listen to what your body's telling you to do, Carrie. Give me a nice big push."

I clench my jaw and push as hard as I can. My feet slip against the seat. "I can't!" I pant. "I feel like I'm just moving down the seat!"

"You can do it," Hope tells me. "Put your feet here." She places each foot up against the inside of my car. "When you push now, you won't move anywhere."

"You've got this, Carrie," River says in my ear.

He puts his hands up, and I grab hold of them.

"Okay, Carrie, give me another big push!" Hope says.

I push with all my might. "ARRGGH!" I yell, breaking off. "It's not working!" I cry.

"You're doing great, Carrie. Just keep going."

"But it hurts!" I whimper.

"I know. But you got this. You're a strong, badass woman. You can do this. I bet you could birth this baby in your sleep."

"In my sleep?" I pant out a laugh.

"For sure." She grins up at me. "You're a woman. We can do anything we set our minds to. Now, let's do this, yeah? Bring this baby of yours into the world, and then we can all go and have a nice cup of coffee."

"Tea, and it's a deal."

"You're on." She smiles up at me. "Now, come on, Carrie. I need you to give me one big, long push."

Gritting my teeth, hands squeezing a tight hold on River's, I push with all I have. But it feels to be in vain. "I can't do it! It hurts too much. I can't take it." I'm turning my head from side to side. I feel like I'm being ripped in two.

"You can," Hope encourages.

"No, I'm tired. I've had enough! I want to go home!"

"And we will, Carrie. I promise we'll go home as soon as this is over. You just need to push real hard."

"I did! It's not working!" I cry.

My face is wet with tears. I'm drenched in sweat. And I'm in the worst pain of my entire life.

River cups my chin, turning my eyes to his. "You can do this, Red. You've endured way worse than this and walked out the other side."

"No …" I cry. "I can't … it hurts too much. I can't take it."

"Is there anything you can give her to ease the pain?" River asks Hope.

"I'm sorry." She shakes her head. "It's too late, Carrie. Your baby's crowning. I can see the top of the head. What I need you to do right now is give me one real big push."

Both my feet are wedged up against the inside of the car. Legs akimbo. My dignity went the moment this baby decided to make an early appearance.

River's eyes fix back on mine. "You can do this because you have to. Olive needs you to push. She needs your help getting out into the world. So, you need to dig deep and do whatever you need to do to get through this."

You can do this, Carrie.

You can.

"ARGH!" I scream, giving one big push.

"That's it," Hope says supportively. "Just keep pushing."

"That's it, Carrie. Keep going."

"FUCKING HELL!" I scream. Channeling River in this moment, I let every curse word I can possibly think of rip. "HOLY MOTHERFUCKING CUNT OF A FUCKING PAINFUL BASTARD!"

"Woohoo!" River hoots. "That's my girl! Keep it going!"

"JESUS HAROLD CHRIST!"

"And the shoulders are out!" Hope beams up at me. "Just one more big push, Carrie, and you're done, all done."

"One more," I pant, exhausted, my body sagging against River's.

"You heard the lady. One more push, and we can finally meet Olive."

We.

On that thought, I pull in every bit of strength I have left. Teeth gritted, I push as hard as I can, screaming out through the pain, "FUUUCK!"

And then I hear the single sweetest sound in the world.

My baby crying.

"You've got a baby girl!" Hope beams, handing my baby over to me, laying her onto my chest.

My baby girl.

I have a daughter.

A daughter.

I stare down at the tiny head covered in a mass of pale blonde hair, and a wave of love like nothing I've ever felt before washes over me. I shift her tiny body a touch, so I can see her face for the first time. I gaze down at her.

God, she's beautiful. Perfect.

Curious dark blue eyes stare back at me.

I press a gentle kiss to her soft cheek. "I'm your mama," I whisper to her.

"She's beautiful, Carrie."

I glance up at River, who is staring down at her with awe and adoration and wonderment.

His eyes move to mine. "She looks just like you."

I look back to my daughter. "You think?"

"Definitely." He presses a sweet kiss to my forehead. "You did amazing, Carrie."

Maybe it's the overwhelming emotion of the moment or maybe just a simple need, but I lift my mouth up and press a soft kiss to his lips.

I start to move away, but his hand cups my cheek, bringing me back to his mouth.

He kisses me softly, tenderly. Gently sucking on my lower lip.

I pull back from the kiss and look into his eyes. He tenderly tucks my hair behind my ear. His eyes on mine.

"Thank you," I whisper.

"For what?"

"For being here. For being you," I repeat the words he said to me the night we learned to trust each other.

"Couple of minutes, guys"—Hope reappears, pulling my attention to her—"and then we'll be moving mama and baby into the ambulance and taking you both to the hospital."

I notice a blanket now covering my lower half. I didn't even realize that Hope had covered me up. I was too busy loving on my baby and the man sitting behind me.

"Can I come in the ambulance with them?" River asks. "If that's okay with you?" he checks with me.

"I'd like that," I tell him.

"So, do we have a name for this little beauty yet?" Hope asks me.

I stare at her for a long moment and then down at my daughter, a smile falling onto my lips. "I didn't. But I do now."

Carrie

Hope Olive Ford is the single most perfect human being ever.

And I'm not just saying that because I'm her mom. It's the truth.

She's amazing.

She's been on this earth for two months, and they have been the best months of my whole entire life.

Tiring. But the best.

I honestly don't remember life before her.

That could be because I'm exhausted.

And I wouldn't have it any other way.

I always thought that, if I could go back in time to the moment when I met Neil, I would run in the opposite direction. But, now … with Hope here, I know that, if given that chance, I would do it all again. Suffer all the pain and humiliation and anguish because it would mean that I got to have her. And she is everything.

I hate Neil for everything, except for her. She is the one thing that I am thankful to him for.

Because she is perfect.

I sometimes have to remind myself that this isn't all a dream. That I'm not going to wake up back in that house, still with Neil.

I could never have imagined the life that I have now with Hope. And River.

River has been amazing since Hope was born. He is completely smitten with her. The way he looks at my daughter … like she's a precious gift that he will protect at all costs, makes my heart ache in the best kind of way. It's amazing to watch this big man be reduced to mush by my baby girl.

He's at my house pretty much all the time. Only going home to shower and change and when he needs to work for orders that come in for his glass art.

He's totally involved. Changing diapers. Helping at bath and bedtime. Rocking her to sleep when she won't settle for me.

Feeding me to keep my energy up. Turns out that Hope is a hungry baby. I feel like she's constantly on the breast.

But, if my girl needs milk, then milk she'll get.

River is even watching her when I'm at work. Yes, I'm back to work. This mama has got to bring home the bacon for her girl.

River offered to watch her when it came time for me to go back to work two weeks ago, which is where I currently am, standing at the counter, waiting on the breakfast order for my waiting customer.

I hadn't even voiced my worries to him about leaving her in daycare with a bunch of strangers.

It was like he knew my concerns without me even having to say a word.

He knows me better than anyone.

Sometimes, I feel like he's the other half of my soul. The part I was missing but didn't realize until that day when I looked into his eyes and saw him. The real him.

It's almost like we're a family.

Except we're not.

River and I … we're together in every sense of the word, except we're not actually *together.*

I've never mentioned the kiss we shared after Hope was born, and neither has he. Just like the time before that when we kissed.

It seems River and I kiss every so often and just never discuss it.

Not that I'm complaining. I love having River in my life. I don't know what I would do without him.

But … my feelings for him have only grown stronger over time.

And I can't help but think about when the time comes that he meets someone. I know he's a prickly jerk at times, but he's also handsome and kind beneath the prickles.

Some woman is going to come along and snap him up.

And then I'll lose him.

But I'm not thinking about that right now. It makes me feel sad, and I'm not going to be sad because I have way too much good in my life right now.

Guy puts the plate out for me. I scoop it up and walk over to my customer's table.

I've put the plate down in front of him when the door chimes as it's opening. I lift my head and see my two favorite people coming into the diner.

Funny how I was just thinking about them both, and here they are.

Although they are both all that I think of lately.

"Enjoy your breakfast," I tell the customer.

Then, I walk away from his table, my smile turning into a beam at my little girl, who is in River's arms.

"Hey." I lean down and press a kiss to her cheek. "What're you guys doing here? Not that I don't appreciate the visit."

"I decided to take a walk. Hope was getting fussy, so I figured a walk into town would keep her entertained."

"Well, hand her over. It's been ages since I last had a cuddle with my girl."

"Which was about … three hours ago," he quips.

"Like I said, ages ago."

River hands Hope over to me, and I hold her to me, pressing a kiss to her nose, breathing her sweet baby scent in.

The door chimes. It's Sadie coming back from the grocery store. We were low on milk.

"Hope's here!" She dumps the grocery bag by the counter and comes over to us, practically hip-checking River out of the way. "Hand her over, Mama. Auntie Sadie wants a snuggle."

Laughing, I hand her over to Sadie, who takes her from me.

"How is my sweet girl doing?" Sadie coos to her. "You've grown already since I last saw you."

That was two days ago. Sadie has been a regular visitor at my house since Hope's arrival. She's baby crazy. And she just adores Hope.

I love that Hope has already got people in her life who love and care for her. She's got a family.

"Did I hear that Hope is here?" Guy calls from the kitchen. "Bring her on in here."

"No way! You're cooking bacon in there. You'll make her smell."

"Fine. I'm coming out to see her." Guy appears, pushing through the kitchen door. "But, if the bacon burns, it's your fault."

I watch, laughing as Sadie and Guy argue over who gets to hold Hope. I feel River tug on my sleeve.

"Got a sec?" He nods to the side.

"Sure. Everything okay?" I ask, following him to a quiet spot around the other side of the counter.

"Yeah, everything's fine. Just …" He blows out a breath. "I didn't just stop here by chance."

"I know. You said you were out for a walk because Hope was being fussy."

"No. I mean, she was. But that's not why I came in the diner to see you."

"Okay. So, why did you?"

"Well, I actually came to see Sadie."

"Sadie?" I glance over at her, confused, and then back to River.

"Yeah … I, uh, I wanted to ask her for a favor."

"Which is?" I'm also kind of wondering why he's telling me this right now.

Then, a thought, like the thudding of a dumbbell dropping on me, hits.

Oh no. He's not … with Sadie, is he?

No. Surely not.

I've never seen an inkling of anything like that between them. He barely speaks to her, to be honest.

And Sadie knows we're not together, *together, but she's aware of my feelings for him. A girl needs someone to talk to about these things.*

And Sadie would never break the girl code.

I think.

"Well … I was going to ask Sadie if"—*I don't think I want to hear this. Would it be childish of me to stick my fingers in my ears right now?*—"she would watch Hope tonight while I take you out for dinner."

What?

"What?"

"Dinner, Red. You and me."

"You want to take me out for dinner?" I say slowly.

"Yes."

"Why?"

He gives me a look that says I should already know the answer. "Because you're my girl, Red."

My heart literally skips a beat. *I'm his girl.*

"I am?" I say through a mouth that feels like it's filled with cotton.

"Yeah. And guys take their girls out on dates."

"Uh, River … did I miss a step or something?"

"Nope. We've kissed twice."

"Yes … but … the first was when I was still pregnant with Hope, and the second was right after she was born. And there's been nothing since. Not even a hint of anything between us. I figured …"

"What?"

"That you weren't interested in me in that way."

He steps closer, and my breath stutters.

"I'm more than interested. Always have been. But you were pregnant, and I didn't want to cross any boundaries. And then Hope was born, and you needed time to adjust to being a mom to a baby."

"She's still a baby. So, why now?" I ask quietly.

"Because I'm done waiting." His hand slides around my waist, pulling me up close to him. "Hope is two months old. It's time to make this thing with us official."

"This thing?"

"Yeah, Red." He leans into my ear and whispers, "I'm taking you out tonight. We're gonna eat. Have fun. And then, afterward, I'll drive you home in my truck, and we'll make out on the front seat like a pair of teenagers."

I lean back to look in his eyes. The gleam of desire there is unmistakable. My whole body heats up. If someone struck a match next to me, I'd go up in flames right now.

"Only make out?" I tease the edge of my lip with my teeth.

His eyes fix on that spot, and his mouth tips up at the corner. "We might get to second base. Third, if you're a good girl."

I press my cheek to his, my lips at his ear. "And, if you're a really good boy, then I might even let you hit a home run."

I step away from him and sashay into the kitchen, grinning, knowing that his eyes are on my swaying ass the whole time.

Carrie

River drives us out of town to a seafood restaurant in New Braunfels. I know he doesn't like being around the people of Canyon Lake. He probably thinks people will stare and whisper if we went out to dinner together in a restaurant at home.

But I don't think he's realized that folks are used to seeing us together now. And that they don't stare and whisper anymore either.

Sadie's at my house, watching Hope. When we left, Sadie was sitting down with Hope and Buddy to watch *Frozen* even though Hope won't have a clue what's going on. I think Sadie just wanted an excuse to watch it herself.

River's taking me to a seafood restaurant. The man clearly pays attention because I love seafood, and most of it is a no-no while pregnant. But, when breast-feeding, seafood is actually a good thing. The omega-3 is good for babies, which is passed on through the breast milk.

Win-win for me and Hope.

It is weird, being all dressed up and out without her.

Normally, I'm in sweats or pajamas right now, at home with River and Hope.

But, tonight, it's just River and me.

On a date.

I haven't been on a date in a very long time. I kind of feel out of my depth. But then I remind myself that it's just River. There are no expectations with him. Only happiness. And excitement for what tonight is going to bring and all the possibilities open to us.

River parks the truck on the street and turns off the engine. "Stay put," he tells me.

I watch him climb out, round the hood of the truck, and then open my door.

He's going old school.

It makes me smile.

"Why, thank you, kind sir," I say with a faux Southern accent when he takes my hand and helps me down from his truck.

He doesn't smile. Or speak. And he doesn't let go of my hand.

He takes our linked hands beneath my back, bringing me closer to him, until our fronts are pressed up together.

My breasts are crushed up against his chest.

Bonus of breast-feeding: big boobs.

I can also feel the definite outline of his length beneath his dress pants. Did I mention he's wearing dress pants and a shirt? He's all smartened up, and he looks divine.

I blink up at him, feeling breathless.

"Did I tell you that you look fucking gorgeous in that dress?" he says in a low, raspy voice.

"Oh, this old thing?" I tease.

It's actually not old. It's brand-new. I went out shopping straight after I finished work at the diner and picked out a new dress and heels to wear tonight. It's not often I get asked out on a date. Especially not by the hottest man in town.

The dress is black lace with a floaty skirt that sits an inch or so above my knees. It's classy with an edge of sexy. The heels are red and strappy with a matching clutch. My hair is down and curled into soft waves down my back. I even have makeup on. It's light, but it's there.

"And, yes, you did tell me. Only a couple of hundred times." I laugh softly, teasingly.

River has made it very clear that he likes the way I look tonight.

He sweeps my hair back over my shoulder and presses a kiss to my neck, making me shiver. "Clearly not enough," he whispers into my ear.

A kiss to my cheek. The corner of my mouth. Then … his lips finally meet mine and kiss me.

My toes curl, my breasts tingle, and my body hums.

"Isn't that supposed to come at the end of the date?" I say, breathless, when we break apart.

Dark, lusty eyes gleam down at me. "No. That was just the starter."

River leads me over to the restaurant, my hand still held by his. He walks at a steady pace because I'm a little out of practice when it comes to walking in heels.

"The restaurant building is a century-old converted post office," River tells me.

He releases my hand and places it on the small of my back as we walk up the handful of steps to the entrance.

River holds the door for me while I walk inside.

The maître d' approaches. River gives him our reservation name. Wild, of course He asks if we would like a drink at the bar first. River looks to me.

"I don't mind," I say.

"We'll go straight to our table," River tells him.

He leads us over to our table, which is by the window that overlooks a courtyard.

"Is this table okay for you both?" the maître d' asks, pulling my chair out.

"It's perfect," I tell him, sitting.

I put my clutch on the table. River sits opposite me.

"Your waiter will be over soon with your menus and to take your drink order," he tells us before departing.

"This place is so nice," I tell River, reaching over to touch his hand that rests on the table.

He smiles, turning his hand over, linking his fingers with mine. "I'm glad you like it."

"Do you think Hope is okay?"

His eyes crinkle at the corners. "She's fine. But you can check with Sadie if you want."

"Maybe I'll just text her."

I get my cell from my clutch and type out a quick text to Sadie.

She responds straightaway.

I smile, reading the text to River. "Hope's having a bottle. Buddy's passed out cold. And Sadie is eating the cupcakes that I left in the kitchen for her. Oh, and *Frozen* is almost finished. They're watching *Moana* next." I put my cell back in my clutch.

"Sounds like Sadie's having fun." River chuckles.

"You know, I think she is. She adores Hope."

"Of course she does. Hope's awesome. Like her mom."

"True." I grin.

The waiter comes over with our food menus and takes our drink order. River orders a Bud Light because he's driving. I order a glass of wine, which will most likely last me the whole night. I've never been a big drinker. Neil wouldn't allow me to—

Nope. Not going there tonight.

I'm on a date with the best man I've ever known.

My past doesn't even come into the equation tonight.

When the waiter leaves our table with our drink order, I open my menu but don't look at it yet.

"Can I say something?"

"Will I like what you have to say?"

I lift a shoulder. "Not sure. But I'm going to say it anyway."

He gestures with his hand for me to speak.

"I do love this restaurant; it's amazing. But you do know you didn't have to drive all the way out of town to bring me here. We could have gone to a restaurant in Canyon Lake."

A frown appears on his brow. But he doesn't say anything.

"I know why you didn't. Because you avoid the people in town. But, honestly, I think maybe you … shouldn't go out of your way to avoid them. I think … well, maybe things have changed now, you know, with us being friends—"

"We're just friends?" He raises a dark brow at me.

I feel my cheeks heat. "You know what I mean," I say quietly.

"I don't think I do, Red. Because I'm very sure that I want to be more than friends with you. I thought you did, too."

"You know I do. I wouldn't be here tonight if I didn't. But I also know that you're changing the subject."

He gives me a slow, knowing smile.

I nudge his leg with my foot under the table. "Ass." I grin.

"That is also true." He chuckles.

"So, as I was saying, I think, since people have seen us together and seen you with Hope … I just think maybe things have changed—you know, changed … how they see you."

"People like that don't change the way they think. And they're not people that I want to be around."

"And I agree. They're narrow-minded sheep, and I'm not saying you should be friends with them. But I just want you to stop hiding in your hometown."

He exhales a slow breath.

"Just think about it."

He stares at me for a moment. "Okay."

"Can I ask something else?"

"No," he says, but I know he's teasing. I can tell by the look in his eyes.

"Why have you never left Canyon Lake if you dislike the place so much?"

He leans back in his chair. "I don't dislike the place. Only the people—barring two now. And where would I have gone if I had left?"

"Where people are nicer," I suggest with a shrug.

His lips tip up. "Is there such a place?"

"Probably not," I admit.

"As strange as this might sound," he says, "sometimes, the devil you know is better than the devil you don't."

"I hope that's not why you're out with me tonight."

That does make him laugh. And I love the sound. It has me smiling from ear to ear.

"Definitely not." He shakes his head, his laughter subsiding. "Although a lot of people from our town might think that's the case for you—that you're out with the devil."

"Well, I'd rather be out with the devil. At least I know what I'm getting."

"That's how you see me? Not like a devil, but that you know what you're getting with me."

"Yes." I smile warmly at him. "And I very much like what I'm getting with you."

"Good."

"How do you see me?" I ask tentatively.

"Right now?" He suggestively raises his brow.

I playfully narrow my eyes. "You know what I mean."

"I've always known what I was getting with you. And I've always liked it."

"Even when you were being an ass to me?"

"Even then." He lets out a breath and picks up the saltshaker. "Say this saltshaker is me." He picks up the pepper with his other hand. "And the pepper is you. To the outside world and even to us at first, we don't seem like we should go together. I'm brash and hard. You're soft and beautiful. But we do go together, Red." He presses the shakers together. "We go together perfectly."

My heart pauses, skipping a beat, before starting back up at a faster pace.

A smile lifts my lips.

He smiles, too.

And this is the exact moment that I know for sure that I'm in love with River Wild.

I'm in love with him.

"You're a closet romantic." I smile, hiding the words that I feel are scrawled all over my face.

He puts the shakers down and eyes me, amusement sparkling in them. "You ever tell anyone, Red, and I'll deny it until my dying breath."

"Your secret's safe with me." I grin.

The waiter returns with our drinks and asks if we're ready to order, but neither of us has even looked at the menu. So, the waiter says he'll come back.

I pick my wine up and take a sip. Then, I read the menu.

I go for the shrimp brochette, and River orders the freshwater trout.

We mostly talk about Hope over dinner—you know, because she's awesome. And River tells me stories about times that he and his gran had together.

Before I know it, dessert is finished, and River is paying the bill.

We step outside the restaurant. The air is pleasantly warm.

We walk to his truck, hand in hand. River opens the passenger door for me.

I watch him round the truck.

Every part of me is tingling with feelings and emotions, now knowing what I feel for him.

I want him.

Like I've never wanted anyone in my life.

He climbs in the truck and turns the ignition on.

"So …" he says, meeting my eyes across the space between us. His eyes are dark and glittering with desire for me. "We have an hour before we told Sadie we'd be back. Do you want to do anything else? Or we can go home now? Whatever you want, Red."

"There is one thing I'd really like to do," I softly tell him, nerves creeping up my throat.

"Oh, yeah? What?"

I bite my lip, delaying, and then decide to just go for it. I take a breath and blow it out. "Go back to your house, River. That's what I would really like to do right now."

Carrie

River opens his front door, stepping aside to let me inside first. He follows me in and closes the door behind him. He takes me by the hand and leads me into the living room. He clicks on a lamp. He lets go of my hand, and I stand and watch as he walks over to a cabinet. He bends down and lifts up the lid. Flicks a switch on it. I hear a scratch, and then music starts to play—"The Power of Love" by Frankie Goes to Hollywood.

River turns to me. The look in his eye makes my insides tremble with anticipation and need.

He walks over to me. Stopping an inch from me, he stares down into my eyes. "Dance with me?"

"I'm not a good dancer," I tell him.

"Me neither. We can be bad together."

He takes hold of my right hand with his left. His other hand slides along my waist and around my back, his fingers pressing gently against me, urging me closer.

I settle into him.

And we start to move together.

Eyes on each other, we sway to the music.

I listen to the lyrics. They're beautiful.

"I like this song," I tell him.

He nods. "Me, too." He leans his face down to mine, brushing his nose over my cheek, making me shiver. He says into my ear, "But I like you more."

I turn my eyes to his. And then we're kissing.

The soul-deep, toe-curling, drive-you-wild kind of kissing.

The kind of kissing that only leads to one thing—sex.

The feel of his lips on mine is like fireworks and symphonies. My skin buzzes with electricity. I can't get enough of him. Feel enough of him.

His hand releases mine. I wrap my arms around his neck. Both his big hands slide down my back and curve over my butt.

He lifts me like I weigh nothing. I wrap my legs around his waist.

We're still fused at the mouth, kissing like the world is about to be hit by an asteroid.

My fingers glide up into the hair at the back of his head, gripping.

He moans into my mouth.

I feel it low in my stomach.

"Take me to bed," I whisper against his lips.

He doesn't need telling twice.

He carries me through the living room and upstairs to his darkened bedroom.

He leaves the light off.

River lowers me to my feet. "Turn around," he says in that sexy, low voice of his.

I turn with deliberate slowness, giving him my back.

His fingers find the zipper on the back of my dress. He drags it down. The sound tantalizingly loud in the silence.

His hands push the dress off my shoulders, down over my hips, letting it fall to the floor. Leaving me in my lacy black underwear and my red heels.

I turn to face him.

His eyes move down my body, the moonlight in the window casting light over us.

"You're so fucking beautiful, Carrie," he whispers roughly.

"And you're still dressed."

I reach out and unbutton his shirt with shaky fingers, taking my time, the way he did with my zipper. When the last button is undone, I slide my hands up his bare chest and push the shirt back off his shoulders.

He frees his arms from it and tosses it to the floor.

I lean forward and press a kiss to his bare chest, over his heart.

He shudders. His hand slides into my hair, gripping it, and he tilts my head back and covers my mouth with his.

He walks me backward, not breaking our kiss once, until the backs of my legs hit his bed.

I sit down on the edge of it. I unbutton the fastening on his pants and lower the zipper.

River kicks off his shoes and removes his pants. Then, he takes off his boxer shorts.

I suck in a breath.

He's still as big and perfect as I remember him being.

The sight of his cock makes my mouth water. I've never had this reaction to a man's penis before. But, with his, I definitely do.

He reaches down and fists his cock.

It's so insanely erotic.

He's so virile and just so goddamn male.

I want to know what he tastes like. How he will feel in my mouth.

I reach my hand out, covering his over his cock, bring my mouth to his dick, and press a kiss to the tip of it.

He sucks in a deep breath. The muscles in his stomach tightening.

I part my lips and slide the tip of him into my mouth.

He tastes salty and musky. I like it.

River leans over me and unsnaps my bra, removing it. I have to take my mouth and hand off him to let him do so.

I don't get a chance to get my hand or mouth back on him because he lowers to his knees in front of me.

He removes my heels from my feet. Then, he hooks his fingers into the elastic of my panties. I lift my hips to give him purchase.

He slowly pulls them down my legs until they're gone. And there's nothing left to remove.

Just him and me, completely bare to each other.

"If there's any hard limits for you … any triggers … tell me. I don't want to fuck this up. You're too important, and I've waited too long to mess it up now."

I swallow back my emotions. I touch my hand to his cheek. "You won't mess it up because I trust you."

He turns his mouth into my palm and presses a kiss there.

"And the same with you, River … if there's anything …"

He shakes his head. "There's nothing I don't want or won't do with you. I want it all. I want all of you, Carrie."

I bring my mouth to his and kiss him again.

The kiss turns molten in seconds.

River's pushing me back onto the bed. I'm scooting back to make room for him.

He lies over me, propped up on one hand. The other slips between my legs.

"Fuck, Carrie, you're so wet."

He runs his finger between my lips. Then, he slides his finger inside me.

I groan at the sensation.

He brings his mouth to my breast and runs his tongue over my nipple, licking it.

His thumb starts to rub against my clit. He sucks my nipple into his mouth. I feel the graze of his teeth over it.

My hands clutch his hair, as I'm overwhelmed with all the sensations flowing through me.

"I won't last," I tell him, knowing I've wanted him so badly for so long. I can feel my body priming to go off like a rocket.

"I need to taste you," he growls. Then, he's moving down my body and covering my pussy with his mouth.

The orgasm hits me with the power of a freight train.

I scream out his name. Body writhing with the power of the orgasm.

I'm still shaking when he lifts his head and moves back up my body.

He takes my mouth with his. I can taste myself on him. I've never done that with a man before—tasted myself on his lips. It's maddeningly erotic. I feel like I could come again. Or maybe it's just him that makes me feel this way.

"I need you," I tell him.

Something virile and wholly male flashes in his eyes, making me shiver with need.

His voice is as dark as his eyes when he says, "You've got me, Carrie. Always."

I reach down and take him in my hand. His muscles ripple from the hard shudder in his body.

"I need to fuck you," he rasps, deep and sexy. "No condom. I want you bare."

I'm on the pill; he knows this. And I trust him. Like I've never trusted anyone before.

"Please," is all I can manage. I want this man more than the next breath in my lungs. I'm starved for him.

Lining his cock with my entrance, he plunges deep inside me, making me cry out.

"Fuck, Carrie," he grits out. "You shouldn't be this tight after having a baby two months ago."

A laugh flies out of me. "Maybe I'm not tight, and it's just that your dick is ridiculously big."

"Say that again."

"I'm not tight," I tease, knowing what he wants me to say.

"Red …"

"Dick, River. Is that what you want me to say?"

"Fuck yeah," he groans. Pulling out of me, he slams back in.

I wrap my arms around his neck, bringing his mouth to mine. He kisses me deep and wet and dirty.

His hand grips hold of my hip, holding me in place.

His fingers are digging hard into my skin, but that only seems to turn me on even more. Knowing how badly he wants me from the strength of his grip and the hardness of his cock.

His hip bone is rubbing against my clit with every move he makes against me. His cock strokes a delicious spot deep inside me.

It's like sensory overload.

"Tell me you're close, Carrie. Because I'm not gonna last much longer. You feel too fucking good."

"I'm close," I pant. "Just keep doing … that … right … there. Yes, oh, yes … please!" I'm hit with an orgasm stronger than the first.

My inner muscles contract around him, squeezing him.

"Fuck, Carrie. You're making me come … so … hard." His hips jerk against mine as he pours himself inside me.

We're sweet kisses against fevered skin. Neither ready to let this moment end.

River takes my face in his hands, framing it. He brushes my hair from my forehead with his thumbs. Staring down at me in the dark.

I smile up at him. "What?" I whisper.

"I love you," he says. The words spoken so simply … easily but with so much meaning.

My heart stutters in my chest. Then, sheer delight ripples through me, blanketing every inch of my skin.

I cover one of his hands with mine. "I love you, too," I tell him.

His lips lift into a beautiful smile, his eyes crinkling at the corners. "I want us to be together. You, me, and Hope. I want us to be a family."

"I want that, too. So much."

God, my heart feels like it might burst. I never believed that I could have something so good, so pure. But I do. I've got it here, right now, in my arms.

River drags his thumb over my lips, presses a kiss there, and then buries his face into my neck, tightly holding me. And I hold him back equally as tight.

Carrie

I finish up in River's shower and wrap a towel around myself. I decided to get a quick one while I was here because no-condom sex can be a bit messy.

I left him lying in bed.

I can't believe that he told me that he loves me.

It's all just so perfect. He's perfect.

And I'm sickeningly happy. Like tooth-achingly happy. I'm like a Hallmark movie.

And you know what? I'm glad.

Because happiness doesn't come around often for people like me. So, I'm going to grab it with both hands when it does.

And it has. With River. And Hope.

I'm so lucky to have them both.

I dry my body with the towel and put my clothes back on, which I gathered up from the floor and brought in with me.

I let my hair down from the band that I tied it up with. And I go back into the bedroom.

River's still in bed. Arms behind his head, he smiles at me.

"You sure I can't tempt you back in?" He gives me a sexy grin, pulling back the cover to show me his impressive and ridiculously hot body.

And it is seriously tempting, but …

"I need to get back to Hope. I'm already ten minutes past the time I told Sadie that I would be back, and I hate to be late."

River slides out of bed and pulls his boxer shorts on.

"You go back home to our girl. I'll grab a quick shower here, and then I'll come straight on over."

I walk up to him, laying my hand against his chest. "You're going to spend the night?"

"Don't I every night?"

"Not in my bed."

"You want me in your bed?"

I tip my head to the side and let a slow smile on my lips. "What do you think?"

"I think I'm getting lucky again tonight."

Laughing, I press a quick kiss to his lips and turn for the door. He swats my ass with his hand, making me laugh even harder.

We head downstairs. River opens the front door, letting me out. I step onto the porch.

He tucks my hair behind my ear. "I'll watch you walk over."

"It's like twenty steps to my house," I tell him.

"More like fifty. And you think bad things don't happen to people—"

"Even in the shortest of distances," I finish for him. "I know."

I kiss him again because I can. One last lingering kiss to keep me going until he comes over.

"I'll be over in fifteen," he tells me as I start to walk away.

Turning, I walk backward and smile at him. "How about ten?"

He smiles. "Ten it is."

I blow him a kiss and then face forward, so I don't fall over on my ass in those heels.

I reach my front garden and walk up the path.

Out of nowhere, I feel a chill on the back of my neck. I glance around, only to see darkness.

I look back, and River is still standing at his door. Watching and waiting.

I get my front door key from my clutch and push it in the lock, turning. I lift my hand in a wave to let River know I'm going in.

He lifts his hand back in return.

I push open the door and let myself inside the warmth and brightness of my house.

"Hey. Sorry I'm late," I say to Sadie as I enter, closing the door behind me.

She's sitting on the sofa, watching some medical drama on TV. Buddy is curled up beside her.

He clambers down at seeing me and wanders over. I pick him up and kiss his head.

"You're hardly late." Sadie chuckles. "And you could've stayed out longer. It's not exactly a hardship, being here with the cutest and world's best-behaved baby and my little Buddy here. And then there are the cupcakes."

"Can't forget those."

"Did you make them?" she asks, getting to her feet.

I nod, suddenly feeling shy.

"They're really good, Carrie. You'll have to make them for the diner sometime."

"I'd like that. How was Hope?" I change the subject. Not because I don't want to bake food for the diner, but it's still hard for me to receive compliments. Seven years of being told I was useless made sure of that.

But I'm learning slowly.

"She was perfect, of course. She had a bottle and then passed right out. I put her down in her room and brought the monitor in with me." She gestures to the baby monitor sitting on the coffee table. "I checked in on her about thirty minutes ago, and she was fast asleep. Haven't heard a peep from her." Sadie slips her shoes onto her feet and picks up her car keys from the coffee table. "So … how was the date?" Her eyes gleam at me.

I bite the corner of my lip. "Good." I nod, feeling a blush creep up my neck. "Really good."

She smiles widely. "I'll ask no more." She winks. "I'm just glad you and River are together. You two both deserve happiness."

"As do you," I remind her.

I'm not the only one with a bad past. Sadie had her very own Neil, too. She deserves all the good the world has to give her.

She shrugs, pulling her jacket on. "My time will come."

I put Buddy down to the floor and walk Sadie to the door. Giving her a hug and kiss on the cheek, I thank her again for watching Hope.

Buddy and I stand in the doorway and watch Sadie walk the short distance to her car. She gets in and turns on the engine. She gives me a wave before pulling away.

I glance over at River's house, seeing it all lit up. Knowing that, right now, he's in the shower, all soapy and wet.

Sweet Lord. I'm getting hot, just thinking about it.

"Come on, Budster."

I step back inside, and Buddy follows me. I shut the door behind us. I go to lock it and then stop because River is coming over. I might as well leave it unlocked, so he can just come straight on in.

I take my heels off and carry them with me down the hall, dropping them just inside my door. I go straight into Hope's room with Buddy at my heels.

Hope's bedroom door is ajar, leaving a glow of light inside.

I tread softly across the floor. Reaching her crib, I stare down at my sleeping daughter. I lean down and press a light kiss to her soft cheek.

"Mama loves you," I whisper, lightly smoothing my hand over her hair. "Sleep well, baby girl."

As I leave her room, keeping the door open, Buddy settles down on the rug in Hope's room.

"Toilet time soon, Buddy boy. But you can chill for now."

I walk into my bedroom and take off my dress and underwear, tossing them into the laundry basket in my bathroom. I grab some clean panties and pull them on, followed by my plain white pajama top and baby-blue shorts. I don't need to stay dressed up for River. He's seen me at my worst when I was giving birth. If that didn't put him off me, then nothing will.

I go in my bathroom and brush my teeth. When I'm finished, I look at myself in the mirror.

My eyes are bright. My cheeks flushed.

I look happy.

When I think back to the person I was not even a year ago, it's hard to reconcile that with the woman I am now. It's crazy to believe that it's not even been a year.

"You did it, girl," I whisper to the mirror.

Switching off the bathroom light, I walk back through my bedroom. I glance at my bed, knowing I'm going to be sharing it with River for the first time tonight.

The thought sends butterflies fluttering into my tummy.

You know, I heard a saying once that said, *Love is like a river, never ending as it flows but gets greater with time.*

That's my love with my River right there.

And it's only just begun.

On bare feet, I walk down the hall, heading to the living room to wait for River, humming away to myself.

And then I'm smiling when I realize that the tune I'm humming is the song that River and I danced to tonight. Right before we made love.

I'm still smiling when I walk into the living room.

The smile freezes on my face at the sight of the person standing in my living room, my heart stilling in my chest.

My visitor doesn't smile. Not that he ever did.

His head tips to the side a fraction. Cold eyes fixed on mine. He parts his lips, and in the voice that still fills my nightmares now, he says, "Hello, Annie."

Carrie

"N-Neil," I feel like I'm choking his name out. My vocal cords strangled by the realization that he's here.

Here in my house.

How is he here?

"H-how d-did you f-find me?" I'm stammering. I can't help it. My body is trembling so hard; I'm rattling from the inside out.

It only gets worse when I see the gun in his hand held at his side.

Hope.

It's my only thought.

Please don't make a sound, baby.

I need him to not know that she's here.

He lifts the gun and rubs the barrel against the side of his head, up into his blond hair, which was always cropped short but has now grown out. It looks messy and unclean.

As the rest of him does. Blond whiskers cover the lower part of his face. His clothes are unclean and crumpled.

This is a man who would beat me for failing to iron out a single crease in his work shirt. And, now, he is wearing a shirt that hasn't seen the inside of a washing machine for a long time.

Even in this terrifying moment, the irony is not lost on me.

"It wasn't easy." His voice is like needles piercing my skin. Every syllable agony to listen to. "I've been looking for you since the day you left. I've been looking all over the country in fact. Smart move, coming to Texas, Annie. I really wouldn't have thought to look for you here, knowing how you hate the heat. You're brighter than I ever gave you credit for. But then I got lucky and happened to stumble across a news article online about a woman giving birth to a baby in her car on the side of the road. With a picture of the woman accompanying the article. And who was that woman, Annie?"

Me.

He knows about Hope.

I feel fear like I've never known before.

I swallow down gravel.

"Me," I whisper.

He laughs a deeply scary sound. "You could change your hair to every color under the sun, Annie, even change your face, and I would still know it's you. And you know why? Because you are mine, Annie."

River. Where are you? I silently call.

"I-I'm s-sorry," I stammer.

"*I-I'm s-sorry,*" he mimics. "You're always fucking sorry, Annie!"

He starts to pace in front of the door, blocking that exit. Not that I can leave without Hope.

I think about if I could make a run for it down the hall to Hope's room and get her from her crib and climb out of the window.

But there's no lock on the door. I wouldn't make it in time.

He stops pacing. "Is the baby mine, Annie?"

I don't know how to answer. If I tell him the truth—that, yes, Hope is his child—he will take her from me. And he will hurt her.

If I tell him no … he might still hurt her.

But he'll hurt me first if he thinks she's not his.

He'll need to punish me. It's his way. And that will give me time … time for River to get here.

"Answer me!" he barks.

And I snap to attention, like a well-trained dog.

"No." I swallow the lie, holding his stare. I need him to believe me. "The baby's not yours."

Nothing changes in his expression. I expected rage and fury. But there's just nothing but emptiness and blankness in those cold eyes of his.

And that terrifies me more than any anger he could direct at me.

He starts tapping the barrel against his temple. "You left me, Annie, to have a baby with someone else?"

"Yes," I say quietly.

He starts shaking his head, chanting, "No. No. No! It wasn't meant to be that way! You're mine! You have always been mine! We were meant to spend our lives together! It was my baby that you were supposed to have!" Spit is flying from his mouth. His eyes bulging. He looks manic. Like a rabid dog.

He lifts the gun, aiming it at me.

My heart stops.

"Neil … please … don't."

"Oh, you're pleading now? You want my forgiveness, Annie? You want me to forgive you for being a dirty whore and having a bastard child with some other man!"

The word is hard to say. I have to force it out. "Y-yes." But I need to do anything to keep him calm right now.

I just need a little more time before River gets here.

"Too late, Annie." He cocks the gun.

"No! Please!" I cry, defensively holding my hands. "Don't do this! I-I'll come home with you. Right now. I'll make this all better."

"And the baby?"

I swallow down the disgusting lie I'm about to say. "I'll leave her with her dad. I'll leave and come home with you."

He's staring at me. My heart is pounding hard in my chest. My pulse roaring in my ears.

Then, he shakes his head, and my heart drops.

"It's too late. You're tainted now, in this body." The gun pointed right at me, he moves it up and down. "You soiled it when you fucked another man and bore his child."

"Neil … please … I'll make it better, and we can be together."

A smile that looks almost sad comes onto his lips. "And we will, Annie. Just not in this life."

I hear a click and loud popping sound. And then a sensation hits me, like I've just been punched in the chest.

No.

God, no.

I look down at my body and see a hole in my shirt. And blood.

There's blood seeping out of the hole.

He shot me.

Stunned, I stagger backward. Reaching out, I grab hold of the sofa, but I can't stay up. My legs give out on me. I slide down the sofa, slumping to the floor.

River, help me. Please.

Neil walks over to me. He lowers to his knees beside me. "I'm sorry it has to be this way, Annie. But you've left me no choice. But this is good, you see. We can be together in death. We'll both be reborn in heaven. You'll be clean again."

I blink up at him. I can't breathe. It feels like water is filling my lungs. Like I'm drowning.

Neil lifts the gun to his head. He smiles at me. "See you on the other side, Annie." Then, he pulls the trigger.

His body drops beside me.

The only thing I feel at the sight of him dead is relief.

Relief that he can't hurt Hope.

Help, I try to yell, but only a gargled noise comes out.

Hope is crying.

Mama's here, baby. I'm right here.

"Carrie! Oh God, no! No! No! No!"

River. He's here.

He's dragging Neil away from me. He's at my side, lifting me into his lap.

"Carrie, baby, it's okay. It's going to be okay. I'm here. I've got you. I'm gonna call an ambulance. Just hold on, baby. I love you, Carrie. I love you so fucking much. Don't leave me. *Please.*"

He's crying. It hurts me to see it.

Please don't cry, River.

His cell is against his ear. He's calling emergency services.

Hope, I try to tell him. *Go to Hope.* But the words won't work.

My lungs are burning. I'm choking to death.

I'm dying.

I know I'm dying.

I love you, I tell him with my eyes. *And Hope. So, so much. Take care of her for me. Tell her every day that I love her.*

I try to gasp in one more breath. To give me one more second with him.

And then—

EPILOGUE

River
One Year Later

"Come on, Hope." I pick her up out of her high chair after cleaning off her sticky porridge-covered fingers.

Hope likes to feed herself at breakfast time and also lunch and dinnertime, and by feed herself, I mean, get the food everywhere except for her mouth.

"Time to go visit Mama."

I strap her into her stroller, hanging her bag of everything I'll need to keep an active fourteen-month-old clean, watered, fed, and entertained. I swear, going out for a few hours with a toddler is like packing for a vacation.

I step outside.

The sky is clear of clouds. The sun is shining. It's a nice day for a walk.

We head into town, stopping by the florist to pick up a bunch of flowers that I ordered earlier over the phone.

I put them in the basket below the stroller and start walking again.

Hope is playing with the hanging toys on the stroller arch, jabbering away to herself in a language only she knows.

Her first word was *Dada*. And she's right; I am her daddy. In every sense of the word that matters.

We reach the entrance to the cemetery.

I push the stroller in, walking past all the rows of headstones.

Until I reach the one that belongs to me.

I park Hope's stroller, unclip the straps, and lift her out. She wriggles to be put down. She's independent. She got it from her mama.

I put her down onto the grass.

She immediately plops down on her butt and pulls her shoes and socks off. She clambers to her feet. The sock goes in her mouth. And she begins toddling around the grass.

I watch her, smiling.

I get the bunch of flowers that we picked up from the basket under Hope's stroller.

I walk over to the headstone. Brushing some dirt and leaves off it.

I lower down to my knees, sitting before her. "Happy birthday," I tell her. "I got you some flowers—bluebells. I know you loved them."

I put the tied bunch down in front of the headstone.

The one that I picked out for her.

I stare at her name engraved deep into that stone.

"I miss you," I tell her. "I will always miss you. But … I have so much now because of you." I look over at Hope, who has found a patch of daisies beside a nearby headstone and is currently chattering away to them. I smile and then look back at her headstone. "I … love you."

I swallow back the tears clogging my throat.

A hand touches my shoulder.

I turn my head, looking up at the one person who makes things so much more bearable.

"Hey."

"Hey, Red." I smile.

"You okay?" she asks, sitting down beside me.

"Yeah." I nod. "Just talking to Mama."

"Happy birthday, Mary," Carrie says.

I reach out and take hold of her hand, squeezing it.

"Sorry I'm a little late," she says to me. "Old Mrs. Parker caught me on my way out of the diner. She was asking how Hope's doing. Wanted to see recent pictures of her. It took a while."

I chuckle at the thought.

But I can't blame Mrs. Parker. Because Hope is awesome.

I think she's stolen the heart of nearly everyone in this town.

Of course, there are a few who will always keep their distance because of me.

But the majority love her.

It's hard not to love her. She's sweet and adorable.

I love her and her mom in a way I never thought possible.

They are both my whole world.

And, because of the sacrifice my mama made for me, I get to be here with them now, being Hope's daddy and living the amazing, wonderful life that we have together.

"Mada!" Hope cries happily when she spots her mom. She comes waddling over to Carrie, who pulls her into her arms and kisses her head.

"Hey, baby girl. *Mama* missed you!"

I chuckle at the highlighting of the word *mama*. Carrie is still pissed that *Dada* was Hope's first word. And, of course, I wind Carrie up over the fact that Hope calls her *Mada*.

Some things never change with Red and me. And I pray to God, they never do.

After coming so close to losing her that day when that sick fuck of her ex shot her … seeing her die right there in my arms … it was the single worst moment in my entire life.

It felt like my life was over.

Watching the paramedics fight to revive her right in front of me …

Even now, just thinking about it almost breaks me.

But my girl is a fighter. And, when they got her heart beating again, putting a tube in her chest, draining the blood flooding her lungs, I got down on my knees and thanked God.

But the nightmare wasn't over.

Carrie was put on a stretcher and transported to the hospital.

I followed in the car with Hope. Calling Sadie on my way. She met me at the hospital along with Guy.

The police were at the hospital, wanting a statement, but all I could think of was Carrie.

She was taken to the operating room.

She flatlined on the table.

She died twice on that horrific fucking night.

If her ex-husband hadn't killed himself, I would have murdered him with my bare hands.

Those doctors got her heart started again and got that bullet out, which was lodged in her left lung. It had missed her heart by millimeters.

When she came out of surgery, her doctor told me that they'd put her in an induced coma to help give her time to heal. Her breathing was assisted.

There were fears that she would never wake up. That she wouldn't be able to breathe alone. That there would be irreparable damage.

It was the longest week of my life. I'd never felt so helpless.

But the strangest thing happened. People from the town started showing up at the hospital, offering support to me. Bringing food. Helping with Hope. Some even just came to sit with Carrie and me while I waited for her to open her beautiful eyes.

It changed how I saw everything.

How I saw people. Especially the people of this town.

After seven long days, Carrie woke up.

I'd never felt such relief.

Then, she started breathing unassisted, and from there on, she made a full and complete recovery.

She's a goddamn fighter, my girl.

When Carrie got out of the hospital, she and Hope moved in with me. They're still with me.

My house became *our* home.

It was hard on Carrie though, having to see her old house and remembering what had happened there every time she left our home.

So, I contacted the owner of the house, who was only happy to sell it to me. The day that house became mine, I had it demolished. I flattened that fucking place to the ground.

I had money just sitting in the bank from my inheritance from my gran. She hadn't just left me the old house. She'd left me a truckload of money. Gran never was a big spender, so her money from her art had accumulated over the years. I never had anything to spend it on. Spending some on buying that house and bulldozing it to the ground was the best use of it. I knew Gran would have approved.

And, truthfully, I didn't just do it for Carrie.

I did it for me, too.

That house was the place where Carrie had died. In my fucking arms.

I didn't need a reminder of that every day.

I just thank God every single day that she came back to me.

We could have moved. Sold Gran's house.

It probably would have been the easier option.

I did suggest it to Carrie even though it would have been hard for me to move. Gran's house had been my safe place since the day I came to live there.

But I would have left for her.

I would do anything for Carrie.

But she said no. She wanted us to stay. She was adamant.

I knew she partly did it for me, aware that it would be hard for me to leave my house.

But I also knew that she was trying to stop that motherfucker from taking anything else away from her than he already had.

Carrie still has problems sometimes with her lungs. It hurts her on cold days, and her breaths falter a little. But, thankfully, we don't have many cold days in Texas.

She's struggled with nightmares and flashbacks from what happened that night.

They're happening less often these days, but the bad memories are still there, affecting her. As are the scars he left on her chest. If I could take it all away, I would. But I can't. All I can do is love her and protect her and make sure nothing bad ever happens to her again.

It fucking kills me that I wasn't there when she needed me most.

I have a lot of *if only*s from that night. I have tortured myself with thoughts of what I should have done.

But I know that having Carrie with me, alive and healthy, is the only thing that matters now.

And, knowing that, I knew I had to let go of my past, too, once and for all.

So, the day she woke from the coma, I closed the door on it.

I didn't want to be a victim any more.

I wanted to be a survivor.

And, to do that, I needed to heal. I had to crush the demons that I allowed to still haunt me.

I don't enforce anymore. To move forward, I needed to stop doing that.

I didn't realize at the time that it was hurting me more than helping me.

I had to pull back for my mental well-being. And for my family.

I need to be healthy for the sake of Carrie and Hope.

And there will always be men and women out there willing to help in the way that I did.

That doesn't mean I've stopped helping with The Avengers of Injustice. I do, but I'm more in the background. I help with the paperwork side of things. Marcus and I have developed a website with a detailed listing of sex offenders around the country, even right down to the "minor" sex offenders, showing their mug shots, listing their locations and offenses. You can search by zip code, making it easier to know when there is a sex offender in your area.

And, if someone decides to take the law into their own hands against those sick fuckers, using the information that I provide, who am I to stop that?

"Want to go into town and get some frozen yogurt, Hope?"

Hope starts happily clapping her hands together, grinning at her mom, showing those cute two front teeth of hers.

"Ugh, frozen yogurt?" I complain, getting to my feet.

I take Hope from Carrie and then offer her my hand and pull her up. I walk over to the stroller and strap Hope in.

I turn back to Carrie, who is smiling at me. I know that smile well. I've traced it with my tongue a thousand times.

She moves close to me, aligning her body with me. We fit together so fucking perfectly. We always have.

She puts her hand on my chest and pats it. "Yes, frozen yogurt. And, if you're a good boy and stop complaining," she lifts up on her tiptoes and whispers into my ear, "I might let you eat it off me in bed tonight."

My dick throbs in my pants.

"Won't it have melted by then?" I tease, my eyes staring down at her as I imagine a hundred scenarios of me and Red in bed with a tub of frozen yogurt … hours of fun to be had.

"We'll take extra to go. And maybe you'll get lucky, and I'll lick it off of you, too."

Jesus fuck. This woman.

I slide my fingers into her thick red hair, cupping her cheek in my palm. "How did I get so lucky to have you?"

"You didn't get lucky, River. We just found each other. Like we were always meant to."

I kiss her with all the love I feel for her.

"Dada! Mada!" Hope complains in her stroller, making us both chuckle.

I swear, that girl is way too smart for her age.

I glance over at Hope and then back to Carrie. "Red …"

"River."

"After we've finished with the frozen yogurt tonight, how about we start practicing making a baby?"

"Don't we do that most nights?"

"I mean, why don't you stop taking the pill, and we try to get pregnant?"

A smile takes over her face, lighting her beautiful eyes. "Really?"

"Really."

She takes my face in her hands and kisses me hard on the mouth. "I would love to have another baby with you."

Another baby. Damn right.

Because Hope is my child. She always will be.

And Carrie is my heart. Forever and always.

"I love you, Red," I tell her, earning her beautiful smile that she bestows only on me.

"I love you, too, River Wild."

ACKNOWLEDGMENTS

RIVER AND CARRIE'S STORY was one of the hardest that I had ever written. It covered delicate and sensitive topics that I hope I did justice. I feel like I bled this story, and I definitely cried it. But I loved every single moment that I spent with these beautifully complicated characters. River and Carrie's story touched my soul. I hope it touched yours, too.

As always, my first and biggest thank you goes to my husband and children, who put up with my crazy ways, my long working hours, and my random outbursts of tears while sitting, writing on my laptop. I know living with a writer isn't easy. Yet you all still love me. And I love you like I never knew possible. Oh, and thank you, husband, for keeping me fed and watered when I slip off for extended periods of time into my imaginary worlds and forget to take care of myself. I would literally die of starvation without you.

My editor, Jovana Shirley—I have the best editor ever. You make my life a million times easier. And you put up with me dropping last-minute things on you and constant delays on delivery and extended deadlines, and you never tell me off. You are an angel. I honestly couldn't do this without you. So, don't ever leave me. Please!

My cover designer, Najla Qamber—As always, just simply amazing! Your talent to produce exactly what I want never ceases to amaze me. You took this stunning photograph and made it even more beautiful.

My agent, Lauren Abramo—You continue to bring amazing things to the table. If it wasn't for you, I wouldn't be seeing my books in stores in my home country or in other countries all around the world. You helped make my dream come true, and I can never thank you enough for that.

My Wether Girls—Our group is my safe place and my man candy slice of heaven! I adore each and every one of you. Long live Micah Mondays, Happy Tuesdays, Henry Hump Day, Mitch Wick Thursdays, and Free for All Fridays!

As always, thank you to each and every member of the blogging world, who work tirelessly to help promote books without ask or complaint. We authors couldn't do it without you. You are truly appreciated.

And, lastly, to you, the reader—You're the reason I get to live my dream. And work in my pajamas! Thank you from the bottom of my heart.

ABOUT THE AUTHOR

SAMANTHA TOWLE is a *New York Times*, *USA Today*, and *Wall Street Journal* best-selling author. She began her first novel in 2008 while on maternity leave. She completed the manuscript five months later and hasn't stopped writing since.

She is the author of contemporary romances The Storm Series, The Revved Series, The Wardrobe Series, The Gods Series and stand-alones *Trouble*, *When I Was Yours, The Ending I Want, Unsuitable, Under Her,* and *Sacking the Quarterback*, which was written with James Patterson. She has also written paranormal romances *The Bringer* and The Alexandra Jones Series. All have been penned to tunes of The Killers, Kings of Leon, Adele, The Doors, Oasis, Fleetwood Mac, Lana Del Rey, and more of her favorite musicians.

A native of Hull and a graduate of Salford University, she lives with her husband, Craig, in East Yorkshire with their son and daughter.